# A SICILIAN-AMERICAN COMEDY

A Sicilian-American Comedy
Joseph J. Corso Jr.
ISBN 978-1-939693-11-2

**Library of Congress Control Number: 2015945215**

For information and for orders, write to:

## Legas

P.O. Box 149
Mineola, New York
11501, USA

3 Wood Aster Bay
Ottawa, Ontario
K2R 1D3 Canada

legaspublishing.com

# A SICILIAN-AMERICAN COMEDY

BY

## JOSEPH J. CORSO, JR.

LEGAS

# Acknowledgements

The author wishes to recognize the contributions of four individuals who made this book a reality. The first is Professor Emeritus Gaetano Cipolla. Dr. Cipolla was first exposed to earlier versions of the book's first two chapters twenty-five years ago, when I requested his help in translating words and expressions from English into Sicilian. I later asked him to publish that material, but he advised that it was too short for a book and too long for other venues he published. Finally, last year, when I revisited the matter, he suggested that I expand the material into a book-length piece. His encouragement motivated me to imagine a third chapter and revise the first two. Again, Professor Cipolla, wearing the hats of translator, editor and publisher, gave his time and expertise to assuring the authenticity of Sicilian, Italian and French passages in the book and moving the project along. His contributions to the finished product have been invaluable.

Secondly, I would like to express my boundless gratitude to my wife, Barbara, who served as a tireless proofreader, making suggestions which improved the sense of many passages and assured the grammatical correctness of sentence structure when the issue arose. Her loving patience and English teacher's acumen were welcome despite my often "grumpy" protestations to the contrary.

Thirdly, I would like to thank our son Michael Jerome Corso, a professional digital artist, for his help in taking materials I possessed, or he found, to create illustrations for the book, as well as his splendid conception and digital creation of the cover artwork.

Lastly, I would like to acknowledge Dr. Susan Zimmerman, Professor of English Emerita, Queens Collage, CUNY. She fired my imagination in her Graduate classes on Shakespeare's *Hamlet*. As she moved between Freud and Lacan, I was so impressed by her presentations that I actually dreamed parts of what became "The Blue Bunny." In a way, she started the whole thing. I think of her often.

I dedicate this book first to Barbara, the one indispensable person in my life, who ultimately made this book possible.

Secondly, I dedicate it to all the generations of my Sicilian families: the Barberas and the Genovas of Vita, the Corsos of Montevago and the Spataforas of Calatafimi and Alcamo.

*"ART IS A LIE THAT MAKES US REALIZE TRUTH"*

*PABLO PICASSO*

# Table of Contents

# THE RED SWAN

# SICILIANA

O Lola c'hai di latti la cammisa
Si bianca e russa comu na cirasa,
Quannu t'affacci fai la vucca a risa,
Biatu pi lu primu cu ti vasa!
Ntra la puorta tua lu sangu è sparsu,
Ma nun me mpuorta si ce muoru accisu –
E si ce muoru e vaju 'n paradisu
Si nun ce truovo a ttia, mancu ce trasu. Ah!


O Lola, white and red as the cherry
In your nightdress white as milk,
When you appear at the window you smile;
Happy he who gives you your first kiss!
There are blood stains upon your entrance door,
But I don't care if I should then be killed;
And if I die and go to Paradise,
If I don't find you there I won't go in. Ah!

# SPAWN OF THE SWAN

Girolamu had begun a long journey to America. First by mule-driven cart from Calatafimi to Trapani: then by boat, stopping first at Marsala, and continuing across the Atlantic to the Port of New York. He was ten years old.

Girolamu's aunt Giuseppina, his father's spinster sister, had arranged to send him to America to live with her married sister Caterina, before joining his older brother Tonio, who had gone before him. Angelina, Giuseppina's twenty year old ward, had been entrusted with taking him to New York City.

The local women of Calatafimi had long ago decided that Angelina had been born to Giuseppina out of wedlock. But heaven help the person who ever publicly said so, as Pippinu, Girolamu's father, would have given them the beating of their lives in the *Piazza Plebiscito* for all to see.

Pippinu was a big, strong, cuddly man, prone to smile a lot and laugh a lot. But if you crossed him in any way, *Jesus*! His unbridled revenge made the angels flee to paradise, until the bloodbath was over.

Turbulent waters rocked the boat throughout the trip. Fearful of the water and upset by the pitch of the boat, Girolamu ate little and slept poorly. Angelina tried to comfort him to no avail.

Inside his threadbare jacket, Girolamu kept a broken pair of eyeglasses wrapped in some yellow muslin which had dark spots on it. He also had a worn book which he leafed through from time to time, and the remains of an old black and white photograph which had been torn in half: his parents' wedding picture. He had taken the half which showed his mother, who was called *Cignu Russu*, in her white gown. Often he would take the picture out, put on the glasses and gaze at his mother for some time, mumbling words under his breath and weeping until he could no longer see.

Girolamu wept because when he last saw *Cignu Russu* she reviled him for what he had done to her. Pippinu, his father, had also blamed Girolamu for the destruction of his marriage. ...

Not many people in the province of Trapani knew of the woman called *Cignu Russu*, until her husband had nearly killed her four months earlier. Calatafimi, where they lived, is not a small village, but local gossip travels quickly, especially when it is a tale of *illecita libbìdini.*

The old pastor of Calatafimi's *Church of the Madonna del Giubino,* Father Angeloti, kept his distance from the matter because the mysterious death of one of his priests at that time had been linked to the quarrel. The local women still talk about *Cignu Russu,* most condemning her, with a few secretly admiring her glamour and temerity.

An only child, *Cignu Russu* was Christened Annunziata Helena and grew up a "tomboy" among the many boys and few girls in her neighborhood. She paid dearly for trying to run with the pack led by fat Vito Marchello. He pulled her red hair mercilessly, whenever the boys wanted to be alone. Annunziata cried but always went back for more.

Finally, one hot day she earned the other boys' respect. When Vito began pulling her hair, she ignored the pain, twisted around and instinctively grabbed Vito's testicles under his short trousers and squeezed and twisted them until he begged her in agony to stop. Annunziata secretly became "Nunzia, the nutcracker" to the boys who had also been bullied by Vito.

Then Annunziata matured as if overnight. The freckles that had dotted the pale skin on her face and extremities were gone and her body grew into the substantial shape of a woman. Her red hair lightened into strawberry with a bright sheen, and she let it grow out until it draped down her back to her waist. She became a source of enormous pride for her parents and they spoiled her, giving her unaccustomed freedom for one of her age and sex.

Around this time, Annunziata received her new name. She had been seen swimming naked in the early morning by one of the old men on his daily walk along the river bank. He did not know the child but, as he told of the sighting, the story and the name found their rightful owner.

Although she denied everything, Annunziata's parents were unsure, but they forgot the incident and accepted the name because it seemed to capture her spirit and beauty; after all, her parents, the Grecos, had also given her a middle name, Helena, which linked her to the Greek ancestry they claimed.

At thirteen, *Cignu Russu* and the fourteen-year-old Occhipinti boy had been caught in a hayloft and her father had severely beaten the boy. *Cignu Russu* confessed to her priest and parents, after a lecture on the hellfire awaiting *buttani.*

Since her mother's "examination" of *Cignu Russu's* body revealed no impropriety, *Cignu Russu* admitted only to letting Occhipinti "kiss my hair." She said this as she stroked her hair in a sensuous way she had, which demonstrated why a boy might long to touch it with his lips.

The plausible explanation relieved everyone. That it represented only a partially truthful play on words amused *Cignu Russu* who had used her handkerchief to quickly wipe away the evidence of Occhipinti's *baciu umidu.* The silk fabric, hidden in the hay, bore stains and the fragrance of *Cignu Russu.*

*Cignu Russu* had taken no notice of the spectacled Occhipinti boy until she had returned from a wonderful holiday at Siracusa with her parents. They had promised her something special for her thirteenth birthday and she asked to visit this ancient city on the Ionian Sea.

At school and at home she had learned about the Greek myths associated with Sicily. Her favorite story concerned Arethusa, for whom the fountain on the island of Ortygia in Siracusa had been named. *A signura maistra* Spaventa had introduced her to the story at school.

It was not surprising that *Cignu Russu* identified with the free, romantic spirit of the nymph. Arethusa, pursued by a would-be lover, the river god Alfeus, threw herself into the sea. Artemis transformed her into a spring, but when she reached the islet of Ortygia, Alfeus, still in pursuit, transformed himself into a river and united with her forever.

*Cignu Russu* spent hours peering down into the freshwater spring, planted with papyrus and teeming with gray mullet, searching for the ghostly shapes entwined in an eternal embrace.

At this point *Cignu Russu* began to search for a partner who could help her theatricalize her fantasy. So she set herself for Michele Occhipinti. Already a scholar, Michele's teachers urged him to prepare for study in Rome.

He needed thick eyeglasses as a child and spent many hours mastering the Italian language and reading classic Italian literature. His parents were peasants with little education, but they left him to his studies, so long as he did his chores and tended their few sheep and cows.

Michele was of medium height and slender with black curly

hair and an olive complexion, in contrast to *Cignu Russu* and her family whose hair and skin were light. When Michele removed his glasses to clean them, his brown eyes revealed a vulnerability that touched the observant *Cignu Russu*.

For his part, Michele had already developed a secret idolatry for her, and it did not bother him that she sparked their relationship. She emerged as his "Beatrice," when he thought about his first feelings for her, and he began to write her love poems in the style of Dante and sonnets that imitated Petrarch.

Head of Arethusa, silver decadrachm, Greek coin of ancient Siracuse, private rare coin collection.

But later, when he no longer had to admire her from a distance, on a marble pedestal, she melted into an object of passionate, carnal desire. His *paradisu* lay in the soft white bosom and fragrant red hair of *Cignu Russu*, and the special kisses they exchanged.

At great risk, they stole away to swim in the evenings and discover each other under the cover of night and water. Michele knew the story of Arethusa and indulged *Cignu Russu* by addressing her as such, while he responded to Alfeus.

*Cignu Russu*, naked and trembling in the water, would always lead the way. "Pretend our hands are *calamari*, Alfeus, yours with an eye in every finger, as you search for my secret cave, and mine to wrap around the slippery *ancidda* before it gets away."

Nevertheless, *Cignu Russu* could not bring herself to let the elusive eel find its way into her secret cave. "Alfeus, be careful," she would say, gently deflecting him. Years of maternal and Church indoctrination about virginity and honor had encroached upon the present like an invisible manacle, protecting her fragile chastity.

But these games did not satisfy them for long. One warm night they stole into a barn and climbed into the hayloft, where they found soft bedding. *Cignu Russu* knew of Michele's frustration and resolved to appease him in a safe way.

After they had undressed and embraced, *Cignu Russu* sensed Michele's desire to penetrate her. She grabbed his hair and pulled his face down into the tuft of strawberry hair between her legs, clamping them around his neck. "*Baciami*, Michele," she whispered, "*Baciami, cu sentimentu!*" As he began to penetrate her "secret cave" with his tongue, *Cignu Russu* slowly turned on her side and grasped Michele's buttocks and drew his *ancidda* into her mouth.

*Cignu Russu* glamorized this embrace in her appropriation of the ultimate union of Arethusa and Alfeus. The violent disunion the lovers later experienced sealed the splendid moment in their souls, like the bonding of metals under intense heat.

Occhipinti, a promising scholar, left the next year to study on the mainland. Eventually he surprised everyone by becoming a priest, returning to Calatafimi as "Padre" Occhipinti when he became twenty-five. ...

After the boat left Marsala, Girolamu began to have a strange dream every night. He found himself standing under a long yellow canopy which resembled those he had once seen in the marketplace in Palermo during *Carnalivari* before Lent. The canopy arched over the ground before him and led to the mouth of a cave. A red, beaded curtain hung from the mouth and moved as wind passed through it.

Girolamu desperately wanted to enter the cave. He had a long knife in his hand and saw that a giant spider's web stood between him and the mouth of the cave. At the center of the web clung a huge spider that had a glowing eye in the heart of its body. The eye stared at Girolamu and he saw his own reflection in its gaze. Girolamu knew he had to escape the eye to enter the cave.

He moved toward the web and lifted the knife to attack the

eye of the spider. As he began to swing the knife, his arm slowed down, as though he were trying to slice through something under water, and his blow fell slowly and harmlessly against the webbing. Girolamu repeated the effort with the same result. The spider's eye glowed more brightly.

Suddenly, a familiar, disembodied voice resonated from the mouth of the cave, swirling the red-beaded curtain: "*Chiù forti, Girolamu! Chiù forti!*" and dozens of black bats burst shrilly from the cave attacking and distracting the spider. Like magic, Girolamu cut through the web in a single blow and ran to the mouth of the cave.

But when he neared the mouth, a ferocious wind whipped through the curtain and blew him back into the sticky web. Then the voice returned saying, "You betrayed me! So to you, little Judas, I give the *Evil Eye* for your evil eye, and wish you all the torment you have given my soul." Girolamu saw the spider moving down the web toward him, feeding on bats from every tentacle-like leg. Girolamu was helpless. And the eye burned red and blinded him.

Each night Girolamu awoke from the dream shivering and wet, the voice's accusation ringing in his ears. His mother would not be part of the life which awaited him in America. ...

*Cignu Russu* married at sixteen, much to her parents' relief. Pippinu Tommaso's handsome face and bright future in Calatafimi, as a gifted carpenter, mason and plaster artisan made him a good catch. He was almost a decade older than his bride, but to all this was to the good, as he had been suspected as a notorious horn-giver in his youth. Pippinu also had light brown hair and blue eyes, so he and *Cignu Russu* made a strikingly handsome couple.

Pippinu's mother, Filippa, had also married at sixteen and gave birth to twelve healthy children before the age of forty-four. Pippinu would see that *Cignu Russu* would be similarly occupied. She seemed to forget Michele Occhipinti.

Pippinu senior and Filippa had many heart aches with their children, because Calatafimi had been periodically plagued with bouts of *pellagra* and *cholera*. Four of their children had succumbed to one or the other disease before they were five years old.

For this reason and others, including extreme poverty, five of the remaining seven siblings began to leave Sicily in 1907, after both parents had passed. Only Pippinu junior and Giuseppina remained.

Caterina, his younger sister, took their youngest brother, with her to America where, through an arranged marriage, she wed a *paisano* from Vita, a small town near Calatafimi.

The four remaining siblings set out for Argentina in 1912, joining other *paisani* who had gone five years before. Any sense of prospective danger was mitigated by the horrible prospect of staying in Sicily.

The Tommasos parented eight children, including twin sons, Peppinu and Vicenzu. Remarkably, only one was lost, the first daughter, whom *Cignu Russu* prevailed upon Pippinu to name Arethusa, after she was still-born. Girolamu, the last, came when *Cignu Russu* was thirty-six, resulting in her only difficult birth. The complications were beyond the skills of her midwife, *Signura* Ravello. There would be no more than seven children.

Those complications were always referenced by *Cignu Russu*, whenever people looked at the odd shape of little Girolamu who, with his dark, curly hair and swarthy skin, resembled no one in his family. His mother insisted he had her nose which wasn't re-motely so.

Then one day, "out of the blue," as they say, *Cignu Russu*'s grandfather, Francesco Greco, then nearly ninety and a notorious storyteller, declared that Girolamu resembled Francesco's father, Pietro, who had died fifty years earlier.

Though incredulous, Pippinu never said so. Yet, at the same time, he felt a slight easing of a dark burden that had been taking some uncertain form in the pit of his soul. After all, in his youth he had often celebrated the "feast of the cuckold," bringing torment to men whose wives strayed to another nest.

With the passing years, Pippinu prospered (he owned a good house and some nice property) and grew fat, losing most of his hair. But he doted on his children and denied *Cignu Russu* nothing for giving him the riches of a family to carry on his name and line.

*Cignu Russu* looked better and better after each child came, as if giving them life (all but dear Arethusa who lived in memory) seasoned her general beauty and burnished her hair, which she kept long to the length of her buttocks.

Before his death at ninety-two, *Cignu Russu*'s grandfather, Francesco, would take young Girolamu to the hills of Calatafimi and would recount the stories of his youth. Francesco brought Girolamu to the *Pianto Romano* where the tall monument to Garibaldi stands. Inside is a charnel-house containing the remains of the heroes of both armies.

He told Girolamu of how he joined Garibaldi's thousand, red-shirted volunteers in the liberation of Sicily from the Bourbons. The old man's eyes gleamed as he reiterated Garibaldi's words: "Qua o si fa l'Italia o si muore!" ("Here we make Italy or we die.")

In another area near the hill, Francesco said "Here are the caves, Girolamu, we *Garibaldini* hid and slept in so we could watch the enemy. At night we raided their camps and I found the captain sleeping in his French decorations and I stuck him like a *porcu*. Francesco illustrated the thrusts with the tip of his gnarled cane pressing against the boy's chest.

Francesco even introduced the fascinated Girolamu to the bats that inhabited the caves. "Don't be afraid of them, Girolamu, they'll sing you to sleep and protect you. They are not your enemy. Do you know they suckle their young?"

Until he left Sicily, Girolamu grew up in those hills and caves, which became for him the playground of his imagination. His siblings were too old to be his playmates, although his sisters doted on him as an extension of their mother's love.

Girolamu left Calatafimi's hills twice before leaving Sicily: the first time when his family made a trip to Palermo before Lent. Everything there proclaimed the festive *Carnalivari*. The scents of fresh fish covered with garlic and herbs baking in makeshift ovens and balls of dough tumbling in large vats of hot oil pulled crowds to the tables where they were sold.

There were games of chance to play, opera arias and folk songs to hear and sing and much purple wine to drink. For a short time before the season of abstinence, carnival license turned the world upside down, for beggars to be crowned "Princes of Trinacria" and for politicians to beg alms in rags. Even the sight of *Signura* Cucinna, the famed local "Madam," parading around as Mary Magdalene was possible. Girolamu could only wonder at these events which confused his five-year-old mind.

On a clear night, under a brightly decorated yellow canopy by the shore, Pippinu began to wade through dozens of raw clams, which Girolamu had never seen, making loud slurping and sucking noises. With each swallow, Pippinu winked at *Cignu Russu* who would not eat raw clams because it was *pocu eleganti*.

Girolamu expressed interest and Pippinu put him on his knee and proceeded to demonstrate, in exaggerated fashion, the noisy art of swallowing raw clams. *Cignu Russu* became upset and said the lesson had become lewd. Finally, she let go of Helena, her youngest girl, and pulled Girolamu away, snapping at Pippinu, *"Basta!"* and flashing her blue eyes which meant the matter had been concluded.

Only a few months later, Girolamu became aware that a "war" had started north of Italy. Over the next few weeks his parents and siblings became sullen and quiet in his presence.

Shortly, Girolamu learned that Italy was fighting against people from "Austria-Hungary," and his three brothers, ages twenty-one to twenty-four (the twins) were to be sent north to the mainland to fight with guns.

*Cignu Russu* became hysterical several times each day, screaming for God's mercy: "Please, Lord, not all three!" The whole family sat in prayer with the rosary every evening. Many candles were lit in *Madonna del Giubino's* chapels by the dozen families about to lose their young sons to war.

The day all twenty-six men left Calatafimi for Palermo in a military truck; they were joined by father Occhipinti who was to be their Chaplin. It was the coldest day of any August Girolamu could remember. The high-pitched wailing and the bitter tears of women, children and some older men were pitiful. For weeks thereafter, hardly anyone smiled or had a pleasant word to say.

The government in Rome had called to service a high number of Sicilian men at least age twenty-one, granting exemptions only to those young men working in northern Italian factories. The Tommaso brothers could find no way out of serving.

Grudgingly, life went on in Calatafimi, and only when the first letters came from the men did any kind of celebration take place. Like most parents and siblings, the Tommasos had written to their sons daily, but who knew when and if any letters would reach their sons from a post office box in Palermo.

The letters from Pippinu, Vicenzu and Tonio lifted the heavy curtain of despair surrounding *Cignu Russu* and her family, if only for a little while, as they were read and reread like scripture.

But the few lines from each boy were virtually identical: "We are all well and pray we will return in good health to Calatafimi soon. Dear mother, father, sisters and Girolamu, you are in our thoughts and prayers every moment we face danger. May God bless and protect all of us through this ordeal. Please write when you can. Love and a thousand kisses, your devoted sons ..." The three signed each letter.

In the first year, six such letters were received by the Tommasos, yet none ever mentioned the letters from home. The same was true of the other families which led each to believe their sons were moving all over Europe, never staying in one place long enough to get mail. There were only four letters received by the Tommasos the following year and but three came shortly before the Armistice in November 1918.

In the years before 1918, while the Great War raged in Europe, life in Calatafimi returned to a semblance of normalcy. Of course the daily lives of all families adjusted to the continuous supplication to God, the Virgin Mary and all the saints for their sons to return unharmed.

Almost every day, father Angeloti would lead the rosary dialogue for hundreds of residents come from every corner of Calatafimi to the *Piazza Plebiscito*. On several occasions, father Angeloti told the crowd that he had received word that father Occhipinti was alive and well among the fighting soldiers. That news did not lighten *Cignu Russu*'s burden.

Even in such times, Pippinu Tommaso was very busy, as the churches and official buildings were in greater need of repair and restoration. This was due to the great influx of families seeking succor and reassurance that all would be well if they kept the faith and steady flow of devotion.

The parish churches and town halls could still afford to pay something (more often grain not *Lire*) for highly-skilled restoration work, so as to provide a more cheerful refuge from reports of the horrors of war reaching every village in Sicily, however outdated.

Pippinu would donate some of his time and skills, when the situation warranted his charity. He considered himself blessed, even in the absence of three sons risking their lives in a war which meant little to the citizens of Calatafimi.

During these years, Pippinu noticed that Girolamu began to exhibit a curiosity about his father's work. Pippinu's other sons never demonstrated much interest or aptitude for fine carpentry, preferring occasional hard labor to fill out their bodies and catch the eyes of local girls, before being called to war.

The young men, under the tutelage of their father, with the tacit blessings of their mother, skirted serious emotional relationships and marriage. Pippinu's well-worn adage: "Never marry! But if you must, make sure she is *brutta comu la morti* (she is as ugly as sin.) She will give you many children but no horns: those <u>you</u> will give to others instead." The hypocrisy in this cautionary tale was not lost on the young men, each of who worshipped his mother above all beings, seen and unseen.

Pippinu began working with Girolamu to teach him the skills needed for practical and artistic carpentry and masonry. Having demonstrated to his father an apprentice's eagerness to learn, Girolamu was given an opportunity when he was eight years old to join Pippinu on a second trip from Calatafimi to nearby Alcamo.

It was to fulfill a modest commission from the local church fathers. The work involved restoring a very old and revered wooden bannister, which was part of a circular staircase leading up to a canopied pulpit. The bannister had very ornate carvings on it representing the expulsion of Adam and Eve from Eden, in high relief.

Areas along the bannister had been chipped or broken off, and the once vivid red, yellow and green colors were subdued by time and dirt. In addition, the effect of the dank, corrosive weather conditions, which seeped into the church plaguing its entire interior of wood and stone, corroded everything.

Girolamu observed whatever Pippinu did: how he did it and with which tools. Two days later Pippinu was preparing to paint a restored section of the bannister. He paused and turned to Girolamu smiling and said: "One day you will go north to Rome and Florence and see first-hand the incredible work of a man called Michelangelo, a Florentine. At home I have a large book filled with pictures of his sculptures, painting and architecture.

"He was a true genius and worked hard all his long life. *I so mani appartinevanu a Diu* (His hands belonged to God). When you are blessed by the Lord, your imagination is rich and it guides your willing hands so you can create or restore wonderful works of art. It's like having magical fingers which do the bidding of your brain to fulfill your plan, step by step, to perfection."

Girolamu never forgot what his father said. It gave him an unexpected sense of purpose he had never thought about. Smiling, Girolamu grasped Pippinu's right hand and pressed it to his lips, kissing it tenderly. Pippinu was moved to tears and embraced his son, kissing the top of his head many times to hide his emotion. The two Tommasos had never connected this way before, nor would they ever again.

21

The day that everyone in Calatafimi fearfully awaited finally came in early November of 1918. A single, dust-covered Italian soldier on a belching motorcycle screeched into the *Piazza Plebiscito.*

He sought out Father Angeloti, asking for the bells to be rung for fifteen minutes summoning the citizens of Calatafimi who had given their twenty-four sons to the war effort. Gradually, twelve families and their friends, neighbors and relatives, including the Tommasos moved anxiously into the *Piazza*, holding rosaries and making desperate signs of the cross.

The young soldier had removed his hat and riding spectacles. His blue eyes were circled with rings of dust and road dirt. His blonde hair, also encrusted with dirt, nonetheless glistened in the morning sunlight. Under his left arm was a thin briefcase containing the names of the living, missing and dead sons of Calatafimi.

As the crowds gathered before the soldier and Father Angeloti, it was apparent that all the blood had drained from their faces and everyone was trembling. The young soldier could have been one of their sons, but he had driven down from Palermo, after a joyous reunion with his own family. No! Today he was the dreaded messenger, the angel of life and death, doling out joy and misery, perhaps in equal measure.

His first words were totally unexpected and bittersweet: "The Great War is over! Troops from the front lines are preparing to return to their homes sometime later this month." A nervous cheer rose from the crowd. "However, today I bring salutations from our government honoring the sacrifices your sons and their families have made these three years." The word "sacrifices" brought forth a common moan.

The people's response was muted, as they were told the protocol of these military revelations: living, wounded, missing in action and dead. The youth continued: "I am happy to announce that the following ten soldiers are alive and well by recent confirmation."

He paused to allow a collective deep breath and proceeded to read off the names, slowly and clearly, allowing the euphoria to subside before moving to the next name. No Tommaso was mentioned. Pippinu drew *Cignu Russu* close *to* him and encircled his trembling children with his other arm.

"We have confirmed that Giuseppe Rincali and Tonio Tommaso, though wounded, are alive and well enough to return home very soon. Now the wails and keening joined the cheers. The Tommasos realized that one wounded son could mean the worst for Pippinu and Vicenzu. One slight ray of hope to feed on: missing in action. Ten more names were read, accompanied by sobs expressing little hope but not yet complete hopelessness.

Nonetheless, the families of the ten cried out to God for mercy in their inconsolable grief: ten young men lying somewhere in a purgatory of mud and fire, bleeding, limbs ripped off by heavy ordinance and praying with, perhaps, their last breath for their mothers and medical aide. None of the names was a Tommaso. The encroaching reality gripped the family like a giant snake squeezing its prey in a deadly embrace.

"The last two soldiers, Pippinu and Vicenzu Tommaso are confirmed to have fallen in combat and died bravely defending their country," the young soldier said very slowly. *Cignu Russu* and her daughters collapsed as one, while Girolamu clung desperately to his father.

Pippinu lost all sense of civility: "Cursed God of death, where are you hiding!? Helpless Holy Mother, did your son not rise from the dead, promising we would, too!? Well my sons are dead now and where is the Christ hiding!? *Lu munnu apparteni a Lucifiru. Diu è mortu! Diu è mortu!* (The world belongs to Lucifer after all! God is dead! God is dead!) We must bury our sons forever, Holy Helpless Mother!"

Father Angeloti tried to calm Pippinu down, as the young soldier, having left papers to be distributed to the families of the twenty-four, put on his hat and spectacles. Without another word, the youth mounted his motorcycle and roared out of Calatafimi, en route to another town or village to bring the horrid tidings of war.

Two days later Father Angeloti received word that Father Occhipinti was in Palermo en route to Calatafimi, alive and well.

Gradually, the stinging pain of the deaths of Pippinu and Vicenzu was ameliorated for the Tommaso women, accepting their death as God's Will and anticipating the happy return of Tonio. Not so with Pippinu who began to drink more heavily, cursing God and His Paradise with every drunken breath.

When All Soul's Day was celebrated inside the *Madonna del Giubino* Church, the families of the "missing in action" soldiers were encouraged by Father Occhipinti to trust God's Plan and continue to hope for good news. News did come a few days later that an Armistice was to be signed in Paris by all parties to the conflict, officially marking the end of the Great War on November 11, 1918, when all arms were laid down.

Within a week of this news, Pippinu sat in a chair outside his house enjoying some tranquility and wine. A small celebration was conducted in *Piazza Plebiscito* by Fathers Angeloti and Occhipinti with little flags of Italy passed out to mark the occasion of the defeat of the "Hun" in Europe.

Girolamu sat with his father while the women prepared an "Armistice Dinner" of *Wiener schnitzel* and *pommes frites. Cignu Russu* had found it in a famous recipe from 1871 her grandmother had left her.

Pippinu had become philosophical about all the brutality of life he recognized. "Girolamu," he began, "This was northern Italy's war, Rome's war. It had little to do with Sicily and nothing to do with Calatafimi: but see the human cost to all of us paying tribute in blood and suffering, while getting nothing but mutilated, lifeless bodies of our children in return. Girolamu shrugged his shoulders not fully comprehending his father's words.

Pippinu knew why so many Sicilians fled the Province of Trapani years before the Great War: Rome's cruel indifference to the plight of the farmers without arable land, land exhausted by the demands for grain from the north.

"My son," Pippinu said, "man is cursed by two things in life: fighting wars and becoming cuckolds. It has always been the rapacious Church of Rome showing the way to war, as with the Crusades, when looting and slaughter of human beings was licensed by the Pope.

As for wearing horns, we have mother Eve to thank for spreading her legs and inviting in that long, slimy phallus she preferred to Adam's little joint. Can you imagine such ingratitude from Adam's rib?

"Is it not curious Girolamu, that the Armistice declared peace on the eleventh day of the eleventh month, the very day and month we celebrate the feast of the cuckolds? There is a lesson in all this, my son. Never go to war: find a way out; and never marry! But if you must, make sure she *è cosi brutto come il peccato.* She will give you many children but no horns: those you will give to others, instead."

"But what horns? What are cuckolds, Papa?" Pippinu realized he had stepped into a *purtusu chinu di merda* and was sinking.

"Girolamu, there is a kind of bird called the cuckoo that lays eggs in other birds' nests. Cuckoo's leave their chicks for the other birds to raise as their own.

As for the horns, they are a sign that you're raising somebody else's chicks without knowing it. They form on the head like painful bumps and grow into red horns like Lucifer's. You are the chick's male parent but not the little bastard's father. Do you understand?"

Girolamu had only primitive ideas about parent's reproductive activities and responsibilities, and, at that, it was limited to what his older brothers had told him from time to time, while laughing loudly. In school one day, a loudmouthed boy had welts on his face for asking a lot of questions at home about babies.

He asked *A signura maistra* Spavenda what she had between her legs. He received some good whacks on his hands from a wooden ruler, and the infuriated teacher made him wash out his mouth with soap. That, of course, was nothing compared to the welts he got that evening from his father. Girolamu decided he was content in his ignorance.

A few weeks later, just in time for the Christmas season, a military vehicle driven by the young blond soldier who brought the welcomed-unwelcomed news in October, delivered Giuseppe Rincali and Tonio Tommaso to Calatafimi. The bells of *Madonna del Giubino* clanged for fifteen minutes bringing dozens of people to the *Piazza*.

Rincali had lost a leg and walked with a wooden crutch. Otherwise, he seemed alright as he was mobbed by his family and friends. Tonio had no visible injuries but there was an obvious vacant look on his face as he was embraced by the family.

It would later be made manifest that he had suffered "shell shock." He would move in and out of moments of tranquility to those of violent screaming, as he held his head tightly and ran to hide behind objects for protection.

Gradually, the violent episodes subsided and Tonio was able to sleep a few hours each night, with only periodic eruptions. The local doctors had little concept of the nature of his malady and, consequently, could offer little help.

Father Occhipinti spent hours with Tonio, trying to get him to talk about his feelings, as one who had also seen first-hand the carnage and heard the shrill shells explode in earth-shaking destruction, causing both physical and mental damage.

25

Tonio kept his silence to everyone. The family knew he was suffering but could do little besides giving him the comforts of home and loving care, while praying for his recovery.

In the spring, Tonio advised the family that he wanted to go to America where there were no wars and plenty of opportunity to prosper. He had written to his uncle, Silvio Tommaso, who had gone to the United States shortly after the turn of the century.

Silvio, like Pippinu, was smart and learned as much English as he could, getting heavy labor work in New York City during the explosion of bridge, tunnel and subway-train building projects before the war. As a bilingual, he became a foreman and was in a position to help many *paisani* from the Province of Trapani get work.

He became prosperous by investing most of his earnings in real estate: six-family tenements in east Kings, and western Queens, Counties. In all, Silvio owned ten dwellings: nine of them producing thirty-six rents a month. The tenth was for himself, his wife, Vita, two single daughters and his three married children who lived free until they saw their way clear to buy their own homes.

Silvio was indeed living the American Dream and Tonio wanted a piece of it. As it turned out, Silvio had become "connected" in New York, working his way up the ladder in another "Family."

The Tommaso's saw Tonio off in Trapani in May of 1919. For *Cignu Russu* this was like the loss of a third son, as no unmarried person the family knew who had gone to America, had ever come back to Sicily. Tragically, a month later the remains of her twin sons were officially returned for burial.

The bodies, unfit for any display, were accompanied by military declarations and medals of heroism and sorrow for the family's loss. Pippinu arranged for a mass and immediate burial behind the Family's garden: *Cignu Russu* did not want her sons resting with strangers in a Church cemetery.

Father Occhipinti had gotten a special dispensation to declare the grave site hallowed ground. This audacious act upset the community, but Father Occhipinti reminded those at mass that the Tommaso's had suffered the greatest loss of any family in Calatafimi.

Of course, the sons still missing in action, who would never return, eventually evened the score. The general grumbling in Calatafimi soon dissipated as life grudgingly moved on.

As he grew, Girolamu had exhibited a remarkable memory and showed it early to his grandfather Francesco by repeating the old man's stories to him almost word for word. "And this is how I stuck the Bourbon *porcu cu la me spata!*" the boy would bellow to the old man's delight, while gently waving a stick at Francesco's midsection.

Girolamu performed the stories at family gatherings. Everyone roared at the tales they themselves had been regaled with for years, and also at the child's inflections, which unerringly mimicked Francesco's.

Girolamu had developed this ability partly because of poor eyesight. He needed glasses to help him read, but *Cignu Russu* would never allow Girolamu to be fitted for them. He began to compensate by memorizing whole passages and pages of schoolbooks he read in bright daylight. Inexplicably, *Cignu Russu* encouraged her son to read, calling him *"u me picciriddu eruditu."*

At the age of nine, Girolamu astounded the neighborhood, and gained some notoriety throughout Calatafimi, when he entered a contest sponsored by the Dante Society and the school districts in the Province of Trapani. The prize included a bicycle and twenty-five *lire*. This would be awarded to the boy who could best recite from memory ten complete and consecutive cantos from Dante's *Commedia*.

The epic poem, hailed by the government as the basis for the standard Italian language, competed with the Sicilian in classrooms on the Island. In a show of resistance, few Sicilian families permitted their young sons to be contestants. Pippinu did not feel strongly about the matter, but *Cignu Russu* wanted her little warrior-scholar to shine.

*Cignu Russu* approached Father Occhipinti for help one Sunday after Mass. The priest had the habit of removing his eyeglasses, smiling and pinching Girolamu's cheek between his thumb and forefinger, which did not please the boy. But Father Occhipinti had become a Dante scholar in Florence before going to Rome and the priesthood. He could be helpful.

"Won't you give my little boy some guidance, Father," *Cignu Russu* asked with a serene smile. Girolamu and his sisters looked expectantly at the priest. Father Occhipinti's face appeared to blanch for a moment. Then he said, *"Sì, signura Tommaso,"* so effusively, he almost choked and *Cignu Russu* had to hide her face in her handkerchief and pretend she was sneezing.

At their initial meeting, the priest suggested to Girolamu

that he use his glasses to read the passages, even before the boy opened the *Commedia*. Girolamu saw for the first time how clear the words became.

Girolamu won the contest easily and *Cignu Russu* enjoyed the following months, reminding everyone in the town of Girolamu's great scholarship, and taking credit for his intelligence, if not his looks. But there were a few mistrusting women who said to each other, *sotto voce* and with a wink, "He has his brains and his looks from his *padre*. ..."

On a rare, calm evening at sea, Girolamu could not sleep and he went quietly up on deck. He walked to the railing and looked out at the water. Despite a brilliant moon, only vast darkness could be seen, and Girolamu felt an overwhelming fear of the unknown within those deep, black waters. He saw himself as a small vessel set adrift on a great, forbidding sea with no anchor and no clear destination.

He decided to read some passages from the *Paradiso* he did not know by heart, to improve his spirits. Girolamu carefully removed his glasses from their yellow muslin wrapping and held them up to the moonlight to see if the lenses needed cleaning.

Suddenly, an inebriated member of the crew grabbed Girolamu from behind, thinking the boy was in danger, and pulled him back from the rail. Girolamu screamed and the crewman yelled back. Several other crewmen and passengers, including an angry Angelina, came on deck to calm everyone down.

At that point, Girolamu realized his glasses and their muslin covering had been lost overboard. Girolamu was inconsolable. He had gotten them shortly after his tenth birthday, and they had been precious to him. His vessel had lost its only remaining compass points. ...

On the day of his tenth birthday, Girolamu left school early because *Cignu Russu* had promised to prepare a special meal for him. She was stuffing green and red peppers with chopped meat and rice and baking them. And there would be a pepper-flavored plum tomato sauce for his favorite macaroni, *fusilli*.

Girolamu's father had work in a nearby village, renovating the local church's hardwood pews. Pippinu wouldn't be home until dark and then they would eat.

But Girolamu wanted to smell the aromas of the kitchen while his mother cooked, and it wasn't often that he could be alone with her. His surviving brother, Tonio, had gone to America and of his three sisters, the two oldest had married, following their baker husbands, two brothers, to Palermo to work and live. Helena, the youngest, worked in the town, running an electric sewing machine at a clothing factory which produced ladies' garments.

It was a sunny, sleepy day in September and the flies were plaguing the livestock and swarming around warm droppings, filling the air with a soothing buzz. As Girolamu approached his house he saw a small, drooping *sceccu* tied to the wooden fence out front.

The poor animal continually waved its tail in an effort to minimize the bites from various flying insects feasting on its shanks. Girolamu saw markings on the animal which indicated clergy. He immediately thought of Father Occhipinti.

Now, Girolamu panicked, thinking something terrible had happened to his mother, and he bolted to the front door. He found it locked, much to his surprise and exasperation. Girolamu ran around to the back of the house. His throat had constricted and he couldn't make a sound.

As he passed the window to his parents' bedroom he heard sounds from within like moaning. The curtains were drawn, which seemed odd because the sun had already slid to the other side of the house. He could only think of death. *Cignu Russu* was dead or dying!

Girolamu had become numb with fear. He wanted to know and he didn't. What if his beloved mother had died? How could he survive? In this moment of terror, Girolamu suddenly remembered something his older brothers had shown him when they declared him old enough to understand.

A chink above the base of the wall, just outside the bedroom, had been found and covered by the scoop of a rusting ladle his brothers had nailed to the wall. Pippinu, one the twins, had said, "If you want to learn more about life than you will in school or in church, look through there very early on a Sunday morning."

Knowing that his parents' bedroom was sacrosanct, Girolamu had refused to look but had sworn a blood oath never to reveal the secret. Now, he felt compelled to look inside out of concern and an immodest curiosity. Girolamu got down on his knees, bent over and very carefully slid the ladle aside.

It took Girolamu a few seconds to focus his eyes but only a moment to absorb the scene. It became a memory that nettled him *comu si caminassi supra na strata di spini finu a la morti* (like walking a thorny road in bare feet to his grave), as Pippinu frequently said. But at this moment, Girolamu knelt transfixed by what he saw and he gazed at his mother as never before.

*Cignu Russu* was propped up by pillows against the headboard of the bed, her head tilted back and her arms spread out along the top of the headboard; her hair draped behind it. The unlaced bodice of her yellow muslin dress exposed her large, white breasts. Although Girolamu had been weaned on those breasts for two years, he did not remember how they looked. The sight of their fullness, which reminded him of summer eggplants swollen by the rain and sun, simultaneously attracted and repelled him. *Cignu Russu*'s legs were splayed, though still covered, canopy-like, by her dress.

Then Girolamu saw the black cassock and the shape of raised buttocks and the dark form flowing under *Cignu Russu*'s canopy. Suddenly, she cried, "*Chiù forti, Michele! Chiù forti!*" Two swarthy hands reached up and pressed against *Cignu Russu's* breasts and the cassock wriggled further under the canopy. Girolamu's mouth felt as though dried cow dung filled it.

Then he heard a sound emerge from under the canopy that shocked him almost as much as the thrill he felt from *Cignu Russu's* ecstatic sighs. It took a moment before Girolamu realized that Father Occhipinti was swallowing raw clams.

Girolamu finally broke off his gaze, ran to get his bicycle and rode, weeping, to the hills and his secret cave. He vomited as soon as he got there and continued to tremble.

He could not fully understand his feelings about what had happened, but he knew his anger was not at what *Cignu Russu* had done - but with whom she had done it. Girolamu had accepted his father's place in her life, but he had never seen them together. Girolamu's imagination had censored any form of carnality between them. But to betray him with a stranger - that could not be forgiven!

That night at dinner, Girolamu sat quietly at the table. His sister, Helena, teased him about growing old. But Girolamu did not smile. He ate without any zest and the food went down hard. The acid in his stomach bubbled up to his throat. He didn't enjoy one bite of the dinner *Cignu Russu* had prepared for him.

How could he, knowing what he did. What she did! It seemed like the memory of a bad dream. Perhaps it was a dream. No, the images were too vivid, the sounds too clear.

At last, *Cignu Russu* brought out the birthday cake: a sweet confection with alternate layers of sponge cake soaked in rum and *cassata* cream loaded with dark chocolate drops and bits of dried lemon and orange fruit. On top sat a thick layer of flaky pastry covered with freshly whipped cream.

The family wished him a *bon cumpleannu a tia,* as each one kissed Girolamu in turn. *Cignu Russu* concluded the ceremony, and although Girolamu tensed when she pressed him to her breast, he closed his eyes and threw his arms around her and squeezed as she kissed his forehead.

*Cignu Russu* handed Girolamu a long kitchen knife and told him to cut the first piece of cake. Girolamu struggled to get the knife through the thick pastry. Pippinu hummed patiently but Helena told Girolamu to hurry. *Cignu Russu* clicked her tongue and shook her head with impatience.

Finally, she said, "*Chiù forti, Girolamu! Chiù forti!*"

The words burned in Girolamu's ears and he lost control. Standing up, he brandished the knife and said, "Like Father Occhipinti did under your dress this afternoon!?" And then Girolamu made the sound of swallowing raw clams.

Everyone but *Cignu Russu* looked stunned. Helena understood the terrible accusation against their mother, but she could not make any sense of the strange sound Girolamu had made. Their eyes turned to her. Pippinu emitted a sound like a helpless man whose mortal enemy had slit open his belly with a *stiletto.*

*Cignu Russu* struck Girolamu across the face, knocking him back in his chair as the knife fell to the floor. The worm of doubt feeding on the fruit of Pippinu's trust sprang into a poisonous serpent, but his muscles were frozen.

*Cignu Russu*'s face hardened and she removed her apron and threw it on the table, turned and walked slowly into the kitchen. His sister's eyes turned to Girolamu who said in a raspy voice dredged up from the pit of his hate, "I saw them together (then turning to his father) in your bed!"

Helena began to moan and weep hysterically. Pippinu's face purpled. Finally, he jumped up and screamed, "*Buttana! M'adurnasti la casa! Mi facisti curnutu! Buttana! T'ammazzu!*" Pippinu ran into the kitchen and beat *Cignu Russu* with his fists until she confessed her shame.

Girolamu ran out and cycled the path he knew, even in darkness, weeping, to his secret cave in the hills. Helena ran, wailing, to neighbor Pizzolato's house down the road, to seek comfort and consolation. While Helena feared for her mother, she knew better than to get embroiled in a domestic quarrel.

Millie Pizzolato offered Helena comfort but little consolation. She and most of the other wives and widows in the area had suspected *Cignu Russu* of illicit behavior. Did she not parade to church on Sundays without her husband, wearing only a small, transparent piece of lace on her long, red hair to satisfy the letter of the law? Who knows how many of St. Paul's angels blushed at the sight of her wicked temptation. She had too much pride. It was only a matter of time before she fell into "*i manu du diàulu.*" Millie Pizzolato entertained such thoughts in her hour of vindication.

Girolamu spent the next twenty-four hours turning over in his mind the phrase that Pippinu had used,"*Mi facisti curnutu!* Suddenly, he hated everyone.

No one witnessed what Pippinu did next to *Cignu Russu.* The older men in the town knew what he would do. Ample precedent existed and a long tradition, regarding married women who "opened their door to strangers." The procedure likely had its origins in the *Inquisition* when priests silenced unrepentant heretics by "Cauterizing the Devil's Lips."

After beating her unconscious, Pippinu stripped *Cignu Russu* of her clothes and carried her to the dishonored bed. There he tied her hands and legs to the bedposts and put pillows under her buttocks to assure easy access to the tainted flesh. He cut off *Cignu Russu's* hair as close to the scalp as he could and draped the strawberry sheaf across her groin. Pippinu took a rag and stuffed it into her bleeding mouth. Then he got the oil of vitriol.

An acrid stench of burned flesh and hair hung about Pippinu's house for three days. Finally, he let a doctor come to tend *Cignu Russu.* Her body had succumbed to the horror of her torture, but she had resisted death with an undiminished fierceness of spirit. *Cignu Russu* needed special medical attention and a hired truck carried her three hours to Palermo.

Father Occhipinti had disappeared. At the dusty taverns where old men sat to have a bowl of *ministruni* and a glass of wine, while they gossiped the hot afternoon away, it was opined that the priest had the good sense to leave Calatafimi far behind. But soon thereafter, his body, or the remaining parts of it, was found in a lime pit, after a sudden thunderstorm.

Occhipinti's tongue and hands were severed and his chest was crushed. His eyes had been crudely gouged, and above each ear a long rail spike had been driven into the temple at a telling angle. The remains of the priest's poor *sceccu* were also left in the pit. Its legs had been broken and its head bashed in.

At the funeral, only the priest's widowed mother wept as the mangled body was laid in unhallowed ground. There were no inquiries concerning his death. Official records indicated that Occhipinti accidentally fell into the lime pit during a severe storm.

*Cignu Russu* survived the surgery but not the shame. Three months passed before she would let her sympathetic sister-in-law, Giuseppina, who lived in Vita, bring Helena to see her at great risk. The widowed and childless aunt and her ward, Angelina, had taken Helena in permanently with Pippinu's blessing. But to him, and by extension, to them, his wife was dead.

Pippinu worked less and less and received few commissions. Girolamu left school and stayed at home with his father to help run the house. It was not pleasant. Pippinu had begun to drink a great deal of wine, but the wine did not make him drowsy and placid. Instead, it sharpened his anger and hatred, which soon spread from *Cignu Russu* to Girolamu.

"I have no peace: my marriage and my happiness are all gone because of you, you ugly, peeping snot! I didn't know about it and I was happy. What if she had been unfaithful for years? Pippinu was content. She warmed my bed, cooked my meals, raised my sons and daughters, kept my house in order. Only that goddamned priest! But he's dancing for Lucifer.

"But what am I to do, *caminari a pedi scausi supra na strata di spini nzinu a la morti?* (walk a thorny road with bare feet to my grave?) I want you out of my sight, you crooked little bastard! That's what you are, you know, a crooked devil-child. My brain burns and horns are searing through my scalp! There is no escape: sooner or later, they all betray their men. It's the feast of the cuckolds, again."

After such harangues, Pippinu would corner Girolamu and attack him, bellowing, *"T'ammazzu!"* But the wine would finally take effect and Pippinu could only manage to raise blue welts on Girolamu's face and shoulders before he collapsed into sleep.

One night, after Pippinu had exhausted himself trying to catch Girolamu and beat him, Girolamu tried unsuccessfully to drag his father to bed. But while in his father's bedroom, Girolamu found a bag on a table next to the bed. His curiosity would not let him put the bag down without examining its contents.

33

Girolamu removed a small carpenter's knife, a prayer book and a pair of familiar glasses with one cracked lens. Then he found something wrapped in yellow muslin. When he unraveled it, he saw what might have once been part of a human tongue and two eyeballs. Girolamu felt his whole body chill, as though he had been unexpectedly thrown into the local river on a February morning. He put the glasses and muslin in his pocket and the other contents back in the bag.

Girolamu always had Sunday dinner with Giuseppina, Angelina and his sister, Helena, walking the nine kilometers to and from Vita. At first, Pippinu joined Girolamu, but lately Pippinu slept off his wine on Sundays and couldn't bear the piety that permeated his sister's house. Girolamu, his aunt, Angelina and Helena were all grateful for the respite.

On one of those Sundays Giuseppina told Girolamu that she, Angelina and his sister were soon going to Palermo to see *Cignu Russu* in the hospital where she was convalescing. Girolamu insisted on going with them. He had longed to see his mother, despite hearing about the violence done to her. In Girolamu's memory, *Cignu Russu* remained the beautiful woman sighing in yellow muslin on his father's bed.

They left on a Saturday morning in a truck driven by Giuseppina's neighbor, Mommu, on the pretext of a journey to a holy shrine outside Palermo. They all saw *Cignu Russu*, scarred, black and blue all over and so thin from loss of blood and appetite, her hair only beginning to grow but without the old luster. They wailed and wept and were reconciled.

Then *Cignu Russu* turned to Girolamu who, despite her battered face and body, wanted desperately for her to call him to her arms and kisses. But her face became a ceramic mask. She shook from the emotion she felt and said in a cold, raspy voice, "You betrayed me! So to you, little Judas, I give the 'Evil Eye' for your evil eye, and wish you all the torment you have given my soul!"

*Cignu Russu* resisted all attempts by her sister-in-law and daughter to soften her heart towards Girolamu. She was adamant in the scorn she felt for her son. None of them knew that *Cignu Russu* had learned of Occhipinti's fate and turned her back on Girolamu from that moment when the spark and fuel of her secret fire died.

Girolamu stayed with his father a while longer, until the house and property became so run down that Pippinu accepted the first offer to buy them from a shrewd *padrone* looking to extend his local empire. He advised his sister that he planned to move to Palermo to be close to his married daughters. This he did, after arranging for his sons' bodies to be moved behind the *Madonna del Giubino Church*. A generous donation to the church assured their exhumation and reburial.

Giuseppina told him that Girolamu should go to America where he could live with their sister Caterina among caring family. Pippinu gave Giuseppina enough money for the passage for Girolamu and Angelina who would bring him, stay a while and return.

During those last weeks, Girolamu spent more and more time up in his cave. He started to spend nights there with the bats. They didn't bother him, and he fell into a fitful sleep to the sound of their high-pitched chatter. Rejected by his parents, Girolamu adopted the bats as his new family.

He was excited about going to America and being with all the Tommasos, but he feared he would never see his beloved mother again. For the first time in many months he prayed to the Holy Mother, asking her to intervene and convince *Cignu Russu* to become his loving mother again. ...

Girolamu spent much time on his passage to America thinking about his father and sisters, but *Cignu Russu* most often occupied his thoughts. He struggled to comprehend what had happened. A deep sorrow consumed him over what he'd done - not out of guilt, but for a loss he couldn't understand. Near the end of his journey, he turned in desperation to Dante. Girolamu recalled the lines he had committed to memory a year ago. He began to revel in the horrors of pain in the circles of hell that Dante recounted in the *Inferno*. While he didn't understand all of the words, the crimes and punishments were vivid and consoling to Girolamu. But when he remembered the pitiful story of Francesca, he thought of his mother and he wept and prayed for her forgiveness.

Girolamu repeated the lines over and over, until he fell asleep:

*"E quella a me: 'Nessun maggior dolore*
*che ricordarsi del tempo felice*
*ne la miseria ...'"*

"Then she to me: 'There is no greater sadness than remembering happy times in misery ...'"

# THE BLUE BUNNY

[Enter GHOST and HAMLET]
HAMLET  Where wilt thou lead? Speak; I'll go no further.
Ghost  Mark me.
HAMLET  I will.
Ghost  My hour is almost come,
  When I to sulphurous and tormenting flames
  Must render up myself. ...
  I am thy father's spirit,
  Doom'd for a certain term to walk the night,
  And for the day confined to fast in fires
  Till the foul crimes done in my days of nature
  Are burnt and purged away.
  But that I am forbid
  To tell the secrets of my prison house,
  I could a tale unfold whose lightest word
  Would harrow up thy soul, freeze thy young blood,
  Make thy two eyes, like stars, start from their spheres,
  Thy knotted and combined locks to part
  And each particular hair to stand on end,
  Like quills upon the fretful porpentine:
  But this eternal blazon must not be
  To ears of flesh and blood. ...

# SPAWN OF SENECA

Heavy rain swept the tar paper roofs of the tenements in patterns, like rhythms of a giant brush spreading a glossy coat. Lathem found it consoling. Looking out the top-floor apartment window of the kitchen to all the little back yards of this block of six-family dwellings in Brooklyn, Lathem believed that everyone was inside, like one large family at a table celebrating his birthday.

The radio atop a refrigerator blared out a news bulletin about "the death of Josef Stalin." Lathem's mother, Sonia, distracted by the radio report, looked up from her cup of coffee and smiled, raising the cup in salutation.

Sonia had been nauseous all morning and understood the signs with some dread. "You know the blue bunny didn't come until almost eleven o'clock, Lathem. We will sing 'Happy Birthday' in two more hours when my little Prince is ten."

The blue bunny had brought Lathem to his mother at the Wyckoff Heights Hospital at eleven o'clock. On his fifth birthday, Lathem's mother had told him the story, and she had told it every year thereafter.

"When mommy was a little girl in Warsaw, she learned how babies were brought to their mothers. Gray bunnies brought little boys to poor farmers; white bunnies brought little girls to poor farmers; but the blue bunny brought princes and princesses to royalty. Lathem, in his country, your father was a Prince, brought by the blue bunny, and you are a Prince because the blue bunny brought you to me. Thanks be to God." She made the sign of the cross and they said, "In the name of the Father and of the Son and of the Holy Ghost, Amen."

Some younger boys at school had been brought by storks or bright angels. Lathem, alone, had been brought by the blue bunny. The boys thought it queer and laughed at him. He had once overheard boys his age teasing the younger ones about not knowing that babies came from mothers' stomachs, "pissed" out from between their legs. Such thoughts made Lathem feel sick.

He would never again tell who had brought him. His schoolmate James was different. James liked the story of the blue bunny, and was happy Lathem was a prince. James' mother had told him he was brought by a "taxi driver." James and Lathem liked each other.

Lathem thought his mother was beautiful and loved to have her hold him close to her, but just when he started to enjoy the closeness, she would thrust him back from her and smile and he would wince: it wasn't her hair, fine and strawberry colored, nor her eyes, calm and dark blue; not her mouth, with thick, soft lips. It was her teeth. Every time, her smile reminded him of the once-white bathroom tile surrounded by yellow stains.

The smells of the bathroom and his mother's inspection of his naked body after the Saturday bath made his stomach hurt. His mother would sway him, asking "How's my little Prince?" and he would almost vomit.

"Lathem," his mother called to him from her chair, "come, let me hug my little Prince." He obediently walked into her embrace, resting his head on her left shoulder, looking away from her face. "Were you frightened last night, Lathem?"

"Yes, mommy, I couldn't fall asleep, thinking about today, and then I started to see shadows on the wall and they moved. I was afraid to sleep alone."

"Lathem, mommy put the night light in your room because you were afraid of the dark. There will always be some shadows." Sonia realized she sounded cross and softened her voice. "Were they the same shadows you saw all the other times?"

"Yes, mommy, the little crooked man with a hatchet came to chop my head off again." Lathem conjured up the horrid image in his mind, able, in the safety of his mother's arms, to flesh out the dark shadow and give the "bogeyman" a swarthy face and gnarled fingers holding an axe and a name he could not utter.

Sonia's eyes stared at the rain pelting the kitchen window. She wondered how she could possibly explain her condition to Lathem. In a few weeks she would begin to show and he would ask. She wanted to find a way to tell him, but not yet knowing how, she gently pressed him closer, whispering, "Mommy would never let anyone hurt you. And God will watch over you." Again, they made the sign of the cross and then Sonia held him closely.

Lathem felt bold in her embrace. "Why did you put me back in my bed?"

Sonia drew him out at arm's length, her muscles taut, and tried to subdue the look of danger that flowed from her deep blue eyes. "Lathem, Girolamu gets very angry when he finds you sleeping next to me. I had to put you in your bed before his alarm went off.

40

Here, let mommy fix your hair. It's almost time."

She took a jar from the bathroom cabinet and rubbed some scented pomade in Lathem's blonde hair. Then she combed a part on the left side and shaped a big wave from the part to his right temple. "Now find something to do for a while. Later we'll start the next chapter in your French reader."

Sonia was teaching Lathem how to read and speak French, which she said was the first language of European royalty. She knew several languages beside English. As an orphaned, Polish immigrant with charity status in 1936, Sonia learned English, Latin and French from the nuns at the Saint Mary Magdalene School in Brooklyn.

With an apparent gift for languages, she taught herself Italian, after deciding to become engaged to Girolamu. Lathem, she believed, had to be prepared for conversations with his mother that his father should not understand. In turn, Sonia spoke to Girolamu in Italian, when the discussion was not for Lathem's ears. She even learned Sicilian expressions Girolamu often used, although most of them were blasphemous.

Lathem pulled out a flat, oblong box from under his bed and emptied the contents on the coverlet. He selected a Hopalong Cassidy comic book. Hopalong was his most favorite hero of all. He didn't sing or romance girls like Gene Autry or Roy Rogers. Hoppy wore a black outfit and had white hair. He could get a dangerous look in his eyes that said a lot about him, a look Gene and Roy never showed, like a man who had secrets. Besides, Hoppy was a little older and wiser, like a father, and although he could be tough, he could also give you a smile that said everything was alright.

Lathem decided that if he could be a sidekick to any one of his western heroes it would be Hopalong Cassidy. Hoppy had a royal look about him. In his black outfit, sitting on Topper, his white Arabian horse, Hopalong Cassidy looked just like a knight from King Arthur's Round Table or a Prince might look, if he had lived in the American West.

When Hoppy appeared at Macy's department store in Manhattan last year, Lathem's mother took him by subway train on a Saturday morning. They waited on line for two hours for the thrill of shaking hands with Hopalong Cassidy. Each boy and girl received a small silver token with Hoppy's face on one side and Topper's on the other.

Lathem trembled with excitement as he approached Hoppy, set off from the crowd in a small corral, realizing that his hero was both older and handsomer than in his movies. When his turn came, Lathem and his mother entered the corral and Lathem offered up his unsteady hand. Hoppy took it firmly, smiling just for Lathem, and said, "Hello son, it's nice to meet you. Here's a gift from Hoppy.

Now you be good and take care of your mom. Goodbye." Lathem, overwhelmed by the authoritative but kindly baritone voice, uttered a barely audible, "I will. Goodbye, Hoppy." Cassidy's voice resonated in Lathem's head all through lunch at the automat and for the entire trip home.

Today, Lathem would celebrate his birthday with his mother, alone, for his father had died just before his birth and he hated his stepfather, Girolamu, who came to live with them two years ago. Girolamu was a short dark man who worked in cement all day--even Saturdays. He did things Lathem detested--like when he pinched Lathem's right cheek between his gnarled thumb and crooked index finger--or when he did the same thing to Sonia's behind.

On Sunday mornings, Girolamu had a bowl of wine and a loaf of fresh baked Italian bread for breakfast. He would break the bread into small pieces, while he mumbled something under his breath then dip the pieces into the bowl of wine until they turned purple.

Girolamu would offer a piece to Sonia who would angrily turn away. She would pull Lathem away, when Girolamu offered the same piece to the child. His offering rejected, Girolamu would get a strange gleam in his eye as he lifted up the piece of bread and said, "*Corpus Christi, Domine nostru Jesu Christi,*" and proceeded to chew the bread like a mule. Then he would laugh and mock Sonia by making the sign of the cross with his left hand as he said, "*In nomine Spirdu Santu et Figghiu et Patri, amen.*"

Every Sunday morning Sonia and Lathem would go to St. Bridget's Church for mass, and then they would light candles for the redemption of his father's soul. Sonia said that for every candle they lit, his father would be warmed when it was cold in Purgatory where he waited to be taken up to Paradise. She said that by the time Lathem was twenty-one, this would happen, so long as he lit the candles and said prayers for his father.

Every November second, All Soul's Day, they lit more expensive candles to shorten his father's stay in Purgatory. Lathem learned at religious instruction for his first Holy Communion that Purgatory was a mystical place where souls of the dead did penance for minor sins until Jesus brought them to Heaven.

Girolamu was working on Lathem's birthday. He could have arranged to be home but he told Sonia tenth birthdays were unlucky, as his had been. But Sonia remembered that the year before there had been a very unpleasant experience when Lathem turned nine. She was relieved that Girolamu would not be home.

Because hers had been a marriage of convenience, Sonia had found it difficult to deal with Girolamu's outburst of carnal passions, after nearly a year of sexual abstinence she had welcomed but did not impose.

Early in their marriage, even when tipsy from wine, Girolamu could not bring himself to so much as touch Sonia's hair, although he made gestures as if to do it. Eventually, as they lay in bed, he worked his way silently from a tentative caress of Sonia's thigh to pressing her buttocks between his legs. Girolamu wept silently at first, yet Sonia could feel his body trembling but did nothing, pretending to be asleep.

Gradually, she allowed him to do what he wished without having to face him. One night, with his head buried in Sonia's hair and his hand cupped around her breasts, Girolamu ejaculated into her buttocks, letting out a moan filled as much with pain as pleasure. Sonia got up to clean herself in silence.

About this time, Lathem celebrated his ninth birthday. Girolamu was home and drinking a lot of wine that day. For the first time, he told Sonia about his mother, Annunziata, called *Cignu Russu*. She was beautiful he said and had a special affection for "my little giant," as she called Girolamu.

Girolamu had come to America at age ten, after something horrible happened to his mother. He said no more, and he said nothing about his mother when sober. Girolamu never mentioned his father or siblings, merely saying he broke off relations with all his family in America when he was twenty-one and had become a naturalized American citizen.

"*Bon cumpleannu a tia,*" Girolamu said in his raspy voice, and pinched Lathem hard for his birthday and made him cry. Lathem ran screaming to the protection of his mother's arms. Girolamu whirled around in anger, stormed off to get his tool bag and returned to threaten them with a hand axe, bellowing in a cold, raspy voice, "*Buttana! M'adurnasti la casa? Mi facisti cornutu! Buttana! T'ammazzu!* I killa you - I killa you bote!"

Sonia, used to these outbursts, calmed Girolamu down and later explained to Lathem when she put him to bed, "Girolamu has a warm heart and he's an excellent provider, he takes good care of us. He says things he doesn't mean when he has too much wine to drink." She said this while holding Lathem to her breast so he could not see her troubled eyes and doubt the sincerity of her words.

Then for five minutes Sonia rocked Lathem in her arms, as she had done since he had begun to sleep in his own bed after her marriage. She rocked him until her warmth and the rhythmic sound of her body depressing and releasing the mattress springs eased Lathem into sleep.

In the middle of the night, Sonia awoke suddenly and muffled a frightened cry. Girolamu was breathing heavily and he threw the covers off the bed and rolled Sonia on her back. She closed her eyes and concentrated on Lathem's face, resigned to a clumsy and painful penetration.

To her relief, Sonia realized that Girolamu was not trying to enter her. She thought she had heard a noise in the next room, but couldn't move because Girolamu had pinned her against the headboard, his hands pressed against her breasts, his face and tongue driving noisily into her belly.

Lathem had been awakened by the terrible nightmare about the crooked "bogeyman." He got out of bed sobbing and frightened and instinctively moved to the door to his mother's bedroom, but found it locked when he tried to turn the knob. Then he heard moaning and a sound that chilled his body like when some boys stuffed ice and snow inside his coat and down his back one winter. It was the sound of a mattress rhythmically groaning.

Lathem stopped crying and tried to fight off an image that began to emerge in his imagination. He suddenly felt sick and ran to the bathroom and vomited down the toilet bowl. Lathem washed out his mouth and went back to bed with his hands on his ears, then he covered his head with the quilt and thought about Hopalong Cassidy until he fell asleep.

Sonia was too tense to feel any gratification and moaned with relief when Girolamu's body went slack as he straddled her leg. She felt liquid running down her thigh and Girolamu's warm breath on her belly. Now she relaxed and reached down, clasping both hands behind Girolamu's head. But it wasn't his head she pressed against her and squeezed between her thighs, until she fell into a reverie.

Later, Sonia got up quietly and went to the bathroom to clean herself. She passed Lathem who was breathing quietly in his sleep. On the way back to her bed, she kissed Lathem's forehead.

Lathem put his comic books away and returned to the window to look out at the rain. He sighed loud enough for his mother to hear. "Lathem, why don't you play with your *Tom Mix Lariat?*" The head of shining blonde hair nodded from side to side. "What about your *Captain Midnight Mystery Code-o-Graph?*"

Lathem turned to his mother and said, "It's broke!" He would not cry but she remembered that he had been angry and hurt because Girolamu had stepped on the premium toy and hadn't even apologized. "I wish my ring would come," he said. "It's almost four weeks."

Sonia had been saving the ring for his birthday. It had arrived earlier in the week, before Lathem had come home from school. "Lathem, mommy has a surprise for you." She returned from her bedroom with a small oblong package the size of a box of wooden kitchen matches but not as thick.

Lathem's eyes glowed at the sight of the small brown box. He handled it like a bar of gold bullion, feeling its heft. He knew that *Straight Arrow* had kept his promise. Lathem let the excitement run through him, enjoying that moment of wonder, when you possess something you're not yet able to imagine. "Mommy, I'd like a bowl of shredded wheat, please," he said.

Sonia gave Lathem his cereal and made herself a cup of hot water with sugar and bay leaves to relieve her heartburn. She looked at her son for a moment, at the soft, blue eyes, long lashes and thick brows that dominated his face. They were his father's hallmark and had first aroused Sonia.

"How should I believe such a story, Mr. Yarmolinsky?" she said to the young man she had first met in her place of business. He had come to repair her typewriter. Now they were lunching on Delancey Street in Manhattan. "Look in my eyes, Sonia, and tell me if I am lying." How should a young Catholic girl from Poland believe anything she heard on Delancey Street. But Lathem Yarmolinsky had been very persuasive.

"At the time of the revolution," he continued, "my family had governed the Borenko Principality in White Russia for five generations. They were Princes and Cossacks. I was next in line of succession. Then the revolution came and my family was all executed. At the age of two, loyal servants smuggled me out and brought me here to live with relatives."

Sonia smiled demurely, saying, "And how did you know such things as a child of two?"

"When I reached my majority," Yarmolinsky said, "I received

official papers establishing my lineage and my rightful claim to
the Principality. Of course, I could never return to Borenko. There
is still an outstanding order for my immediate execution by the
Communist Regime."

Sonia looked into Yarmolinsky's blue eyes and believed him,
even though the papers he showed her were in Russian and beyond
her immediate comprehension. Years later, Sonia, using her gift for
learning languages, studied some Russian and found the papers
somewhat misleading and inconclusive. She put them away, and

47

then determined that Yarmolinsky was a lovable opportunist who should spend many years in Purgatory, and she would see to it.

"Lathem, finish your cereal," Sonia said, when she saw that he had left a piece of soggy biscuit in his dish. We don't waste any food - you know there are children starving in Europe."

Lathem did not know any such thing, but he had come to believe it because his mother repeated the remark if he left so much as a crumb of food in his dish. Lathem ate the last mouthful and put the dish in the sink, as he had always been told to do. Sonia caught him up in her arms again, saying, "You're such a good boy, Lathem."

Sonia made herself another cup of hot water with sugar and bay leaves and looked out at the teeming rain: although nearly ten o'clock, the sky remained dark. Again, she considered how to tell Lathem she was going to have a baby. Sonia wasn't happy about it, but Girolamu had, in his crude way, made it clear he wanted his own child and she could no longer deny him.

"Why did you think I would be unhappy, Sonia?" Yarmolinsky asked.

"I didn't want to have a child in wartime. I'm afraid for it and us," Sonia said.

Yarmolinsky held his wife closely. "There is no bad time to bring children into the world. Just think, in his lifetime he may be able to reclaim Borenko and reign a Prince in my motherland."

After wiping a bit of bay leaf from her tongue with her napkin, Sonia bit her lower lip, then said, "Lathem, please come here. Mommy wants to talk to you."

Sonia had decided to use a direct approach with Lathem. She had something important to tell him, she whispered. Sonia had said nothing to Girolamu. She had not yet seen her doctor, but Sonia was fairly certain she had been "caught" because she and Girolamu had relations thirty-eight days ago, shortly after her last period.

Now she was two weeks late for the first time since she had been expecting Lathem. Sonia had worn a heavy Tampax under her nightgown for the last ten days, so Girolamu would leave her alone. She didn't want him to know until she had sorted things out, and gotten a sense as to how Lathem would take the news.

"He died bravely, Mrs. Yarmolinsky," the young army adjutant nervously explained to Sonia, handing her a little box that contained a Purple Heart Medal. She didn't hear his words. She put her hands on her swollen belly and thought, Dear God, why

48

have you filled me with life only to visit me with death? Please give me a son for my pains: his father's son.

"Lathem, *Aimerais tu avoir un petit frere ou une soeur?* Would you like to have a little brother, or sister, come to live with us?" Sonia asked again.

The subject had never been broached before and Lathem had no immediate thoughts about it. Maybe it would be nice to have a baby in the family. But Lathem hadn't shared anything with anyone but his mother and sometimes with his friend, James. She had centered her attention on him alone, until Girolamu came - and still Sonia doted on Lathem. What would happen if another child came to live with them? He said, "I don't know. I mean, *Je ne sais pas.*"

Sonia pushed him gently out at arms-length and looked at him intently, believing he must need some reassurance of his prominence in the family. "Lathem, my little Prince, I think the gray or white bunny is going to bring us a little brother or sister for you."

"Not the blue bunny?" he asked with a touch of surprise and hopefulness.

"No," Sonia replied. "Remember the blue bunny only brings princes and princesses to royalty. Someday, when you have children of your own, the blue bunny will bring them to you because you are a Prince."

A thought tried to form in Lathem's mind but was beyond his capacity to define. "*Quand viendra le lapin gris ou blanc,*" he asked.

Sonia pulled him back into her arms with a sense of relief, saying, "*Pas pour pres de neuf mois.*"

Lathem, too, felt relief: nine months - a long time. "*Je peux attendre,*" he said. Sonia squeezed him and kissed his forehead. "Mommy loves you, Lathem. Don't ever forget that, my little Prince."

Lathem went back to his bed and pulled out another box from underneath containing a large pad of white paper and a sharpened number 2 pencil. Drawing had become one of Lathem's favorite pastimes. Often in the evenings, after finishing his homework, he would lie on his bed and draw pictures of a secret place, a cave you entered beneath a river where he would swim from time to time to be alone.

In that cave rested a solid silver box and that box contained something he alone in the world possessed. What the box contained was never absolute because it changed. But that something which belonged to him made him able to face all the things in life he feared, even Girolamu, knowing it waited always there for him, gleaming and pure and perfect.

Today, on his tenth birthday, Lathem would add another chapter to his adventures because when he opened his secret box he would find a *Straight Arrow Golden Nugget Ring*. The nugget sat high on a gold band and a tiny lens on the side of the nugget provided a view of the Indian's hidden gold mine and secret cave. There the golden Palomino Fury waited for his master and Straight Arrow made golden arrows, the arrows of justice.

Digitally created by Michael Corso from author's private collection. "Golden Nugget" ring in silver box, belonging to Lathem Tommaso, 1953.

For a moment, Lathem's train of thought reverted to the image of Sabu, as the little thief of Bagdad, who had also used the golden arrow of justice. With it he killed the evil Grand Vizier Jaffar who wanted to steal the beautiful Princess from Ahmad, the man she loved. *The Thief of Bagdad* was one of Lathem's favorite movies.

He and James sat through it twice one Saturday last year at the Rivoli, which showed only old movies until the evening. They managed to change seats and avoid the fat "matron" in white with her flashlight who herded the children out after each show.

At half past 10 o'clock, Sonia put on her raincoat. "Lathem, mommy's going down to Nudelman's bakery to get tea biscuits and apple turnovers." They were his favorites. "Why don't you take a nap, I'll lock the door."

Lathem put his pad and pencil away and lay down on his bed and the rhythm of the rain on the roof made him drowsy and he closed his eyes. The sound of the rain gradually trailed off, then stopped.

Sunlight burst out yellow-bright like the huge lamp the photographer had used the day before for his ten-year-old picture. Lathem was drawn to the window. He heard birds singing as they flew, making shrill sounds like the scales of a flute. Eventually, a rainbow emerged, arching over the back yards like a giant slice of the multicolored confection he paid a penny for at Hymen's candy store on Knickerbocker Avenue.

Lathem opened the kitchen window and leaned over the wooden safety bar to take in the glistening-wet fig trees which dotted the yards. Fresh figs were his favorite fruit. He could taste their soft, purple-red and sweet centers just by looking at the budding branches, hidden under sheets, paper and curved linoleum for the winter. Now he could smell the clean scent of *grass-after-rain*, something fresh and green. He had to shade his eyes as he looked up to the sky which had become a transparent blue.

Something flew past Lathem into the kitchen. It lighted upon the spout protruding from the sink and looked like a crumpled piece of blue-tinted paper the size of a small pocket handkerchief. But it moved. Lathem wasn't afraid; often he had played in the back yard with ants and worms and once with a small mouse.

He cupped his hands and scooped the object from the spout. It came willingly. Lathem crossed from the kitchen into the next room, which served as his bedroom, and sat on his bed to view

51

the object away from the bright light. As he opened his hands, the object unruffled into the distinct shape of a pale blue butterfly whose wings were segmented and floppy.

Amazed, Lathem bent down to look more closely, when the butterfly hopped down the crevice between the bed and the wall to the floor. Lathem bounced from the bed to the floor, lifted the draped coverlet, and lying on his left ear, stared into the darkness.

He blinked as his eyes adjusted, then opened his mouth in awe. Two bright eyes stared back at him. "Come here, little fella," he said as he stretched his left arm out to its fullest length, beckoning with his fingers, "I won't hurt you. Honest!" The eyes slowly grew bigger and Lathem felt something warm, moist and furry brush against his fingertips.

Although perplexed, Lathem moved back to give it room to continue forward. As it neared the edge of the bed and light, Lathem stared in absolute wonder, confronted with a miraculous metamorphosis: a blue bunny.

Lathem drew the bunny into his cradled arms and up to his face to feel the touch of blue fur. He sniffed the pleasing scent of white powder and baby oil. How strange, he thought. It didn't make a sound. Only its blue eyes flashed when Lathem held it closer to him. Lathem admired the long, floppy ears, segmented like the butterfly's wings. He was so happy with this surprise, the best one since his mother had given him three little yellow chicks to care for on his fifth birthday.

Suddenly, the bunny bolted from Lathem's arms into the next room, his mother's bedroom. Lathem moved after it quickly, but saw nothing as he scanned the darkened room and then the bed where he had lain in his mother's arms the night before. Lathem remembered the warmth of her body going through his thin pajamas to his back and legs as he fell asleep in the soft cradle of her breasts and belly.

When he switched on the table lamp, he noticed a lump in the middle of his mother's bed, between two pillows and under the covers near the headboard. He carefully sat on the bed and inched closer to the lump. Spreading the pillows apart, Lathem was amazed to see the face of a child, a fair-skinned baby with dark blue eyes. Was it a prince or a princess?

The blue-eyed baby did not stir or make a sound, but the eyes flashed as Lathem carefully pulled down the cover. The child wore a little dress of light blue, trimmed with white lace. Lathem lifted the dress and looked between its legs. It was not a prince! It must be a girl, a princess, although he wasn't sure because often he had put his bare feet under his mother's nightgown as he curled up in bed beside her and he felt warm fur between her legs.

Lathem wanted to lift the baby from the bed and hold it close and kiss it. As he leaned over the baby he saw a shadow appear on the wall above the bed. It was a crooked little man holding a hatchet above his head. Suddenly, the shadow spoke in a cold, raspy voice, *"Buttana! M'adurnasti la casa? Mi facisti curnutu! Buttana! T'ammazzu!* I killa you - I killa you bote!" Trembling, Lathem stared at the shadow which seemed to move closer to the baby.

"Here, son, use this!" a deep baritone voice called from the entrance to the bedroom.

Lathem turned to see Hoppy smile and toss him a golden crossbow, primed with a golden arrow. Lathem took the bow in mid-flight, aimed and shot the arrow into the shadow. The shadow tried to wriggle free but the arrow pinned it against the wall. It soon stopped moving and then disappeared.

"I killed you!" Lathem said in a voice dark with feelings he did not understand. He turned to thank Hoppy but Cassidy had disappeared.

Sabu about to shoot golden arrow of justice into Jafar's head. *The Thief of Bagdad*, 1940.

Just then, Lathem heard a noise from the kitchen. Was mommy back? He turned and listened, hearing what he thought sounded like water flushing in the bathroom. Forgetting the baby and crossbow, Lathem moved slowly back toward the kitchen, on tip toes, afraid to know what had made this noise.

He realized now that the sound was the bath tub swallowing the dirty water after a bath. "Mommy?" he called. There was no answer. He darted back to his mother's bedroom. The baby, the crossbow and the arrow were gone. Lathem was shaken, disappointed and puzzled, as he returned to the kitchen.

After a moment he heard a laugh, a girl's high-pitched laugh he had heard at school countless times. It, too, came from the bathroom. It frightened him. He moved toward the closed bathroom door. Another trill of laughter pierced his ears. He knocked lightly on the door with a trembling hand: silence, then more laughter. Lathem gingerly turned the doorknob and quickly pulled it open and was immediately engulfed in wet steam. He fell back on his heels.

Recovering, Lathem stared into the evaporating mist and gasped in astonishment! She stood in the tub, tall, dripping, glistening, white, and naked. Not a child, but not yet a woman like his mother.

Her face turned to him, freezing him with eyes the deep silver-blue of anthracite coals he had admired at the Brooklyn Museum. She had breasts like his mother but they were just beginning to swell to lavender nipples. As she put her right hand up to her hip like a jug handle, her legs parted and Lathem could see wisps of strawberry fur.

"Who are you?" Lathem whispered. The girl flashed her phosphorescent eyes and moved them peripherally right, as if in warning. Lathem heard a noise in the hall and the jingling of keys. "Mommy," he thought, "Oh no!" The girl turned and faced Lathem, beckoning him to her. Then she spread her legs and put her hands on her hips, throwing back her head with its wet, dark red hair. Lathem's heart tried desperately to punch its way out of his chest.

"What should I do?" He rushed into the bathroom, slamming the door behind him, as another cadenza of laughter rang out and a key turned in a lock. The girl pulled Lathem into the tub and the soft cradle of her breasts and belly.

Something seized Lathem's stomach, violently contracting his abdomen. It seemed like all the fluids in his body suddenly burst out of every orifice and every pore in his skin, like the spray from an open "johnnie pump," leaving him drained. Then Lathem was standing in the tub, alone, soaked from head to toe, his hands spread across the yellow-stained wall tile.

Sonia walked in singing out "Happy birthday, Lathem, my Prince!" He straightened up in bed, rubbing his eyes, disappointed yet glad to see her. Sonia put her package down on the kitchen table and ran to hang her dripping raincoat in the bath tub to dry. Then she came to Lathem's bed and drew him into her arms against her soft chest, damp with rain.

He too was wet, clinging to her, and Sonia clasped him closer, murmuring, "My dear baby ... my Prince ... my baby ... happy birthday." When she thrust him back from her and smiled, Lathem blinked his eyes then smiled back. After a moment, he kissed his mother on the lips, and she laughed, kissing him back. Sonia beamed as she said, "Thanks be to God."

Lathem put his left hand on his mother's, which lay across her belly, and raised his right hand as in a benediction and made the sign of the cross slowly, speaking in a new, confident voice, *"Au nom du Pére et du Fils et du Saint-Esprit. Amen"*

# THE WHITE BUTTERFLY

# M'APPARÌ

M'apparì tutt' amor,
il mio sguardo l'incontrò
bella sì che il mio cor,
ansioso a lei volò;
mi ferì, m'invaghì
quell' angelica beltà,
sculta in cor dall'amor
cancellarsi non potrà;
il pensier di poter
palpitar con lei d'amor,
può sopir il martir
che m'affanna e strazia il cor.

M'apparì tutt'amor,
il mio sguardo l'incontrò;
bella si che il mio cor
ansioso a lei volò;
Marta, Marta tu sparisti
e il mio cor col tuo n'andò!
tu la pace mi rapisti,
di dolor io morirò.

## SHE APPEARED TO ME

She appeared to me, all full of love,
My gaze met with her image
so lovely that my heart
yearningly flew toward her;
her angelic beauty
wounded me, made me fall in love,
sculpted in my heart by love,
it can never be erased.
the thought of being able
to share my love with her
can soothe the pain
that troubles me and tears my sheart.

She appeared to me, all full of love,
my gaze met with her image,
so lovely was she that my eager heart,
yearningly flew toward her;
Marta, Marta, you disappeared
And my heart just followed yours!
You've taken away my peace,
I will surely die of pain.

# SPAWN OF OVID

## "... This Thing of Darkness I [*Don't*] Acknowledge Mine"

William Shakespeare, *The Tempest*

*Signore e signori, benvenuti a bordo di questo volo Alitalia 687, servizio non-stop da JFK all'aeroporto Leonardo da Vinci, Fiumicino..."*

My mother, Sonia, told me when I was nine years old that on the day of my birth, November 11, 1953, my father, Girolamu, came to the hospital maternity ward "stinking drunk." He had begged her to have her doctor induce labor and deliver a few days before Armistice Day. She knew why he asked, but would not alter nature's course.

Mom was exited and wanted him to know that, in addition to being healthy, I had a distinct black mole on my chest, which she said resembled an Egyptian scarab, a sign of royal lineage. She had told Lathem, my half-brother, who was ten and at our bedside, that he had the lineage of a White Russian Prince. Lathem was Mom's son from a prior marriage. His father was dead.

Sonia was prone to much fantasy about modern European royalty and ancient Pharaonic succession. Pop was more down to earth. His first wine-soaked words, as he burst into the room, were "*Dov'è questo meraviglioso bambino? Lasciatemi vedere mio figlio!*" Pop looked at me and laughed, saying "*O Dio crudele!*" He came closer to the bed and Mom made a gesture for him to hold me. He recoiled, snapping, "What a brute! It has such a beastly face, like a little brown *surici* with a long, hairy nose and big ears. Does it have a tail, too? This is not my son!" Of course, this rant was delivered in a mixture of the Italian and Sicilian languages, which both my parents spoke. Pop's English was not very good.

After my Mom's implied infidelity was publicly declared, Pop bolted for the exit. Mom had clutched me closely to her breast, and that is the only thing I'm sure I sensed at the time. ...

"Ladies and gentlemen, welcome aboard Alitalia's flight 687 from New York's JFK airport to Rome's Leonardo DaVinci at Fiumicino. We especially welcome business class passengers to our new Magnifica Class service which includes flat-bed accommodations and five star dining service, most capably delivered by our friendly and efficient stewardesses. ..."

In later years, as a teenager, Pop's family's accounts to me of my resemblance to the old man were summed up by: "You're the spitting image of him." The son-of-a-bitch didn't fully accept me as his son until Mom died twelve years later.

On my birthday, as he ran from the maternity ward, he screamed for all to hear: "What a curse! It's the feast of the cuckolds, again." And he was right.

I sit comfortably on the Alitalia flight to Rome. Pop is in the hold of the plane, returning to his homeland for the last time. He is to be buried in a narrow plot with his beloved mother, Annunziata, Helena, Tommaso, known as *Cignu Russu*.

I now had the leisure time to reflect on my life, while we were en route to Palermo from Rome and, eventually, to Calatafimi. Looking back at the past at different points in one's life seems to be a universal preoccupation, especially in times of emotional stress.

A colleague of mine in graduate school summed it up best, I thought: "We live the first half of our lives as best we can, and then spend the second half reexamining, or trying to relive, the first half." Perhaps Fitzgerald said it most poetically in *Gatsby*: "So we beat on, boats against the current, borne back ceaselessly into the past."

In my case, I was also trying to resolve my feelings for two women: Rachel, my American friend and lover, and the mother of our child, Sylvia; we are not married; and Marta, my Sicilian beauty, whom I have craved and lusted for in a fantasy of over thirty-four years; she was just widowed.

So, this memoir that I'm piecing together constitutes an expedition into my past, an autobiographical journey of excavation: it also concerns the present and the hoped for resolution of my love-life issues. Perhaps by holding them in tandem and looking back for lessons learned to apply forward, I'll be able to resolve the current dilemma.

I have read that writing "biography" is a misdemeanor offence, but that writing "autobiography" is a felony. We shall see.

Personally, I always use Mark Twain as an example of what works best for me: Twain successfully published the autobiography of President Grant; other books of a similar nature, but without the same popularity, caused his publishing company to fail.

But what we've seen of Twain's own autobiography, which was not published in his lifetime, is a loosely held together narrative which jumps all over the place. Twain's initial approach was to "Start at no particular time of life. Wander at your free will all over your life; talk about the thing that interests for the moment; drop it at the moment its interest starts to pale." Yet it is the most wonderful memoir of its kind I ever read.

It has not been without its critics still it is brimming with Twain's inimitable, good humor and wisdom about American life by one of its sharpest observers and satirists.

So, as we learned in John Ford's film, *The Man Who Shot Liberty Valence*: "When the legend becomes fact, print the legend." Hell, it worked very well for Ronald Reagan.

The first order of business was to organize my material. After some thought, I returned to Fitzgerald: he had outlined actual sources for the nine chapters in *Gatsby* on the endpaper of Andre Malraux's *Man's Hope* in 1938. I had my original copy of *Gatsby* with me, so why not try something similar.

Here I pause briefly to note that the novel is with me because I intend to embark on my 75th reading of the text in twenty-five years, since I became a *Gatsby Groupie*.

For over twenty years I have offered courses at community colleges in New York State on Fitzgerald and *The Great Gatsby* and Hammett and *The Maltese Falcon*, among others. Most often it was "*Green Light/Black Bird*: Fictional Symbols of the Elusive American Dream." I taught in Queens and Nassau Counties in what was a part-time career for me.

My dog-eared copy of *Gatsby* has a couple of blank pages before Chapter I, but I cheated by taking out my little notebook and scribbling in material. I then edited and neatly entered my final thoughts to the blank pages in the novel: for posterity, of course. I labored for a good hour and here is my distillation:

The 1950s: <u>Decade of Adventure and Discovery</u>
The 1960s: <u>Decade of Death and Rebirth</u>
The 1970s: <u>Decade of Liberation</u>
The 1980s: <u>Decade of The French Connection</u>
The 1990s: <u>Decade of Social Eruption and Baptiste's Choice</u>
The New Millennium: <u>Sing: I Am (Bushed) by the Supremes</u>

Then I ordered dinner. I chose *Prosciutto e melone*, then *Rigatoni a la Norma*, followed by *Veal francaise*. I requested a half-bottle of *Chianti Classico*, 1999 vintage and a bottle of *Acqua minerale con gas*; no coffee or dessert: just *Gatsby* and that mysterious green light.

## SONGS FROM
## THE THIEF OF BAGDAD (1940)

Sea song
I never know why men come back from sea
The sea is cruel, but the sea is free
The cause of this vast purity must be
That men at sea are few and far between

Hardship is all she ever gave to me
And yet I ask why men come back from sea
The sea is cruel, but the sea is clean
Oh, poor brown earth, how kind you might have been.


I want to be a sailor
I want to be a sailor, sailing out to sea
No plough-boy, tinker, tailor's any fun to be
Aunts and cousins
By the banker's dozens
Drive a man to sea or highway robbery!

I want to be a bandit, can't you understand it?
Sailing the sea is life for me,
is life for me.

# The 1950s
## Decade of Adventure and Discovery

## Who/Where Did I Come From?

At the present age of forty-seven and one-half, I find myself at a loss for many vivid memories of my very early life, or any lineage tracing my forebears back more than three generations. In place of a completely fabricated tale full of fantasy, I submit the following quasi-scientific, genealogically broad statement of my origins.

The very first human diaspora was not a single event during a single epoch. It was the evolutionary march of *homo sapiens* out of Africa, and in all directions, about fifty thousand years ago.

I gave a DNA sample to a study of the male Y chromosome at Stanford University several years ago. A geneticist, Dr. Cavalli-Sforza, reported to me that my male Tommaso ancestors migrated from east Africa to the Iberian Peninsula, some forty to fifty thousand years ago.

He concluded this (pardon my oversimplification) because every male parent passes the Y chromosome intact to every male child he fathers, going back to number one. So my male forbears belonged to an African tribe that spoke a "click-click" language. It's possible.

Less scientific history tells me that a *Sicani* tribe wandered from the Iberian Peninsula to invade Sicily several thousand years ago. The *Sicani* became the oldest inhabitants of the island with a recorded name. Eventually, other tribes called Elymians and Sicels came from the west and east of the island to lock the *Sicani* in the middle, around one-thousand BCE.

Twenty-five hundred years later, as confirmed by modern history, Princes of Aragon and Madrid, from the emerging nation we know as Spain, ruled Sicily for four centuries. By that time, Spanish culture had been saturated by a vital Arab presence.

The Arabs had already established themselves on the western side of Sicily before the Aragonese began to rule in the thirteenth century. In fact, the town of Calatafimi rose in the twelfth century during the Arabic period. The city's Arabic name was *Kalat-al-Fimi* then.

What does all this mean? Actually, it means very little. It hasn't a feather's worth of reliable narrative. But, for millennia before and after Jesus of Nazareth, many colonizing peoples came, saw and conquered Sicily, making it the most bastardized of places.

In fact, Sicily became the crossroads where a sea of mixed gene pools washed up upon the land to continue their evolutionary journey from muck to man. Today, as a result of this extraordinary crossbreeding, Sicilians are truly citizens of the world.

Ergo, for centuries the Tommaso DNA could have been lurking in the bloodstreams of the vilest scum of the earth, or merely slaves, servants, peasants, farmers or other miserable peoples who groveled in chains, begging for the invisible largess of the aristocracy. The chances of royal blood in my DNA are infinitesimal, unless some royal cock created another bastard by crowning the mother's husband with horns.

And who's to say my ancestors did not worship Allah and read the Koran instead of the Bible? With a few different paths taken, I could be Abdullah Hussain instead of Jerome "Silvio" (my Godfather's name): although the Arabic "beautiful servant of God" would be a stretch for me. My complexion is dark and my hair black and curly. My features are perhaps those that only my mother could truly love: especially my blonde, blue-eyed, fair-skinned, mother. I see that this reads like a diatribe against the uses of fiction and fantasy. If so, I need to make a correction. My brother, Lathem and I were children of fiction and fantasy, entirely because of our mother, Sonia. I realize I need to put my child's memory back in place. Too much of my youth's faith in the imagined world has worn away for me to be subjective anymore. So, let's try again.

Mom said she believed her sons came from royal lineage. As children, we two believed it as well. Lathem was brought by a royal blue bunny with claims to a White Russian Princedom lost to Stalin.

I was an ancestor of the child floating in a basket down a tributary of the Nile into the doomed court of Akhenaten: found by a barren woman and raised as her son to be a shepherd. He bore a black mole on his chest resembling a scarab (as I do) and was destined to bring the wisdom of monotheism to the Jews. You see, harmless.

## The Thief of Bagdad

What was extraordinary was that Lathem and I bolstered each other's memories of epiphanies first experienced by Lathem, then experienced by me and re-experienced by him. For example, he saw Korda's film *The Thief of Bagdad* (1940) when he was eleven, with Mom and his best friend, James (1954).

When I was eight (1961), Mom, he and James took me to see the film at The Thalia Theatre, a revival movie house in Manhattan. It was an overwhelming experience: the story, the mechanical toys, Sabu, the thief, Conrad Veidt's Jaffar, Rex Ingram's Genie, the sets, the costumes, the color and, perhaps most of all, the music.

I instantly became a lifelong fan of Miklos Rozsa (as were Lathem and James), whom I did not know by name. But his musical signature animates films as diverse as, *Knight Without Armor, The Lost Weekend, Spellbound, The Red House, Quo Vadis, The Naked City, Double Indemnity, A Double Life, Julius Caesar* and *Ben Hur*, among so many others.

Perhaps the most insightful comment about the *Thief* score came from a *Films In Review* article published after the picture was released, which I found years later. The piece referenced Max Steiner's music for the film *King Kong* as analogous to Rozsa's, in that each score resembled a "symphony accompanied by a movie." In the case of *Thief*, Rozsa's score is so full of vocal music and Wagnerian-style leitmotifs that an "opera" would be a more apt referent than a symphony.

Operas are traditionally filled with larger than life characters, exhibiting extreme emotions through music created from a grand and colorful palette of solo songs, duets and choral pieces.

However, *Thief* is not an opera but a melodrama which uses dramatic music very effectively. Let me briefly explain the difference, using a single opera to make the point.

Puccini's *Turandot* (1926), is arguably the last opera masterpiece in the Great Tradition of Italian opera, composed between 1775 and 1924, when Puccini died. This opera looked back to Italian Romantic *melodramma*, typified by Verdi's *Aida*. It was the end of this type of *melodramma* which helped pave the way for films, first silent, then with sound and music, which appropriated the *melodramma* for mass consumption. The following quotations from a book on *Turandot* make this connection clear.

> In nineteenth-century *melodramma* it was for the
> music to provide the tragic events. The deepening
> of character, and then with Verdi, of emotional, political
> and musical events. It was for melody, timbre,
> harmony to give a tragic sense to the banal verses ...

From *Andrea Chenier* onward, the functions are
reversed: the plot comes to the fore; the "story-
telling" [*romanzesco*] seizes the attention, while
the music declines to a subsidiary task ...
Comparison with the immanent stylistics of
commercial cinema, which provoke tears and laughter
using devices whose efficacy is proportional
to their elementarity, proves once again opportune.

(W. Ashbrook & H. Powers: *Puccini's Turandot: The End of The
Great Tradition*, Princeton, New Jersey, 1991, p. 7)

... if the operas of the Great Tradition are
in one sense **museum pieces**, nonetheless they
cannot be hung on walls; like other manifestations
of the temporal arts, they must be produced ...
Italian opera in the Great Tradition lives
on in production – and in the affections of the
opera-going public the tradition shows no signs of
coming to an end. ...

But if the Great Tradition has survived in that
sense, with the great opera houses of the
world as its museums ... its latter day socio-cultural
role was absorbed by another medium. As Rubens
Tedeschi has pointed out, it was no coincidence
that the last decades of grasping after vital
new work in the Great Tradition coincided with
the first decades of the movies.

(W. Ashbrook & H. Powers: *Puccini's Turandot: The End of The
Great Tradition*, Princeton, New Jersey, 1991,   p.4)

... Before the spread of the film, the genres were
ready – adventurous, spectacular, pathetic – and
the recipes to cook them were in place, the principle
– the doling out of effects – as well as the choice
of plots. The *melodramma*, in short, opened the way
for the film, which was to become, in the twenties
and afterwards, the *melodramma* for everybody....
(Rubens Tedeschi: Addio fiorito asil, Milan,1978, p.4)

The conclusion is that "Puccini's heirs, then, were D. L.[sic] Griffiths [sic] and Cecil B. De Mille ..." (Ashbrook & Powers, p.5) I would add to that list, among others, Victor Fleming, director of both *Gone With The Wind* and *The Wizard of Oz*, in 1939; Zoltan Korda, Ludwig Berger, Michael Powell and Tim Whelan, directors of *The Thief of Bagdad*, 1940; Busby Berkeley, director of *Gold Diggers of 1935*; Frank Capra, director of *It's a Wonderful Life*, 1946; Vncente Minelli, director of *An American in Paris*, 1951, and Francis Ford Coppola, director of the *Godfather* Trilogy released in 1972-1990.

So American's embraced something akin to opera but home-grown and low brow: the singing and dancing Hollywood musical comedy, exemplified by 1933's *42nd Street*. That film gave Americans a national, inexpensive and readily accessible kind of popular melodramatic entertainment, smack in the midst of the Depression.

The Hollywood operetta (McDonald and Eddy) with its last vestiges of European influence had a brief vogue during the 1930s and early 1940s. Such films as *Naughty Marietta* and *Rose Marie* helped many people smile through hard times but the dark clouds of war in Europe soon relegated them to quaint nostalgia.

Thanks to Hollywood, opulent American cinema theatres like The Roxie and Radio City Music Hall in Manhattan, New York City and Grauman's Egyptian and Chinese in Los Angeles, California, superseded The Metropolitan Opera House, and similar venues, as home to America's chosen mass media theatrical entertainment.

In the 1940s, it is estimated that half the American population went to the movies every week. That's about sixty million people laying out nine million dollars every week: four hundred fifty million a year. That's very popular and very lucrative *melodramma*. But establishing and sustaining colorful and indelible illusions about American life was never so cheap.

In my dad's youth, people paid fifteen cents to see the first run of *Gold Diggers of 1935*, a Busby Berkeley film with a score by Harry Warren and Al Dubin. The climax of the film was a long music and dance sequence featuring the song "The Lullaby of Broadway."

This sequence was imaginatively staged by Berkeley as a stand-alone scenario within the film. It reflected the influence of *avant-garde* German Expressionism on Berkeley's design. It is melodramatic and represents a new and unique American art form. "The Lullaby of Broadway" won the Oscar that year for best film song.

On the other hand, I read in an issue of *Opera News*, about thirty years ago, that the Metropolitan Opera's operating budget was greater than the cost of running most "third-world countries." Met ticket prices were "higher than the moon," which is exactly where we planted the American flag that same year.

Following *The Thief of Bagdad*, we all went to the automat for dinner. There, we feasted on pot pies, BLT and grilled cheese sandwiches, apple pie, milk and coffee. All the while we discussed the film enthusiastically.

There were two particular moments in the film I wished I could recall in detail. The first is when Sultan Ahmad pretends to be a Djinn (Genie) in the Princess's private gardens and they exchange the most romantic words; the second is when the Djinn takes Abu to steal the all-seeing Eye from a temple on the roof of the world. The Djinn describes the roof and its support then he describes where the all-seeing Eye is exactly.

We all put our heads together and through a herculean effort, spearheaded by Mom's and James' nearly photographic memories, we managed to write down what was said by the lovers and the Genie.

In this current age of electronic wizardry, I managed to obtain a laser disc copy of the film in the early 1990s. After multiple viewings, I was able to verify the incredible accuracy of our first effort. Anyway, here's the exchange between Ahmad and the Princess in her garden:

Princess: Who are you?
Ahmad: Your slave.
Princess: Where have you come from?
Ahmad: From the other side of time to find you.
Princess: How long have you been searching?
Ahmad: Since time began.
Princess: Now that you have found me, how long will you stay?
Ahmad: To the end of time. For me there can be no more beauty in the world but yours.
Princess: For me there can be no more pleasure in the world but to please you.

I committed those words to memory and used them on more than one occasion, to feed to, and respond to, young women. Of course, that was before the 1970s when women no longer tolerated such "sexist romantic bullshit" (their words not mine).

However, there were some women I met who still wanted to pleasure me. This began when "Wee Willy," had become *Gugghiermu lu Conquistaturi.* But that's in another "section."

A few years ago, I got an idea for a TV commercial for either fine watches and/or diamonds. The deal is the viewer would be looking at a knoll above a tranquil brook, all in black and white. The words quoted above would be spoken by one male voice and one female voice, just below the knoll but out of sight.

As the last words are spoken, the camera climbs over the knoll and we are in the suddenly Technicolor presence of two white-haired but handsome seniors, appropriately dressed. He is giving her a beautiful watch, or a diamond watch, or a diamond ring. Then there's a voice over talking about eternal love as they kiss. All that set to Rozsa's music. It brings tears to my eyes, every time I think about it.

The other sequence in *Thief* was between Abu and the Djinn flying to the place where the all-seeing Eye rests. Abu plans to steal it to find his friend Ahmad (they've been separated) and become a hero.

Abu: Where are we now?

Djinn: Above the roof of the world.

Abu: Has the world got a roof?

Djinn: Supported by seven pillars and the seven pillars are set on the shoulders of a Djinn, who's strength is beyond thought; and the Djinn stands on an Eagle; and the Eagle on a Bull; and the Bull on a Fish; and the Fish swims in the sea of Eternity. . . .

Abu: Where are we going?

Djinn: On the highest peak of the highest mountain of the world, where Earth meets the Sky. In there is the Temple of the Goddess and in the Great Hall is the Temple of Light where the Goddess sits; and in the head of the Goddess is the all-seeing Eye.

These lines are brought to life by the great Rex Ingram who excelled as the Djinn.

Lathem relived his first indelible viewing and somehow became another version of me but more articulate and animated. We were acting like identical twins, thanks to our Mom. I thought I had a preview of heaven that day. It could not get better than this. Of course, I was wrong.

# Beauty and the Beast

There was a second time this kind of synchronicity happened between Lathem and me. When Lathem was twelve (1955), he was watching a local independent channel 9, WOR-TV, one weekday after school to see a foreign language film. The channel showed 1940s Italian and French films due to limited live programming.

That particular day, a French film, Jean Cocteau's black and white version of *La Belle et la Bete* was shown. Lathem was excited because Sonia had been teaching him French for three years at home, and he was studying it at middle school as well that year. He understood from Mom that French was the language of European royalty (Czarist Russia) and the *Lingua franca* of international business transactions.

Lathem called to Mom and told her the film was on. She stopped what she was doing, checked to make sure I was still asleep (I was a deep sleeper), and went to sit beside him. Mom had never seen the film before.

There were many commercial interruptions, but English subtitles were furnished, so the actor's real voices and their French pronunciation were heard. What a delight the film was: a combination of reality (18$^{th}$ century French style) and fantasy with a beautiful, faithful Belle and a ferocious but kind Beast.

There was minimal dialogue still Lathem was so proud to hear the words and translate them in his head before looking at the subtitles. When the film neared the end and the Beast turns into the handsome Jean Marais who sweeps Josette Day's Belle up and away toward the sky, Lathem and Mom were frozen in an ecstasy forged by *cine-magical* fantasy.

They both began to cry and hugged each other in a moment of synchronistic emotion. They never forgot the experience.

Now we fast forward to 1962 when I was turning nine and Lathem and James were nineteen. Cocteau's film was appearing at The Thalia Theatre in Manhattan. Once again, the four of us trekked to the borough of beaux arts and settled in for another wonderful experience. The print being shown, the program read, was new and the film was full length with an improved sound track to highlight Georges Auric's musical score.

To say that we were all mesmerized for more than ninety

minutes would be a serious understatement. We were bewitched and enchanted by cinematic artistry at its best. The sets, costumes and human candelabras and fireplace figures that blow smoke into the room where Belle first meets the Beast, were better than anything I had seen in Disney films.

Although *Pinocchio*, which I had seen in 1960, as part of a Disney retrospective, was still my favorite; I enjoyed *Snow White, Cinderella* and *Song of the South*. But it was Jiminy Cricket and his song, "When You Wish Upon a Star" that always got to me.

Truthfully, *Pinocchio* was easier to understand for a seven year old than some of the stuff my nine year old brain was wrestling with from *La Belle at la Bete*. I did enjoy Auric's atmospheric music which added another dimension to the film. Years later, Disney's animated version of the same tale, borrowed a few things from Cocteau's film.

As we headed for the inevitable automat, the adults I was with were still emotionally exhausted, dropping comments like "profound," "unmatchable," "not for young children" and *"Saviez-vous qu'ils sont vraiment amoureux?"*

This last remark from James caught Mom unawares and she automatically replied *Josette et Jean?* James countered with *"Non, Marais et Cocteau!"*

Lathem went into a spasmodic crouch, bellowing laughter I had never heard from him before. Mom put on a nonplussed face and shook her head. I put on an idiotic grin, looked around and started to whistle *La Marseillaise*.

Having laid this scatter-shot foundation for the Tommasos of Brooklyn, New York, I will now proceed with my life's story as I have been told of it and as I recall it. I intend to focus on events that were most memorable to me, meaning those that concerned my family both in America and Sicily.

As Margo Channing said: "Fasten your seat belts: it's going to be a bumpy night."

## SO DEAR TO MY HEART

So dear to my heart
That September-y day
When that old shady lane we strolled
Was just turning scarlet and gold
So dear to my heart

So dear to my heart
That December-y day
When the first touch of frost and snow
Had painted each tree in the road
So dear to my heart

I still can picture the flowers in the showers
And that picnic in July
And I still treasure each and ev'ry hour
Of those years that had to fly

They're locked in my heart
In a corner apart
While I tenderly hold the key
As long as I live they will be
So dear to my heart

# So Dear to My Heart

Walt Disney was inspired by his own film, *So Dear to My Heart* (1949), to recreate, or repeat, a part of his own revered past. That film, which was closely supervised by Disney, represented his first major effort to bring alive the happy childhood he recalled in Marcelline, Missouri. That was where he and his brother Roy lived a bit like *Tom Sawyer* for a few years. Disney's memory of those years, and his desire to recapture them, ultimately became the inspiration for Disneyland.

I mention this only to point out my connection with Disney's animated and live action-animated films which deeply affected my life as both a child and an adult. Actually, I had to catch up a lot, because the first Disney film I saw in a movie theater was 1959's *Sleeping Beauty*.

Mom had taken me to other movies before because Pop did not usually go and Mom would never leave me with him or a baby sitter. She loved the movies and went as often as possible. It was one of the ways she learned English years before and could indulge her penchant for fantasy. Happily, I was always described as well-behaved when with Mom in a movie house.

Lathem and his friend James had been going to movies on their own since before I was born (1953). I was five and one-third years old at this time and taken to the RKO Madison Theatre on Myrtle Avenue on the Brooklyn/Queens border by Mom.

She wanted me to join her and my brother, Lathem and his friend James, both sixteen. They wanted to see the film because they loved Tchaikovsky's ballet music which was used extensively in it. Mom thought it would be fun to go as a family (without Pop), and she loved everything Russian, especially the music composed before the 1917 revolution.

This is my first vivid memory of its kind: going to a movie theater with Mom, Lathem and James. But I remember other things about the day, including how Lathem and James looked, looked together and looked at each other. They were certainly a contrast in size, color and speech. Of course, time has tinted this memory, and I remember it through the filter of all the years after.

Lathem was tall and slender with a tan complexion, and a shock of light blonde hair which almost covered his bright blue eyes. He had a soft, pink mouth and spoke quietly and dressed plainly in loose-fitting clothes.

James, on the other hand, was shorter with a touch of stockiness in his frame which was constantly animated. His skin was fair and his brown eyes penetrating when he looked right at you. He had a very prominent Roman nose and thinning black hair.

His hands were large and muscular from years of piano playing; his fingernails were always manicured. James loved pink and yellow sweaters, tight pants, and loafers. He had a high-pitched laugh that made me think of the sound horses make when they emit whinnies but with a British accent, if that's possible.

Lathem and James together, side-by-side, suggested Mutt and Jeff. But when they looked at each other with a mischievous gleam in their eyes, I learned to anticipate an eruption of laughter and perfectly pronounced French obscenities (I was later told by Mom), recited up and down an improvised musical scale.

They were so far ahead of their fellow French students that they could have taken over the class from Professor Brody at Manhattan's *L'ecole de Francais en Amerique*.

Of course, there were also a few moments when I caught them looking furtively at each other with warmth and affection. Although Mom chided them on their inappropriate use of French, she thrilled at hearing her son speak it so beautifully, just as she had taught him.

I distinctly remember a beautiful waltz in *Sleeping Beauty* that became a love song with words, whose I didn't know. Actually, I didn't know anything about Tchaikovsky or songs at the time, but I'm trying to avoid repeating that so and so told me each time I was informed by someone.

I'm learning that a wandering narrative is like a finished brick wall: who cares who laid every brick or applied the mortar, so long as it holds tightly, whether the line is straight or curved or zigzagged.

The story of *So Dear to My Heart* begins with Mom taking Lathem and James to see it in early 1949, when they were six. They each responded to the film with enthusiasm: Mom loving the strong religious overtones depicted by Granny, Beulah Bondi; the boys responding to the music, especially by Uncle Hiram, Burl Ives, and the "stick-to-it-ivity" of an adorable Bobby Driscoll as Jeremiah. All three were entranced by the few animated sequences, which heralded the film's moral in song: "It's What You Do With What You Got" that counts.

# The Days the Music Died

The title song was of particular interest to Lathem. It was introduced during an animated opening sequence. The song set the stage for a journey back in time to the land of grand nostalgia. But Lathem told Mom he knew the voice of the singer. It was the same voice Lathem heard on the radio two years earlier singing a song that lathem grew to love: "Linda." It was evident that Lathem had both a fine ear and memory for music.

Mom recalled the popular song of 1946-47, and was convinced that Lathem was right. However, she could not recall any reference to "Buddy Clark" in the film's credits. James was so infatuated with Burl Ives' rendition of "Lavender Blue (Dilly Dilly)" that he had no opinion to offer.

Well, it turns out that Buddy Clark died in a small plane crash in Los Angeles on October 2, 1949. He was only thirty-seven years old, and at the height of his popularity, even challenging Bing Crosby for the "Crooner's Crown." Mom and Lathem heard the radio report the following morning and were devastated. It was like losing a distant relative you didn't know but admired. They cried all day.

Almost ten years later, on February 3, 1959, just two days after we all saw *Sleeping Beauty*, Lathem was again devastated when he learned that Buddy Holly had died in a plane crash. Holly was touring with Richie Valens and the "Big Bopper," when the tragedy occurred.

The loss of these people and their talent would be assessed as "irreplaceable," and Holly would be acknowledged as one of the most influential rock artists of the century. It was indeed "The Day the Music Died," as Don McLean so eloquently wrote in 1971.

Despite his deep interest in classical music and Jazz, thanks to James, Lathem had become a big fan of Holly and his "Crickets." This happened after Lathem heard a 45 RPM copy of "That'll Be the Day" in June of 1957 at *The Record Rendezvous* on Myrtle Avenue. This local venue was convenient for access to the "pop" music of the day.

## The Day the Music Was Born

However, it paled beside the store in Manhattan, where James had taken Lathem just after Valentine's Day the year before (1956). *Joseph Patelson*'s was the deluxe venue for classical music on the eastern seaboard. Lathem had never seen anything like it.

It happened that Lathem had been begging Mom for a phonograph with which to play records since he had turned twelve (1955). Mom finally prevailed upon Pop to give her the needed twenty-five dollars for the player as a Christmas present for Lathem. She had seen models advertised in the daily paper and knew the range of cost.

Lathem and Mom went to a local audio/video store under the "el" on Myrtle Avenue near the Rivoli Theatre. There, Lathem looked over the monaural players in the price range Mom specified.

Finally, he chose a Voice of Music monaural phonograph in a square box construction. He was influenced by this player's inclusion, free of charge, of a ten inch 33 1/3RPM "demo" record with music on both sides.

It had narration by George Fenneman, a well-known radio and television announcer. One side of the record had popular selections like Nat "King" Cole singing the Gershwin song, "Our Love Is Here to Stay." The other side had classical selections like the final minutes of Shubert's *Symphony Number Five*.

However, the deal maker was the added inclusion, free of charge, of the 45RPM recording, *Santo Natale*, sung by David Whitfield, a big hit the year before. (1954) To make things impossibly bright, the dealer threw in an almost new 45RPM spindle.

It was the experience of listening to the "demo" record that threw Lathem into aural ecstasy, especially the Ravel with four minutes of the opulent *Daphnis and Chloe,* and the taste of blazing brass from Stan Kenton's *Artistry in Rhythm*. Now, he was desperate to find the original recordings, and James took him to Carnegie Hall where James studied piano, to discover the musical magic at *Joseph Patelson*'s.

## FOOL'S PARADISE

You took me up to heaven, when you took me in your arms.
I was dazzled by your kisses, blinded by your charms.
I was lost in a fool's paradise.
Good and lost in a fool's paradise.

When you told me that you loved me, I gave my heart to you.
And I wondered if there could be any truth in love so new.
I was lost in a fool's paradise.

The whole world was my kingdom
And your love the gem in my crown.
Then I saw you glance at a new romance
And my love came tumbling down.

Well you treat me kind of coolish and may never let me know
That you think I'm being foolish because I love you so
I'll still get lost in a fool's paradise.
Lost with you in a fool's paradise.

## THINK IT OVER

Think it over what you just said
Think it over in your pretty little head
Are you sure that I'm not the one?
Is your love real or only fun?
Think it over, just think it over
My lonely heart grows cold and old

Think it over and let me know
Think it over and don't be slow
Just remember all birds and bees
Go by twos through life's mysteries
Think it over, yes just think it over
My lonely heart grows cold and old

Think it over (over and over) (repeat)
My heart grows cold and old

Think it over and think of me

Think it over and you will see
The happy day when you and I
Think as one and kiss the blues goodbye
Think it over, just think it over
My lonely heart grows cold and old.


This present day, a year after Holly's hit, "That'll Be the Day," (1958) Lathem had returned to The Record Rendezvous with James to pick up a 45 RPM recording of Holly's "Fool's Paradise," backed with "Think It Over." The record was a gift for James whom Lathem said should listen carefully to the lyrics of each song. They had quarreled the day before over a very personal matter.

These two precocious teenagers were trying to tamp down powerful, hormonal forces within their bodies, and also trying to come to terms with their romantically-tinged sensuality. They could feel the mutual gravitational pull but were wary of the puritanical world of Brooklyn they inhabited, both at home and at large.

As they walked along Myrtle Avenue to Koletty's ice cream parlor, they burst into French, conversing matter-of-factly, as though they were strolling in Montmartre, to the astonishment of passers-by.

# The 1960s
## Decade of Death and Rebirth

My own encounter with *So Dear to My Heart* took place in 1964. The film was rereleased about a year after Lathem's death. I was eleven and wanted desperately to see it, but I wanted to see it with Mom. She was still in deep mourning for Lathem and James had suffered a "nervous breakdown." I didn't see him for 18 months, but Mom kept in touch with his mom, Dolly, and assured me he was coming along.

She and Dolly had become friends always talking about their boys and happy they were friends. I had formed an opinion, however incomplete, that Mom preferred Lathem to have a close relationship with a nice male more than any kind of relationship with a female.

However, one year we three were invited to James' house for Thanksgiving. It was known that Pop did not socialize: the better for all concerned. However, once in James' home, his father and brother gave us the cold shoulder. They even left the room when the boys were speaking French to each other. Only James' sister Angie was cordial all afternoon.

The next day James' mom called our Mom and tearfully said that we were not welcome back there again. She was very apologetic and Mom knew it was not her choice.

The extent of the tension in James' home was unknown, but every so often James would visit us and try to cover up blue welts on his arms. He never said a word to Mom but I knew he and Lathen had no secrets between them.

## Draft Beer Not Boys

Lathem had been advised to join the New York State National Guard, rather than run the risk of being drafted, as the fighting in VietNam was escalating.

This was the advice of his English professor at the university. Dr. McGovern told Lathem he had a bright future, and should not risk losing his life by fighting in a senseless and unjustified war. Lathem was a straight A student pursuing a double major in English and Theater and, of course, continuing his study of French.

When consulted by Lathem, James reluctantly agreed with the professor and Lathem joined the Guard with Pop's written permission. Lathem already knew that James had failed his exam at Whitehall Street, after getting a draft notice. They did not discuss why James had failed, but Lathem understood when James smilingly said that he was told, disdainfully, by an army sergeant that "Queens don't have to go to war."

Lathem had attended the university for two years before being called to the obligatory six months active duty with the army at Fort Dix, New Jersey.

As a nation, we learned later what few people knew at the time: college educated males, primarily white, were given special consideration in both the draft and for joining National Guard units, while drafted men of color were disproportionately represented "in country."

## Hammett's Flitcraft Parable

I've delayed telling how Lathem died for as long as I could. But I must preface this episode with a reference to Dashiell Hammett's story about Charles Flitcraft in Chapter Seven of *The Maltese Falcon*. This episode does not appear in any film versions.

Sam Spade had taken Brigit O'Shaughnessy's case to find her missing sister: a fiction Spade never believed. At this point in the story Miles Archer, Spade's partner, had been gunned down while shadowing one Floyd Thursby, supposedly Brigit's nemesis. Thursby himself had also been shot dead. In addition, Joel Cairo had come calling on Spade looking for a "Black Bird" tied to Brigit as well.

As Spade and Brigit sit in his apartment waiting for Cairo to phone, Spade starts to tell her a story about one of his early cases as an operative with a detective agency in Seattle. A man named Flitcraft had gone out to lunch one day and did not return to his real estate office. Flitcraft missed a golfing engagement he had arranged shortly before he went to lunch.

"He went like that, Spade said, "like a fist when you open your hand."

Joel Cairo called and agreed to come to Spade's apartment to see Miss O'Shaughnessy. Then Spade returned to Flitcraft.

Mrs. Flitcraft came into the detective agency in Seattle because "... somebody had seen a man in Spokane who looked a lot like her husband. I went over there. It was Flitcraft, all right. He had been living in Spokane for a couple of years as Charles – that was his first name – Pierce."

Flitcraft had established a new life for himself with a new family. His new life resembled his old one to an astonishing degree: well-to-do businessman, family man, secure, comfortable and predictable suburban lifestyle. Even his new wife was more like the first than not.

Spade interviewed Flitcraft who said he had no regrets over what he'd done, as he'd left his first family in excellent financial health.

Here's what happened to him. Going to lunch he passed an office-building that was being put up — just the skeleton. A beam or something fell eight or ten stories down and smacked the sidewalk alongside him. It brushed pretty close to him, but didn't touch him, though a piece of the sidewalk was chipped off and flew up and hit his cheek. It only took a piece of skin off, but he still had the scar when I saw him. He rubbed it with his finger — well, affectionately — when he told me about it. He was scared stiff of course, he said, but he was more shocked than really frightened. He felt like somebody had taken the lid off life and let him look at the works.

Spade tells us that Flitcraft had an epiphany: his previous life had been built on the assumption that "The life he knew was a clean orderly sane responsible affair. Now a falling beam had shown him that life was fundamentally none of these things. He, the good citizen-husband-father, could be wiped out between office and restaurant by the accident of a falling beam. He knew then that men died at haphazard like that, and lived only while blind chance spared them."

Flitcraft was disturbed because he had gotten out of step with life. The beam convinced him to adjust his life accordingly, and as randomly as the beam had fallen he randomly walked away from his former life.

Of course, as life has a way of doing, no more beams fell in Flitcraft's way for a while allowing him to slowly, almost imperceptibly, return to the illusion of the well-ordered universe he had left behind.

Sam Spade had been relating this story to Brigit in hopes of giving her some insight into his method of casework, without revealing to her that he already knew she had killed Miles Archer and could not be trusted.

Spade's brain, keenly attuned to dodging falling beams, could measure their intensity, like a seismic machine. The sudden appearance of desperate people all linked to some black bird, made Spade wary of their stories and seeming cooperation. He listened to Brigit, Cairo and Gutman talk about the black bird, and knew each of them was willing to double-cross the other, however allied they were before. Spade armed himself against other beams they were likely to throw his way. He had pegged them all right.

In the end, only Spade's extreme and conscious self-denial of Brigit's sexual allure and his unwillingness to play the sap for her saved him from another falling beam: "I won't because all of me wants to — wants to say to hell with the consequences and do it — and because — God damn you — you've counted on that with me . . ."

If not thinking about randomly falling beams gets us through life we are most fortunate. For the Tommasos, beams reigned down periodically: many with terrible consequences. Despite many funerals, the family always managed to return to God's good order over life, until the next catastrophe struck.

It's important to note that randomly falling beams are but one of two types of deadly "beams." Disasters like the 1906 San Francisco earthquake occur randomly. But others, like the surprise attack on Pearl Harbor in 1941, were intricately planned and executed by one nation to harm another. In today's society, natural and nation-made beams are falling continually, but only the nation-made ones are preventable with early, reliable intelligence and response, something we missed in 1941.

## Beam Number One

What I've written down about Lathem's death is based on hearsay, interviews with military personnel, consultations with lawyers and a limited review of official U. S. Army documentation of the incident that resulted in Lathem's death.

I say limited review because almost half of the incident report's contents were blacked out. All of this information was gathered over a period of eight years: from the official army closure of the case (1963) until my own assignment to Fort Dix in 1972.

The relevant part of the report read:

. . .as a regrettable but unintended consequence during a Night Infiltration Course where the subject soldier, in the midst of a "low crawl" operation with 7.62 MM live rounds from a M60 machine gun firing overhead, suddenly stood erect, without his protective helmet and raised his rifle into the air. As a result of this violation of army regulations, the subject soldier, standing six feet one inch tall, was struck multiple times in the neck, unprotected head and arms by regular and tracer rounds and severely wounded. His M1 weapon had its stock splintered as well. . . .

In another section of the report the following appeared:

"Official papers were drawn up to proceed with a court martial action for failure to follow orders and destruction of government property. This action was suspended at thirteen hundred hours, 20 August 1963, when the subject soldier was pronounced dead."

The family was devastated upon learning of Lathem's fate, first at eleven-thirty PM by phone: "He was seriously wounded during a training exercise and is hospitalized on base." The second notice came after we arrived at Fort Dix at one-thirty AM in Mr. Farante's car: a doctor Grillo met us and said, "The medical team did its best but he was too far gone. Had he lived it would have been in a vegetative state, that's how bad the brain damage was. We're very sorry for your loss."

Mom had screamed and fainted after hearing "brain damage." Pop caught her and put her on a chair holding her with trembling tenderness like a dozen eggs in an earth quake. He had tears in his eyes, as much for his frustrated ignorance at what was said, as for Mom's condition or Lathem's death.

I understood enough and remember weeping and yelling, "Oh God, no!" three or four times, until Pop pulled me into his embrace and I just kept crying until exhausted. Mr. Farante cried too and left to call his wife who was awaiting some word from us.

I must have fallen asleep at some point, and woke to find myself propped on a small sofa in a dark room. I could make out Pop standing by a bed looking down at Mom who was asleep. She had been given a sedative to deal with her shocked state. I suddenly remembered why we were there, but Pop caught me before I said anything.

He pointed to Mom with his left hand and raised the index finger of his right hand to his lips. I thought I saw something in Pop's eyes that was new: a look of genuine concern for Mom. I understood the gesture, closed my eyes, and went back to sleep.

I find it hard to describe how I felt, after Lathem died, but I kept thinking that I lost a part of my body. Many a day, I'd be aware of looking for something, while I turned around, as though I was incomplete. But what I eventually wound up missing was Lathem's presence above me in our bunk beds every night: the comforting sound of his breathing always reassured me that I was not alone and need not be afraid.

Inside my head I never stopped talking to Lathem, even though Mom said he was in Heaven. I then told him all my secrets and felt a little better. But that silence above each night as I lay in bed was going to make my memory of his loss indelible.

Mom had pulled out all his pictures and covered every available space in the apartment with them. Most were in black and white, but a few of the largest had been studio portraits in color for his sixteenth and eighteenth birthdays. These included one picture from each group with me, one with Mom and one with James. All of those were framed. There were no pictures of Lathem in uniform.

Pop didn't believe in pictures of any kind. He especially hated the ones with James. Mom warned him against anything happening to those pictures. He would smile that wicked smile of his, and make the sign of the cross backwards with his left hand. Mom would look him in the eye, and tell him: "Puoi andare all'inferno, dove tu appartieni!" ("You can go to hell where you belong.")

## The Emperor's Red Butt

The aftermath of Lathem's death was an intermittent nightmare punctuated by the loud buzz of talking and even laughter at the wake. Mom had decided to have a closed casket with a colored photograph of Lathem beside it. The viewing would be limited to one afternoon and evening.

Most of the people who came were in Lathem's circle of young male acquaintances at the city university. They were joined by one of Lathem's professors, Dr. McGovern. A bunch of French students from *L'ecole de Francais en Amerique* also came to the wake. There was also one soldier from Lathem's platoon who had received a pass to attend.

The result of this mélange of mostly young males started out as quiet respectfulness, ultimately rising to almost raucous laughter, as the afternoon melted into evening. There were many stories about Lathem, with and without James, circulating that day. Apparently most of them were funny.

Mom continued to be lightly sedated, enabling her to greet all these people with some dignity. The Farante family came to pay their respect. Mom kissed and hugged them for their genuine sympathy and great assistance.

She was overwhelmed when Dolly, James' mother, came to pay her respect. Dolly had her own tale of woe to exchange with Mom, as James had fallen into a catatonic state, after hearing the news. He had to be hospitalized in the psychiatric wing of a hospital in Manhattan. All Dolly could do was repeat "Otherwise, they say he's in perfect health. I don't understand it!"

I did not know what to make of all this business but I found myself saying hello to the soldier who was present. He had said a few words to Mom before taking a seat in the back of the room.

His name was Morton Fox, according to his name tag. That name sparked my curiosity and so I said: "Hello, Mr. Fox." What ensued was one of the most interesting encounters any ten year old child could have with an adult.

Actually, Mr. Fox was younger than Lathem had been. He successfully came down to my level to tell funny things about himself and Lathem. Mr. Fox said "Call me Mort: all my animal friends do, like Mr. Cat, Mr. Mouse, Mrs. Goose and especially Mr. Pierre, my orangutan."

I took the bait and enquired about Mort's orangutan. This is the tale he told me.

Once upon a time, long, long ago, an orangutan named Pierre and his English master traveled in the Kingdom of France whose Emperor was the vainest of men, always fussing about how his clothes looked on him. He cared about nothing else.

He drove his tailors crazy every time a ball or other public event came along. "I must have something new, beautiful and full of color to greet my subjects," the Emperor demanded.

Well, one day two strangers came to town and asked to see the Emperor, representing themselves as the greatest tailors in the kingdom. These tailors were dishonest men who believed they could play a trick on the Emperor, and be paid gold for doing nothing.

They convinced him their clothes would make him more popular than he had ever been, but the Emperor must understand one thing: the clothes would be magically invisible to anyone who is unfit for his job or is "hopelessly stupid." In this way, the Emperor could identify people who could not be trusted or were not faithful to him.

The Emperor agreed to pay the tailors 500 pieces of gold for the suit, 250 pieces now and the rest when the suit was ready. The tailors asked for a small house where they could work in privacy, as it would take two weeks to finish the suit after taking the Emperor's measurements. All they asked for was given them, including the best food and wine in the kingdom delivered to their house.

After two weeks of eating, drinking and sleeping days away, the tailors sent a message to the Emperor that the suit was ready. Would the Emperor please come to their house in secret to try it on? The Emperor did indeed come alone on horseback. When the tailors opened a large box, they asked the Emperor to look at the color, fabric and workmanship of the suit.

The Emperor saw nothing but an empty box, and was about to say so, when he remembered the tailors' decree: the suit will be magically invisible to those who are unfit for their jobs or hopelessly stupid. After a few moments pause, The Emperor said *"Formidable! Magnifique! Merveilleux! Parfait! Un costume digne d'un empereur!"*

The Emperor was sweating heavily as the tailors removed the suit from its box. "Do you approve of the cut, my lord?" asked one of the tailors. *"Oui,"* replied the Emperor. "And do you approve of the colors and fabric, my lord?" asked the other tailor. *"Oui,"* replied the Emperor.

Having collected the rest of their fee, the tailors suggested that the Emperor call for a festival on the coming Sunday, so that he could parade before his subjects in his new suit. They made sure that a proclamation would be posted in every square of the kingdom on Saturday with the following decree:

The Emperor commands your attendance at his Grand
Parade on Sunday. Later, a festival will be held
inside the Castle. The Emperor will be wearing his
new and brilliant suit of clothes for the parade.
Be advised that this suit has magical properties and

will be visible to all except those who are unfit for
their jobs or hopelessly stupid. Anyone wishing to claim
he or she cannot see the suit will report to the royal
sheriff for the consequences.

This decree would be read by court squires every 20 minutes
to alert the host of subjects who could not read.

On the following Sunday morning, the tailors arrived at the
palace with their large box. They were admitted to the Emperor's
dressing room, while everyone else was dismissed. The Emperor
came forward from behind a tall screen, wearing nothing but his
crown.

The tailors opened the box and carefully removed the suit.
They were well prepared for this moment, keeping solemn faces
as they helped the Emperor put it on. The tailors did not look at
the Emperor, nor did he look at them.

The Emperor was whisked away to his carriage, as all his
courtiers and servants bowed very low with their eyes closed,
until he passed and they could see his large bare bottom waddling
down the hall. No one made so much as a peep, until the Emperor
was in his coach and beginning his journey through his subjects.

There were loud huzzahs and well-rehearsed exclamations of
"What a gorgeous suit, the color of the sun, it dazzles!" The Emperor took a deep breath and sighed, all the while smiling broadly
and raising his hands full of royal lace napkins, revealing his hairy
armpits. But his subjects managed to cleverly turn guffaws to huzzahs as they flung handfuls of confetti at the royal coach.

Well, among the people in this crowd was a visiting Englishman. He was an organ-grinder, holding a male orangutan, named
Pierre, who shook his rump in tempo with the music his master
played. As they waited for the Emperor's coach to pass by, a group
of young boys gathered around the organ-grinder and clapped their
hands, while laughing at Pierre's shaking rear-end.

As the coach was rolling by, the Englishman, who did not
know any French, looked at the Emperor and smiled. He whispered
something to Pierre who howled and laughed. The Englishman
looked at one of the boys, who seemed confused and red-faced at
what he had just seen, and nudged him saying, "'im bare ass, eh?"
The boy repeated what he heard, *"embarrasser?"* He screamed at
the Emperor *"Oui, c'est vous qu'embarrassez tout le monde! L'empereur
ne porte pas de vètements!"*

Suddenly, all the boys took up the cry as one: "*L'empereur ne porte pas de vêtements!*" Within a minute the cry was taken up by the crowds who now pointed to the carriage, screaming with laughter: "*L'empereur ne porte pas de vêtements.*"

I looked at Mort and said, "And?"

"Oh, you want a moral," he said slyly. I shook my head up and down.

"Well, let's see; how is this: sometimes it takes a stranger to remind you that faith is what you believe in but can't see, not what you're told is there but you can't observe."

My puzzled look invited another response. "Okay, strike one, but two strikes left," he said.

"Sometimes, a stranger can show you the wisdom of your language by saying what you see in his language." I blinked. "Strike two," he said.

"Like Mighty Casey, my back's against the wall. Here goes: Never take a male orangutan to a parade in a foreign country, especially if he's looking for a female in heat.

"Now, what happened when the boys yelled that the Emperor had no clothes caused the coach to stop and the Emperor to blanch. He turned bright red all over, especially his buttocks. Pierre got one look at that fat red butt and flew to the carriage screeching, ready to assault the Emperor.

"No one was sure what happened after that. All I read was that nine months later the Emperor died of what Shakespeare called the 'French disease.'"

Mort said all this with a straight face as my face was turning purple-red. "What happened to Pierre," I forced.

"Oh, Pierre; well, Pierre was killed by one of the royal guards, and the royal taxidermist stuffed him. Then the royal portrait painter painted Pierre in the act of assaulting the Emperor's butt. They called it *Emperor and the Orangutan*, after a Greek inspired myth, *Leda and the Swan*. Of course it was never put on view.

"But the courtiers and servants of the late Emperor had private viewings from time to time. This was done to remind them that in French history only once was the ascent of man devolved briefly by a member of the lower order of primates, just long enough to assail a royal asshole with devastating accuracy and asinine pleasure."

When he had finished Mort was beaming and flashing his white teeth like Burt Lancaster used to do. "Of course, I managed to pick up the stuffed Pierre at an auction," Mort added. "It sits in my menagerie of stuffed animals. Someday I'll show them to you."

I told him I liked his story, at least the parts I understood, although I remembered something like it from nursery school which was very similar. In any case, there may have been wisdom in much of what Mort said, but I can remember Lathem proclaiming "It's What You Do With What You Got," from *So Dear to my Heart*, a lot better than all that business about Pierre.

Before I let Mort go to return to Fort Dix, I asked for a last thought about Lathem. He considered the question for moment, and then he said that Lathem was very smart, like himself, and they got along very well.

In fact, they had made plans to combine Lathem's interest in music and opera with Mort's interest in local food from around the world. One idea was *The Opera Lover's Cook Book* and *The Classical Music Lover's Cook Book.*

He mentioned a few early thoughts that they were tossing around before the tragedy. For example, Italian food could be dressed up with selections like *Baccalà Boccanegra, Tagliatelle a la Tosca, Rigatoni Rigoletto, Ossobuco Otello, Bucatini Butterfly* and *Chicken Cio Cio San.*

For Wagnerians they thought of *Wiener Schnitzel Wotan, Sauerbraten Siegfried* and *Brunhilde Brats.* For the French he mentioned *Calamari Carmen, Mussels Manon* and *Frites a la Faust.* I picked up on the heavy use of alliteration which fascinated me in my college years, but the rest sailed over my head.

This was also true of the classical music meals. The ideas they tried out, included, *Chicken Tchaikovsky, Roasted Lamb Ravel, Beethoven's Brisket, Milanzane Mozart, Braham's Bavarian Rabbit* and *Stroganoff a la Stravinsky.*

By this time, I could see that Mort was wistful and teary. He said there was one other thing he wanted to tell me but couldn't. Having told him my age, he promised he would tell me in eight years when I was eighteen.

He gave me a card with a phone number on it. "Call this number when you are eighteen. Someone will tell you where to find me."

I thanked him and said good night. I would not forget him in eight years or twenty. But I didn't ask him to make good on his promise. In 1972, as I was stationed in Fort Dix myself, I learned the truth about Lathem's death.

# MAMMA

| | |
|---|---|
| Mamma solo per te | Momma, only for you |
| La mia canzone vola | my song flies |
| Mamma sarai con me | Momma, you will stay with me |
| | |
| Tu non sarai più sola | you'll not be alone any more |
| Quanto ti voglio bene | how much I love you |
| Queste parole d'amore | these words of love |
| Che ti sospira il mio cuore | that my heart is whispering to you |
| Force non s'odono più | maybe are no longer used |
| Mamma ma la canzone mia | Momma, but my most beautiful song |
| Più bella sei tu | is you |
| Sei tu la vita | you are my life |
| E per la vita | and for the rest of my life |
| Non ti lascio mai più | I'll never leave you again |
| Sento la mano tua stanca | I can feel your tired hand |
| Cerca i miei riccioli d'or | looking for my golden curls |
| Sento e la voce ti manca | I can hear and your voice whispers |
| La ninna nanna d'allor | the lullaby of back then |
| Oggi la testa tua bianca | today your white head |
| Io voglio stringere al cuor | I want to hold to my heart |

# Mama

I must talk about Mom, the only woman in my life, until I met Marta. Mom did everything for me with love and dedication, but I must say I had doubts.

What I doubted was her unconditional love while Lathem was alive. He was the center of her universe and why not. Lathem was beautiful, bright and devoted to her. Mom loved her first husband and her first son by extension. Pop never treated her like a lady. I think he was afraid of her all those years I was growing up.

On the other hand, I've had a face since I was born that "only a mother could love." It was to Mom's credit that I never sensed revulsion in her eyes, arms or manners when she took care of me. I just knew that I was second. This belief hurt me more, because of Pop's indifference to me.

For the record, I must say that my Mom was one of the most intelligent persons I have ever known. She had a decent secondary education with the nuns at The Saint Mary Magdalene School in Brooklyn. As an orphaned immigrant, she became a charity case.

In addition to English (she was a native Pole), she learned Latin and French. Later, after marrying Pop, she mastered Italian and Sicilian on her own. She taught Lathem French and gave me a good foundation in Italian. Yes, she had fantasies about Russian Royalty and Egyptian Pharaohs, but they always seemed harmless to me.

Mom had such hopes for Lathem. He seemed the incarnation of her greatest attributes in a male body. She never talked about his death, but it clearly sapped the life from her body and mind.

I had to wait until I was stationed at Fort Dix in New Jersey in 1972 to learn the truth about his death. The army said it was an accident with unintended consequences: friendly fire during an exercise.

His head was almost blown off by tracer rounds of ammunition fired overhead. For some reason, he stood up screaming something that no one supposedly heard. He was tall and was cut down instantly.

Mom was never the same after Lathem died. She gradually became more and more listless, spending hours looking out our street-side window watching life passing her by. I had a hard time getting her to go to a movie with me. When she finally agreed, it was because *So Dear to my Heart* had been re-released by Disney, and it was showing at the RKO Madison in our neighborhood.

Mom told me that she and Lathem were convinced that the

male voice singing the title song in the opening belonged to Buddy Clark. Clark had died in a plane crash in 1949 and Lathem was very upset when he heard the news. Mom brightened up a bit when she thought to let me listen to some of Clark's singing before seeing the film. She was sure we could settle the matter once and for all.

Lathem's collection of music was as he had left it. When he started listening to classical music and jazz, Mom asked Pop to make a bookshelf deep enough to hold the many long playing records he already owned. They were to be part of Lathem's legacy to me. She was pleasantly surprised to find Pop willing to do so. She gave him the measurements and said it would replace the chest of drawers in our space.

We rarely saw any of Pop's handiwork around the apartment. He had enlarged the space we were allotted in the cellar, after reaching an agreement with Mr. Farante, the owner. Pop renovated the space for his purposes and no one was allowed in there. Pop had installed a dehumidifier in there to keep his work safe from the cold, dank atmosphere. He kept the space under lock and key. Even the occasional rat or mouse who tried to enter were caught in big traps and disposed of.

Pop had finished the bookshelf only weeks before Lathem died, and Lathem was so impressed with it he suddenly hugged Pop who didn't respond but didn't recoil. After Lathem had loaded his stuff onto the shelves, he called us all together, especially Pop.

Lathem beamed as we looked on smiling and he said, "I think we're finally a family now." We three wept while Pop fought back tears. It was the only moment like it we knew before Lathem went off to Fort Dix and death.

Mom spent part of her lonely days walking around the apartment with a yardstick, as she developed a master plan for maximizing my space. The area that Lathem and I shared was very small with room only for bunk beds and a chest of draws. Across from the beds were closets and draws built into the wall which held coats, jackets, toys, comic books and such. Mom knew there was no space in our room for the bookshelf without another move.

One evening, Mom sat down with Pop and me and said she had a plan to change things around so we could make the most of the space we had. She and Pop went at it in Italian but kept it civil. Once in a while Mom would say something in English she wanted me to fully understand. That would really piss Pop off, but she returned to Italian to calm him down.

Mom's plan was to first have the upper bunk bed altered. She said this could be done by having Pop construct a lightweight closet in the space the mattress once occupied. The closet would rise to the ceiling and the new structure would be reinforced with brackets between the posts and the bottom of the closet which would sit on metal slats.

In this closet, I would keep all my personal stuff like underwear, socks, folded shirts and pants, games, small toys, etc. but nothing very heavy. The ladder in place would allow me and Mom to remove or replace items that were clean, etc. On my headboard Pop could create a place for a reading light, so I could study and read, before I had a desk of my own.

Secondly, the new bookshelf would become my property, along with all its contents. It rose almost to the ceiling and was three feet wide. It had six shelves within, thirteen inches apart: two at the bottom would hold up to 130 LPs each (Lathem had accumulated 125 when he died), while the third shelf would hold Lathem's Phonograph and his portable radio with his plug-in for his head phones.

The additional shelves would hold cardboard accordion envelopes for 150 45RPM records (Lathem had already purchased 50 45RPM records), and related paraphernalia.

The last piece of Mom's plan was a big one. She wanted to move their bedroom into the last railroad room that faced the street. Then the former bedroom would be converted into a living room with the television set, a couch and a small desk, lamp and chair for me to use from middle school through high school and college. A bookcase would be needed for my all the books I would accumulate over these years.

Mom knew how well Pop did in the construction line. He was one of the few people in the Hod Carrier's Union who worked forty to fifty weeks a year. He was very lucky in that way. She also knew how cheap he could be when he had to part with any money. But she was now relentless in getting him to spend some of it.

Mom said she wanted a new bed with a queen-size mattress for their bedroom, one they would share. I couldn't possibly know how clever Mom was pushing all the buttons Pop would respond to positively.

She was not only willing to share his bed again but also willing to have his handsome handiwork displayed around the apartment. Of course he put up a fuss, but there were no obscenities. This was all being planned for me his only son.

## IT'S WHAT YOU DO WITH WHAT YOU GOT

You gotta start with whatcha got
If whatcha got ain't such a lot
To make the most of whatcha got
Here's what I recommend
You start by a-tryin' and applyin' your best
If you try, there ain't no denyin'
There's a way to feather your nest, Hey!

You gotta add how watcha do
And multiply by whatcha do
You think you can't win
But you do
And you get that dividend

It's what you do with whatcha got
Never mind how much you got
It's whatcha do with whatcha got
That pays off in the end

It's the means you applieth
That raises your stock
Look what David did to Golieth
With a little old hunk of rock

Now, looky here, son. Stop a sittin'
You can't sit and 'spect to get it
Now, the road to fame takes muscle
Lots of work and lots o' hustle
So start right and hit it

Now if at first you don't succeed
A lot of spunk is what you need
Or someone else will take the lead
So try, try, try again

Just get up when you fall down
And don't be forlorn
Look how Joshua busted that wall down
With a little old measly horn

It's whatcha do with whatcha got
And never mind just how much you got
It's whatcha do with whatcha got
That pays off in the end
That pays off in the end

And so Mom and I searched out Lathem's LP of Buddy Clark's songs now in my collection. We were going to a Saturday matinee showing of *So Dear to my Heart* in a couple of hours. So we played sides one and two, listening to all of the tracks including, "I'll Dance at Your Wedding," "Linda," Mom's favorite, "How Are Things in Glocca Morra," "Girl of my Dreams," and "Baby it's Cold Outside."

We both enjoyed the film, but left undecided about Buddy Clark's contribution, if any. Our eyes concentrated on the credits but no one named Clark appeared. I did come away with the moral of the film which is "It's What You Do With What You Got." I've never forgotten the film or the moral.

In fact, years later I did some research and found out who did sing the title song. I never knew that Dick Haymes had a brother Bob. He did and it was Bob Haymes, under the name Bob Stanton, who sang the song in the film.

Robert William (Bob) Haymes was Dick's younger brother. His claim to fame was writing a song, "C'est Tout," which became "That's All" in 1953, with refined lyrics by Alan Brandt. It was recorded by Nat Cole and became a standard, with additional covers by Bobby Darin and Frank Sinatra.

I own a VHS copy of the film and I came to the conclusion that Haymes' rendition sounds like Clark, and a bit like Crosby, but it's Haymes' voice. I thought of all those tears Mom said she and Lathem shed when they learned that Buddy Clark was dead. It's that fact and legend thing again, but this time I print the fact. That was the last movie Mom and I would see together.

That night Mom reminisced about a film she had seen many years ago, when she and her first husband were celebrating the three-month anniversary of their marriage. It was called *Balalaika* and was released in December 1939, after the invasion of Poland by the Nazi's that September. She then talked about coming to America and movies.

Mom learned to love American films, after coming here in 1936, as an immigrant who spoke only Polish. Sonia Lisak was an orphan in Warsaw at that time. A well-informed friend of her aunt, with whom Sonia lived, understood that rumored Soviet Russian talks with the Nazi's could result in the Nazi's unopposed invasion of Poland.

Mr. Bittleman urged Sonia's aunt to consider immigration to America, as he was planning. By August 1939, when the Russians

and Germans signed a neutrality pact, Sonia had already been in America for three years, brought by the Bittlemans.

After Mom studied English in The St. Mary Magdalene School for two years, the nuns encouraged her to see English language films they thought appropriate for an eighteen year old girl. These were primarily the operettas filmed by MGM with Jeanette Mc-Donald and Nelson Eddy.

They were approved by Holy Mother Church (through the Breen office), for general viewing, as all crimes and sins were ultimately punished. The most famous incident was John Barrymore's shooting of Eddy for the ill-fated and illicit love he shared with McDonald, Barrymore's wife.

This happened at the end of *Maytime* their best and most autobiographical film. Apparently, murder in response to adultery, or assumed adultery, appeared to be sanctioned. However, the ghostly images of McDonald and Eddy are reunited in MGM heaven as the film concludes. The studio got the last shot when true love conquers death. How operatic!

Mom had seen that one at a local theatre that specialized in "rerun" rather than "first run" features. She absolutely loved the film and all the glorious music provided by the two leads. However, her very favorite film operetta was the aforementioned Balalaika.

In early 1940, Mr. Yarmolinsky took his young bride to see the film. He concluded that the picture was a nostalgic swan song to the Czarist Russia that once was. However, the film enabled him to note that Nelson Eddy played the role of Prince Peter Karagin, a White Russian Cossack, while Yarmolinsky's ancestors actually lived it.

On the other hand, Sonia accepted Yarmolinsky's story because she identified closely with Ilona Massey (McDonald and Eddy were separated for a couple of films), the blonde Hungarian actress playing a pro-Bolshevik nightclub singer.

Mom nearly swooned when Eddy delivered a powerful reading of "The Song of the Volga Boatman." However she had already turned her back on Stalin once he allowed the Nazi's to invade Poland and partition the country with the Soviets.

I had just recently celebrated my twelfth birthday. (1965) Lathem had been killed over two years ago and Mom had successfully engineered the major change in our living space. I was still uneasy with Pop but he surprised us both when he offered to celebrate my birthday, after the fact, on November 15.

That day would be a unique experience because Pop actually took me to Little Italy in Manhattan. There, at a very nice restaurant on Mulberry Street, we enjoyed fried *calamari* and baked clams, with a side order of muscles in red sauce. Those were the appetizers. For the next course, we consumed *Bucatini all' Amatriciama*, followed by Veal Cutlet *Parmigiano*.

Of course, all the while we were chewing warm, crisp pieces

of *Pistaluna* bread, dunked in the various tomato-based sauces. Pop had ordered wine for himself and a "coke" for me to drink. Throughout this process, I nodded my approval, even if I was unfamiliar with the food, and I ate everything.

Food and family make a strong bond for Sicilians, and I was getting my first real taste of both. When I inquired, in my own awkward way, what accounted for this change in Pop's behavior, he said he would tell me later: about three years later, it turned out.

## Beam Number Two

Five weeks later, just before Christmas, Mom would suffer what I was told was an "aneurism bursting in her heart." All I know is that on that cold day I walked home from middle school, I found an ambulance outside our apartment building. The ambulance was surrounded by neighbors, and I discovered that my world was truly shattered.

I would never see my beloved mother alive again. Mrs. Farante spotted me approaching and ran to me. All she could say was "Your mother ..." before she embraced me and held me tightly. I started to cry but I wasn't hysterical.

She brought me to one of the medics. They talked while I looked at a covered body they were pushing into the ambulance. I heard Mrs. Farante say "His father's not home. He should be with his mother. Can we go in the Ambulance? I'll stay with him." The medic assented.

After telling her husband what she was doing, Mrs. Farante got into the ambulance with me and held me close to her the entire way to Wyckoff Heights General Hospital.

It had been only two years since she was my mother alone. Only two years to understand I lived with a saint who did love me. I will always cherish her memory and the knowledge that for much of her brief life, for the sake of her sons, she suffered many fools that were not worthy of her intelligence and beauty.

It has never been possible for me to put into words how this loss affected me. But no day passes without my expecting to feel her loving arms around me, kissing me "Good morning" and "Good night." In the history of human calamities there is no greater loss than a child's mother in the prime of her life.

I was unprepared for the events of that evening when, after

shock, I saw terror and fear in the eyes of my father. The realization set in that Mom's devotion to him had been so central to his ability to function.

She made his lunch and dinner every day, and kept a spotless home. She gave him his own space, and the freedom to pursue his joy in solitude working downstairs. She bore his derision of her first son, and exempted him from having to be a father to either of us.

His ability to breathe, speak, walk, think and be sensitive to other's needs had to be learned or relearned, if Girolamu Tommaso was ever to rejoin to the human race. He was falling fast and I did not know how to catch him.

I have been an atheist most of my life but that night I think a miracle took place in our apartment. My father waded through a tar pit of despair. He sat me down and prayed to Sonia in *paradisu*, in Sicilian, not just for undeserved forgiveness but also for the ability to be both mother and father to their son.

He made a promise, he told me, and asked for a pledge and sign of support from her. He also swore to forgive the trespasses of his relatives, and beg their forgiveness for his own against them. That was the first step to mending the road on which their son would travel to the welcoming arms of *La Famiglia*.

Even if I understood little of what he said, he wanted me to witness his saying it. When he was through, he held me in his arms and cried, saying only "*Figghiu miu.*"

That night was unusually warm for late December. There was a severe thunderstorm with flashes of lightning and booms of thunder. A howling wind whipped the rain against and over the building for hours. When morning came with very bright sunlight, there was no sign of rain or any other disturbance.

Before making any funeral arrangements, Pop picked up the phone and called Don Silvio, his uncle. When he finally reached Don Silvio, they talked and they wept, agreeing to reconcile.

The next morning, Don Silvio sent four people, including a woman, to attend to us and make the funeral arrangements. In this part of Brooklyn and Queens, Don Silvio could make miracles too.

Mom had her first husband buried in a small cemetery behind St. Mary Magdalene Church. The nuns at the school had arranged it, gratis, so she and little Lathem could be near the plot.

However, there was no way the entire family could be buried there. Mom brought Lathem there every day to say a prayer for his father's soul. Then they would light candles in the church to hasten Yarmolinski's ascent to Paradise from Purgatory.

Pop bought a burial plot when I was born, and so that's where Lathem's remains were buried. It was in St. John's Cemetery off Fresh Pond Road in Queens. Mom was laid out at Caratozzolo and Sons, before the funeral mass at St. Margaret's Church near the cemetery. The headstone in place had read:

### Lathem Yarmolinsky Jr.
Beloved Son
March 5, 1943 – August 20, 1963

Now, it included:

### Sonia Yarmolinsky Tommaso
November 30, 1920 – December 20, 1965
Beloved wife and mother
Reunited in Paradise Forever

I didn't know until years later that the headstone markings were part of Pop's promise to Sonia. One of Don Silvio's employees at the family's Headstone Masonry shop accomplished this overnight.

A crew from the shop pulled out the headstone and moved it into the shop. By Thursday morning, the twenty-third, the completed headstone was back in place. Mom wanted space left for one more name, when the time came but it wasn't Pop's. When it came to eternity, she wanted to be with her sons alone. Pop later told me that he understood, because he did not intend to be buried in America.

## A Nun's Story

There was one incident at Mom's wake I want to mention. Many people from the Tommaso family came during three days and nights of viewing, leaving Mass Cards. Some had already sent flowers in Mom's memory.

They were happy that we displayed some pictures of Mom and the family whom they had never seen. The only picture Pop was in was taken on their wedding day. I had never seen it. Mom was so beautiful and he was like a stuffed, dark penguin. He had found it among her things tucked in a sewing basket. Pop and I had assembled the pictures and pinned them to an easel for viewing on one side of the casket.

During those three days and nights, I took every opportunity to stand next to the casket and admire my mother. Every night, as we were leaving, I would say a prayer, stand on the kneeling step and lean in to kiss Mom good night. No one stopped me. On the last night, I was happy to see Pop do the same thing.

The room was loaded with colorful but tasteful floral arrangements arriving every hour. The largest and most beautiful was a big heart of three dozen real red roses on a circle of four dozen real white roses. The golden sash across the heart read: "For Our Beloved Niece, Sonia, Granted Eternal Rest – The Family of Silvio Tommaso."

Each day and night members of the extended Tommaso family came to express their sorrow and pay their respects to Mom, a stranger. Pop and I were surprised that these people found time to stop by just a few days before Christmas.

I had never known an extended family before, and was both afraid of, and attracted to, this demonstration of love and respect. Of course, we were yet to learn the extent of Don Silvio's control over events.

One member of each family signed the memory book and wrote their addresses, so that we could send out thank you cards to all who came. I looked at the book every so often to see the names.

Beside the Tommaso's there were the Genuas, the Gennas, the Lorenzos, the Espardas, the Mellanis and the Coronas. The Monsaldos and other neighbors signed including, the Sigismundis and the Gargiullos and a Polish family named Liesch.

Most of these neighborhood people were familiar to me by sight, but I doubt that I had ever exchanged a word with any of them. They barely recognized Pop and had to be introduced. Luckily, most of these people spoke Italian and/or Sicilian.

On the last afternoon of viewing, a nun from The St. Mary Magdalene School paid her respect. Sister Carmeline introduced herself to me and Pop. She spoke in English, but then switched to Italian, when she realized Pop did not understand her. She was one of Mom's Latin and French teachers at the school.

It was important for her, she said, to let the family know something about Mom in the years before she met Pop. The Sister said Sonia never discussed her problems but lived in a world of happy dreams. This temperament allowed her to smile even when life was harshest.

"Sonia was a beautiful and intelligent young woman when she came to the school at age sixteen. She was a refugee charity case. She was generally quiet but quickly exhibited an enormous capacity to learn, particularly languages. We gave her a good basic secondary education and then allowed her to pursue the mastery of English, Latin and French. She accomplished that by age twenty-two, when she left us."

Sister Carmeline, who was well on in years, paused to catch her breath. She was a slim, diminutive woman with a pleasant face and generous smile. Her voice was sweet and modulated to keep any student attentive. She commanded attention with her crisp articulation of English, albeit with a hint of a Scottish accent.

Her speech made each word part of a musical phrase she built to entice the ear of any listener. Her Italian was so good, we thought her a native. It was almost impossible to imagine her doling out any kind of corporal punishment. I, for one, was willing to give her the benefit of the doubt.

She slipped gingerly into a chair, realizing she had been standing for half an hour and talking, and continued with her story.

"Sonia left us to take a job as a stenographer in Manhattan, having also mastered Gregg Shorthand. We had placed her in a fine Manhattan home for single Catholic women with three other girls.

"In those days the Depression was still with us and she was fortunate to get a decent job. The combination of her beauty and a quick demonstration of excellent clerical skills opened doors for her."

Sister Carmeline paused and asked for a drink of water which I quickly got for her. She emptied the paper cup and resumed.

"One day at the office, her typewriter stopped working, and within an hour Lathem Yarmolinsky showed up to fix it. She confided to me that they took to each other instantly.

"But she made him sweat for a few dates, and spend some money, before they started 'keeping company.' He didn't mind having to come to Brooklyn to see her from the Bronx where he lived.

"We had our doubts about him because he was so smooth. I thought he was a Jew and said so to his face. He denied it immediately, reciting the Russian Orthodox rites he knew as a child. As I said, he was very smooth.

"They quickly talked about marriage which seemed a bit premature. But we at the school understood that America was one of the few places in the world that was safe from the war in Europe. Here a couple could work hard and be happy, especially if they were blessed with children. We knew Sonia had no obligation to accept our judgment anyway, so we gave them our blessing."

Sister Carmeline's eyes had moistened at those memories and she paused again, asking for more water.

"On October 13, 1939, Father Pappalardo married them in the rectory, rather than debate whether the ceremony would have to be in front of the rail, due to Yarmolinsky's not being a Roman Catholic. The couple didn't mind, as they were on their way to Coney Island for an abbreviated honeymoon."

The nun stood up, winced and held her back, saying "It's either arthritis or sciatic nerve pain. I can't sit down for too long.

"Anyway, Lathem was drafted in 1942. They were distraught then, but three weeks later Sonia realized she was expecting a child. Lathem had one more weekend to spend time with her and asked us to look after Sonia.

"She wanted to stay in their little apartment in Brooklyn because the rent was cheap and the location good. We arranged for her to have charity obstetric care at St. Luke's hospital. Then the terrible news came about Lathem's death in Europe.

"We brought her back to the school for the last weeks before little Lathem was born. Thank God, she had an easy delivery and her son was born healthy.

"She had saved some money while she and her husband worked. She needed every bit of it to get by for the rest of the year. The army sent her some money too, but she was still forced to leave her apartment in early 1944. We gladly took her and little Lathem back, and she stayed with us until 1951.

All those years she did excellent administrative work at St. Luke's to cover the cost of their room and board. Little Lathem had his schooling with us gratis. He was extremely bright, God rest his soul.

"It was during those years that we became very close, and she confided her dreams to me. Although she loved to read, it was the movies that fed her love for fantasy.

"But post-war movies were not the same as those she remembered, especially those made after the Atomic Bomb was used. She didn't care for science fiction films.

"However, at this time early TV in New York had several independent stations with little live programming. They featured instead many films from the 1930s. Sonia relived her Depression-era youth, viewing those Jeanette McDonald and Nelson Eddy movies that fired her romantic imagination.

"She somehow managed to separate the fantasy world of Hollywood from the real world atrocities committed during the war. Her personal sorrow was sublimated into raising her son in an imagined world where they were assured a safe life.

"Then God sent you, Mr. Tommaso. We were so grateful that she had a family again and a new home. God bless you both. Pray to her often, for surely she sits near the throne of God with the other angels."

With that, Sister Carmeline said a last prayer at the casket and slowly walked out of the room. Pop sat down and put his head in his hands and silently wept. I stood beside him, crying too, and holding his trembling shoulders.

## Per Sempre

A mass for the dead and a burial the day before Christmas Eve: impossible? No! Don Silvio arranged or supervised everything to be done. Money opens many doors, but with Don Silvio favors were never forgotten. His track record spoke eloquently for itself. He was one hell of a CEO!

Our lives now were undergoing rapid and extraordinary changes. Pop had gone to see Don Silvio after the funeral as a penitent pleading for mercy. His uncle was a tall, well-built man, often called "Cesar" because of his resemblance to Cesar Romero, the actor, right down to the signature moustache. He was handsome in the Latin way with a full head of silver-and black-streaked hair. Don Silvio was also what was called a "natty" dresser. If someone wanted to stick a five carat word into Don Silvio's Italian silk tie it would be "Elegant."

Don Silvio's wife, Vita, had married him nearly fifty years ago when he was still a "Diamond in the rough." Vita buffed the persona of the young man to a high sheen, even teaching him how to pick shirt collars and ties while showing him how to knot the ties. She introduced Don Silvio to a little ritual she had shared with her father Pietro. He was a municipal clerk and wore a suit and tie every day he worked.

Each morning, little Vita watched her mother, Antonina, knot Pietro's tie and say: "Today Pietro, the world outside is yours, but tonight you return to us. That is our destiny. We belong to each other."

Pietro would lean down to Antonia's ear and whisper *"Per sempre"* and kiss Antonino's hair. When she was eight years old, Vita usurped her mother's place, and performed the ritual with "Pappa." Once married to Don Silvio, Vita introduced him to the ritual by insisting he wear a suit and tie every day he went to work.

*"Oggi, Silviu, lu munnu di fora ti apparteni, ma stasira tu ritorni nni mia. Chistu è u nostru distinu. Semu distinati a stari nzemmula."* ("Today Silvio, the world outside is yours, but tonight you return to me. That is our destiny. We belong to each other.")

Don Silvio would lean down to Vita's ear and whisper *"Per sempre,"* but Vita would pull the handsome young man's mouth down to her warm, moist lips.

Vita fashioned a partnership with Don Silvio, which he honored in both their intimate and public lives.

## The Brothers Tommaso

Don Silvio's love for his brother Pippinu, Pop's father, ran deep and colored his response to Pop's supplication. Don Silvio later confided to Pop what happened to convince him to accept Pop back into the family.

Pippinu had lived with his daughters, Pop's sisters, Filippa and Agata since 1922 in Palermo. Don Silvio went back to visit his brother every other year between the wars, and every year thereafter. During these visits, Don Silvio also saw his sister, Giuseppina, and would make an effort to see *Cignu Russu* as well. Giuseppina and his niece Helena tried to persuade Don Silvio's sister-in-law to soften and see him, to no avail.

On Pippinu's eighty-first birthday (1946), Don Silvio came for the first time in eight years. He found Pippinu was confined to bed, probably his death bed, and the brothers had a very serious talk.

Don Silvio told Pippinu that Girolamu, unmarried, was living alone in Brooklyn, working steadily but without the love of family around him. Initially, Pippinu's face hardened but then it became sad and he wept.

"My dear brother," Don Silvio said, "what did that child ever do to deserve so harsh a life for all these years? Love his mother and yet tell you she was unfaithful? You ignored the obvious signs and blamed a ten-year-old child for your horns. I trust your revenge was complete.

"So why do you persist in blaming your only healthy, male child for your weakness? Is that what you want on your head, when Jesus comes again to judge you?"

Pippinu let out a long painful breath of air, signaling the collapse of his rock-hard resistance. "What can I do?"

Don Silvio said, "Let me be your right hand to bring Girolamu back into the family, and rest easy because it will be done."

In 1947, Pippinu died peacefully in his sleep, but Don Silvio would act as his surrogate in the matter of Pop's restoration to the family. Not even Don Silvio would have dreamed that nineteen more years and my Mother's death were needed to accomplish the task.

Don Silvio never despaired and felt justified in his continued support of Pop's employment; something he never told Pop, but I learned from Pinu at Don Silvio's wake. I kept it to myself. Thankfully, all those years, Pop had a strong work ethic and back to match.

## Don Silvio and the Great Compromise

In his early seventies, Don Silvio appeared to be much younger. He was a self-made man who used brawn and brains to build a little empire across the Queens-Brooklyn border, with a few tentacles stretching cross country and to Europe. His reputation was founded on trust, a willingness to share good fortune and to offer compromise where all parties could get something they wanted.

Don Silvio did not smoke and drank only red wine in moderation. His family adored him and he lavished love on them. But he insisted that his five children and four grandchildren be well educated and seek careers of their own.

The only exception he made in a moment of weakness was to promise his oldest son, Pippinu "Pinu" Tommaso, he would be heir to the Family business. Pinu was unfortunately nothing like his father. Other males in the family were known to refer to Don Silvio as "the big, sweet wind east of Chicago," while Pinu was "the light breeze downwind from the Newtown Creek."

Don Silvio's wife, Vita, invited Pop and me to spend several days at their home; they lived in Queens and we stayed for the holiday and over the weekend. Assuring no disrespect, they said mourning should be suspended to celebrate our reconciliation and, of course, the Lord's birth.

The circumstances were problematic for Don Silvio. Proceeding as he wished to was extremely unorthodox when a family member had just died. However, he considered in a cool and objective way that only two people, Pop and I, would be truly grieving a personal loss. Everything else had been planned over the last weeks, involving a long standing tradition for many members of the family. They had already arranged to be there, and food and help had been ordered, not to mention the outlay of many thousands of dollars.

Don Silvio fashioned a compromise. Each party to the compromise: Don Silvio and the family, Pop, me and Mom (Pop had informed his uncle about his sacred commitments to his late wife) would benefit from proceeding as Don Silvio intended it.

Mom was given the headstone she desired, as well as a perpetual memorial, via a special annual mass, on the day of her passing. Members of the extended Tommaso family all paid their respects to Sonia Tommaso at her three-day wake and funeral. Her casket was the best available at the time, and stately, becoming a well-loved member of society.

After her burial, the myriad floral arrangements, which filled the viewing room at the funeral parlor, were all donated and delivered to St. Mary Magdalene Church in Sonia's name. Her greatest wishes for my future would be granted when Don Silvio became my Godfather.

Pop would be welcomed back to the family as part of a ritual his uncle would conduct during the holiday weekend. Don Silvio would offer Pop employment which took advantage of his best skills and assured a lucrative retirement. Pop's plea for help in raising me would be addressed in several specific ways to be determined.

I, too, would be welcomed into the family where the sincere love of dozens of relatives would make every effort to compensate for my personal loss. Don Silvio's patronage would assure that my future would contain fewer obstacles than most people are plagued with.

Achieving these goals gave Don Silvio comfort in leaving all plans for the holiday intact, despite its flying in the face of long-standing tradition. After Pop explained to me what my Godfather had done, I wondered if President Johnson had as much wisdom and authority. But I still missed Mom.

## The Christmas Feast

Vita assured us that they had extra bedrooms, now that all their five children owned spacious homes of their own. In fact, the rec room in the full, finished basement of the house would hold eleven children in as many warm sleeping bags that night on plush carpeting.

That Christmas Eve, the Tommaso family shared the biggest feast of food, drink and music I have ever experienced. All Don Silvio's immediate family, which numbered eleven, was joined by the other branches with Tommaso blood: the Genuas, Gennas, Espardas, Mellanis, Lorenzos and Coronas, which numbered twenty-eight. Vita's widowed sister and her daughter made a round thirty.

The children under ten years of age, numbering eleven, had their own dining room and four older male servers. The main dining room had a huge table that sat thirty-two people comfortably. Adults were served by a staff of eight women, one more attractive than the other, although all were dressed very conservatively.

Vita Tommaso had planned the meal with the help of her three married daughters and two daughters-in-law. To lend a hand, Don Silvio had invited master chefs from renowned Italian restaurants (the family owned interest in), one each from Brooklyn and Queens.

The meatless menu consisted of appetizers: hot and cold vegetable and cheese Antipasti, Fried *Ciuri di cucuzzedda* and steamed stuffed *Cacuocciuli*. Then a macaroni dish, *Linguini* in Crab Sauce. This was followed by thirteen varieties of seafood.

Traditionally, seven varieties of fish were served, but Don Silvio served seafood for all the apostles and Jesus. He could afford it.

The list included, *Baccalà* sautéed in Tomato sauce, baked *Nuci di coccu*, boiled *Purpu*, steamed Mussels in Red or White sauce, Baked Clams, Broiled and Baked Shrimp, Broiled Lobster Tails, grilled *Tunnu*, baked *Piscispata*, fried *Merluzzu*, baked *Salmuni*, *Ancidda* sautéed in garlic and olive oil, and fried *Calamari*.

All manner of side dishes adorned the table: boiled, roasted, mashed and fried potatoes; toasted beets, fried zucchini, stuffed, baked mushrooms and artichoke bottoms, freshly boiled, breaded and fried *Carduni* and *Sparaciu*.

To have a general toast to the entire family's heath, Don Silvio provided ten bottles of *Asti Spumante* for the adults and made the toast himself. But first, he acknowledged Mom's passing, expressing regret that the family had not had the pleasure of her company all these years.

He noted that to all who knew her, as he had heard, Mom was a beautiful person, and a devoted wife and mother with a loving heart. He finished by saying that this Christmas celebration would become a perpetual memorial to her, which the family would institute with a high Holy Mass in her honor every December twentieth. Only then did Don Silvio raise his glass to wish the family "*Bon Natali e filici Annu Novu.*"

With the food came bottles of the best white and red wines, from Sicily, Tuscany and Napa, California. These vintages included a Chianti wine bottled near Arezzo, birthplace of Petrarch, from a winery which the family owned under a commercial name.

There was also some special after dinner Port, distributed by a winery in the Napa Valley in which the family had a controlling interest. Don Silvio told Pop that the family was in negotiations with Robert Mondavi to establish the Napa Valley as home to the best wines in the country; perhaps even the world.

Of course, milk, soda and fruit juices were provided for the children, while imported Italian and German beers were available to adults.

During breaks in eating (the entire meal lasted six hours), Don Silvio directed his oldest grandson, Silvio, to put the stereo on and play Nicola Paone's recordings from the album, *Songs My Mother Never Taught Me*, and the album of Louis Prima's *Italian Songs*.

Every hour or so, we'd be treated to Paone's "Signora Maestra," "U Sciccareddu," "Blah, Blah, Blah," and "Uei Paesano; complemented by Prima's "Angelina," "Felicia No Capiscia," "Zooma Zooma Baccalà," "Please No Squeeza Da Banana" and "Buona Sera."

These recordings were a revelation to me, partly because I had never heard them, yet I picked up many of the Sicilian and Italian words. But it was even more fun watching Pop react to them. He laughed like I never saw before, and actually sang along with many of them.

But during one break, Don Silvio whispered something in his grandson's ear and in a minute I was having another epiphany because of "the Voice." I was sure I had heard the name "Frank

Sinatra" before that day, but I had no conscious recollection of who he was. Mom played Bobby Vinton's "Blue Velvet" and "Roses Are Red" after Lathem died. No Sinatra.

Within fifteen minutes I was hooked. It's always been difficult for me to explain that certain magnetism Sinatra possessed, and what made him the best singer of American songs we've ever had.

However, Benny Green, a highly respected British musicologist and critic, said it best when Sinatra announced his retirement (somewhat prematurely) in 1972:

> What few people, apart from musicians, have never seemed to grasp is that he is not simply the best popular singer of his generation . . . but the culminating point in an evolutionary process which has refined the art of words set to music. Nor is there even the remotest possibility that he will have a successor.
>
> Sinatra was the result of a fusion of a set of historical circumstances which can never be repeated.

I won't apologize for this digression because *Songs for Swinging Lovers* and *A Swinging Affair* just concluded. We already consumed the *Nsalata* and some fine *finocchiu* and *provolone*, while Sinatra was finishing his set. Now it's time for dessert.

Enjoyable eating is all in the pacing, allowing enough time for good digestion, which permits Italians to consume the volume of holiday food described above. On the other hand, having quarts of *Brioschi* or bottles of Alka-Seltzer (for the new generation) within reach will provide relief to the over-indulgers in the party.

In any case, Don Silvio's house had nine commodes on three levels in operation, which precluded any lines or long waits. All children and young adults had to go to the top floor to do their business.

After our servers quickly cleared our table, they miraculously changed the soiled red table cloth for a new green one, and desserts flew to the table. Much fresh *Ricotta* was in evidence in dozens of just-filled *cannoli*, two large *cassata* Cakes and a giant Cheesecake. Bowls piled high with deep-fried and sugar-powdered *Sfingi* followed.

Hot demitasse coffee flowed freely into lemon-peel-rubbed lips of little cups, and four bottles of rare Anisette circulated to sweeten the brew.

At this interlude, Don Silvio's grandson prevailed upon him to play some Bobby Darin recordings, especially "Mack the Knife," so the younger generation could be heard. "As long as the singer is Italian, it's alright," Don Silvio would say and wink.

I had made some effort to taste everything in moderation because I had been told what tradition called for at Midnight and thereafter. Most of the party would go to and from Mass in big limousines provided by Don Silvio. That time was used by the staff to do a thorough clean up and prepare the first meal on Christmas Day.

As we band of Catholics returned to Don Silvio's house, the brisk night air faded into the warmth within. That warmth was permeated with the delicious, distinctive smells of cooked pork and fried peppers and onions. The *sasizza* was served up in thick, individual links, just the right size for the mini-loaves of *Pistaluna* bread rushed over from a local bakery the family owned.

That day, we ate, as cousin Nick would say at all our holiday meals with the family, "Like we were going to the chair!" When I was informed of its meaning, I puzzled over its aptness.

Years later, I realized it did happen to at least one member of the Family. However, his execution was delayed so long by legal maneuvering that he survived. New York State ceased capital punishment in 1963. He's an old man now, still serving time.

This meal was what I waited for, as Mom had raised me to be a carnivore, stressing consumption of protein from the concept that *carne fa carne*. Pop was enjoying the pork too, but I noticed a look of concern in his eyes. He seemed nervous about something.

## A Godfather for Me and a Return to La Famiglia

I did not know that Pop was going to be placed front and center that morning, after the children were sent to bed, except for me.

He was to publicly acknowledge and beg forgiveness for his familial apostasy, and express his undying fealty to Don Silvio and the family. Finally, he was to ask for help in raising me. That would be the effect of his asking Don Silvio to become my Godfather.

Pop was nervous but got into a good rhythm in his speech quickly. He maintained eye contact with everyone in the room,

111

especially Don Silvio. I was so shaken by all this that I heard only words and did not fully comprehend what Pop was saying.

"I am also very sorry that I turned away from my brother Tonio. I understand he could not join us tonight because he still suffers from his wounds from The Great War. I will go to him tomorrow to personally beg his forgiveness and ask him to reunite with me in brotherhood.

"Finally, I pledge to visit my father's grave site in Palermo, and see my mother, who I understand is still alive in Sicily at the age of 92. I will plead with her for some kind of reunion of our immediate family, while we still have time to share our love in this life. The graveyards bury both the living and the dead, when we are strangers to our dying loved ones."

At some point, Pop walked over to Don Silvio, kneeled and kissed the green emerald stone in the ring that graced Don Silvio's right ring finger. Don Silvio whispered something in Pop's ear and Pop gestured to me to come forward.

Don Silvio presented his right hand to me and looked benignly in my eyes. I sensed I needed to repeat what Pop had done. After I kissed Don Silvio's ring, he put his right arm around me and said for all to hear: "Jerome Tommaso, I am your great uncle by blood, but today I become your Godfather, too, for the rest of my life. God bless you on the day of Jesus' birth for you have truly been reborn."

Well, we all had a good cry over this ceremony and then we laughed. Pop said I needed to go to bed and Vita Tommaso took me by the hand and up the stairs to our room.

Over the weekend Pop filled me in on plans that were made for us. Don Silvio had more than a dozen two-family houses in Queens that needed some maintenance work, and continual oversight, to keep his tenants happy and the properties' values high. Pop was fifty-six and had all the skills required for this work. Don Silvio suggested that Pop retire from the construction line and become his full-time employee.

Pop did not know that from the time he turned his back on his family in 1931 Don Silvio made sure that opportunities to work were always there for him. Don Silvio had great influence in the labor unions going back to the twenties.

He would never have upset his family by openly doing such a thing. But in considering Girolamu's case he gave weight to the following: Girolamu's genuine love for his mother, *Cignu Russu*; the harsh denunciation of his mother by the other stateside Tommasos; Girolamu's innocence in giving Pippinu horns and Pippinu's acknowledgement of it before he died; and Girolamu's responsibility for his family, including raising another man's son.

All these factors were seen as mitigating any desire for the family's retribution or benign indifference. Don Silvio acted alone and now felt vindicated. It was not necessary that anyone else know. Don Silvio was indeed a wise man. He always told his son Pinu that he intended to die in his own bed from natural causes. And he did.

Part of Pop's compensation would be free rent in another of Don Silvio's homes in Queens, near where we lived in Brooklyn but just inside Ridgewood, Queens. This was a two-family Brownstone house with a finished basement. Each apartment had two bedrooms, a bath, and three other rooms. We would live on the first floor and have use of the basement as well.

The upstairs apartment would be occupied by Don Silvio's widowed sister-in-law, Mary Milano, thirty-eight, and her fifteen year old daughter, Rose. They, too, would pay no rent and share access to the basement. A cleaning service would come every other Saturday to keep the house "spic and span."

Mary would keep an eye on me every day and make sure I ate well and got off to school. Rose was a good student in her second year at Grover Cleveland High School. She would be available to help me with anything related to my schoolwork.

All these matters were settled very quickly, because Don Silvio, Vita and their children and grandchildren who did not work or have school, would be flying to the Grand Cayman Islands on December 28 for ten days of sun and relaxation.

Don Silvio wanted his whole family to be able to satisfy their social obligations to in-laws. So, he did not have the family over for New Year's or Thanksgiving. He did want to entertain the family for Easter Sunday, July Fourth and Labor Day (in Forest Park) and Christmas Eve and Day. All other holidays and weekends he refrained from entertaining large groups.

Of course, if you were in the neighborhood on most Sunday afternoons, you were always welcome to say *Sabbinirica* and sample Vita's matchless meat balls, a plate of macaroni, a glass of Chianti wine and warm, crisp *Pistaluna* bread.

Don Silvio was a busy man and absent most days of the week

and some nights. But Vita insisted he be home most Sundays to have the afternoon meal with Pinu and his family.

The day after Christmas, Pop and I went to see his brother Tonio in Brooklyn. Tonio was nearly seventy-one, and had endured more than forty-five years of continual migraine headaches. His World War I shell-shock injuries seemed acceptable, compared to the loss of their older brothers, Pippinu and Vicenzu in 1918. But Tonio's life, and that of his family's, was a living death with little relief in sight.

Tonio had not seen Pop since 1931. He had lost all memory of the years before he and his twin brothers went to war. That day, Tonio, in a drug-induced state, met two strangers and we saw an old man who probably would have pulled the plug if he could. Don Silvio had paid for the best of care, but the general prognosis was "Hopeless."

## Beam Number Three

Two days later, Don Silvio and his family flew to the Caribbean. Tonio went down to his basement that day to check on an electric connection for his outdoor Christmas ornaments. The connections shorted out and Tonio was electrocuted. There was no investigation by police, and the matter was classified "accidental death."

The wake was limited to one night with a closed coffin. Pop and I went but only the immediate family was present and a priest to lead a final prayer. Pinu and a small entourage made an appearance when the priest left. The funeral was a quiet affair with only a handful of family members present including Pop. Pinu Tommaso handled everything in his father's absence. Don Silvio was informed but did not return home early.

Tonio's $150,000 life insurance policy was paid without question. His family was moved to a different part of Brooklyn into another of Don Silvio's properties. Shortly after his return, Don Silvio visited Tonio's family with Vita. They expressed their personal grief over Tonio's death, acknowledging the family's own years of suffering. Don Silvio hoped they could return to a normal life. He offered his continuing assistance whenever needed.

I asked Pop why this death and the family's response was so different from Mom's. Pop said that Tonio might have killed himself, and his family faced a lot of unkind publicity and legal issues. Don Silvio wanted above all to protect the living, Tonio's family, from shame and snooping. His family would be welcomed back into the fold, after years of absence due to his illness.

Pop did not want to be the one to let aunt Giuseppina know about uncle Tonio's passing. However, Don Silvio had a letter sent to his sister immediately. Angelina and her daughter, Michela, went to see *Cignu Russu* as quickly as they could.

The old woman, now a slender shadow of her former beauty, took the news in stride. Amazingly, she asked about Girolamu and his son, Jerome. There was a defiant gleam in her eyes but it was meant for death to observe. She asked her sister-in-law and niece, Angelina, and grandniece, Michela, to tell Girolamu to come as soon as possible and bring her grandson to her. She said she would defy death as long as she could, so they should hurry.

I must pause here to clarify some facts about people I just mentioned. Aunt Giuseppina, now nearly eighty-six, was the first of three generations of women with Tommaso blood to bear a child out of wedlock. Her daughter, Angelina, was sixty-five; she gave birth to Michela out of wedlock when she was thirty; Michela, now thirty-five, gave birth to Marta out of wedlock in 1955. This chain of events upset Don Silvio no end.

On his last visit, he read them all "the riot act." He told Pop that the women were given a final warning: if Marta became pregnant before age eighteen and was not lawfully wedded, Don Silvio didn't care if it was another virginal conception by the Holy Ghost or a rape by the village idiot, he would cut them all off, not leaving one *Lire* in their bank accounts! That was the good news. The bad news was that Marta was only ten at the time.

I had yet to meet any of these people, but before you think this situation represented a new flowering of *Lesbos*, or an imitation of the *Mosuo* matrilineal society in China, I assure you any similarities are strictly coincidental.

The *Mosuo* society is made up forty thousand inhabitants of Luga Lake in southwest China. The women cherry-pick men in their society to have free sex with: the children born of these matings are raised by the women. The *Mosuo* language has no word for "Father" or "Husband." The women like it that way. I dare say the men like it as well.

The Tommaso women are apparently hot-blooded until they

115

have a child to care for, in which case they dump the fathers and raise the children, *in famiglia.* The reluctant support of Don Silvio also helped. The fact that in this case all children were females was an uncontrollable outcome.

I use the surname Tommaso lightly. After four generations, the Tommaso gene pool had been almost washed out. In a way I was lucky because I could marry Marta one day and not be concerned about congenital disasters. But I'm getting ahead of the narrative.

Once again, my Godfather's grasp of human nature impressed me. However, as I grew older, I began to see a pattern in his decisions. They showed that it was always a King Solomon's balancing act between preserving the interests of the Family and those of the family: that was his real skill.

By the middle of January, a truck belonging to the family's moving service came by and had all our belongings out and packed within ninety minutes. We spent some of that time saying good-bye to the Farantes who were saddened to see us go. But they were happy we were moving to better quarters only a few minutes away.

By that evening, everything was moved in and put where we wished in our new home. Pop tried to tip the movers but one of them held up a thick right index finger and moved it from right to left. Then he shook Pop's hand. I could hardly catch my breath. All I could think of was that my Godfather knew how to get things done.

As each month passed, my grasp of Italian improved. Mrs. Milano and Rose spoke to me in Italian at my request. Rose, who was an excellent student, read, wrote and spoke Italian as well as her teacher, Miss Strunza.

Pop spent more time with me in the evenings as we conversed in Italian. He would tell me stories about his childhood. Many of them were passed on to him by his grandfather, Francesco Greco, his beloved mother's father. I would describe these stories as generally ribald and occasionally raunchy, in the best tradition of Boccaccio. We'll get to one of those eventually, but I want to talk about Marta and the first time we met.

## I Meet Marta

I met Marta in Calatafimi, Sicily in April, 1966; this was nineteen months before the second most important development of my young life.

At twelve and one-half years of age my engagement with the arts was growing rapidly, thanks to James. But I was four feet nine inches tall and weighed eighty-nine pounds. And to be perfectly honest, my penis, at tumescence, measured less than three inches.

I knew I was small, as did most of my male schoolmates. The gym, the pool and the locker room at school were circles of hell to me. On top of all that, I was dark-skinned with black curly hair: not very attractive to white American girls. This was what I looked like when I met all the women from Aunt Giuseppina to Cousin Marta.

I was off from school most of the week leading up to Easter Sunday and the week after, so Pop and I flew to Sicily on the Saturday before Palm Sunday for a week. Don Silvio arranged to cover for Pop during that period and get the plane tickets.

When we finally got to Calatafimi, it was in the early afternoon, following a long taxi ride from Palermo. In Palermo, we had visited grandfather Pippinu's grave site, leaving flowers and a plant to signify our visit. My aunts, Pop's sisters, still refused to see us.

The Tommasos (I knew no other surname and Pop didn't explain relationships) all lived in one stand-alone, four-story walk-up, building: on a street facing a busy thoroughfare. It sat behind a half wall with a narrow street running in front of the building, parallel to the thoroughfare.

Because of their ages, Giuseppina and Angelina occupied the apartment on the first floor. This they now shared with *Cignu Russu*, the matriarch of the family at ninety-three, who had recently moved in to be close to them and more easily accessible to her son and grandson. All had been arranged by Don Silvio.

Aunt Helena, who had shared the first floor apartment moved to the second floor. Michela and Marta occupied the third floor. The top floor was currently vacant and would be our quarters for the eight days we were there.

After our leaving, the floor would be rented to young marrieds with lots of energy. The deed to the property had been signed over from Don Silvio to Giuseppina, with the understanding that all the family live there rent free.

Aunt Giuseppina and Cousin Angelina did some cooking, but most meals were prepared by Michela, who had been well schooled by her mother and grandmother. Since Aunt Helena lived alone, and had the biggest kitchen, all meals were cooked and served on the second floor, as long as Aunt Giuseppina could make it up one flight of stairs with Angelina.

The routine called for breakfast in your own apartment, then congregating on the second floor for the rest of the day. That apartment had a dining room which could accommodate twelve people. There were two TVs on that floor and a new radio, all compliments of Don Silvio. Everyone in the building, except *Cignu Russu*, had lunch and dinner together. *Cignu Russu* took all her meals in her small bedroom on the first floor, usually alone.

Pop and I didn't mind the climbs up or down. Since we were not prepared to make breakfast, Marta was at our door at eight AM to invite us down for breakfast with her and Michela. At eight AM, Marta was bright, loud and quite beautiful. On Palm Sunday, I was up, washed and ready to go down with her when she knocked on the door.

That first evening, Pop and I went to see his mother, *Cignu Russu*, right after the evening meal was served. Marta cleared away the dishes and received a hug and kiss from *Cignu Russu*, who recognized and loved her kindred spirit in the flesh. I stayed outside the room, giving Pop the privacy I know he wanted and needed.

Until Pop emerged, about an hour later, I spent most of that time conversing with Marta, outside, in front of the building where we could be seen. Marta had just turned eleven (March 10 was her birthday) but resembled many sixteen year old types I knew in Brooklyn and Queens. She was taller than I by five inches. I was only eight pounds heavier than she was.

But what a face and what a body! Marta already had the breasts of a grown woman, although I noticed that the flatter the stomach the larger breasts appeared to be. And she had a flat stomach, I imagined.

She was all olive-brown from her toes to her forehead. Her lovely face was surrounded by thick light brown hair, which hung down the left side of her face to the top of her left breast in soft, elongated curls. I imagined she was olive-brown in all the parts of her body I couldn't see.

Marta's eyes were deep brown, except in bright sunlight when they were translucent, her nose was small and graceful as it descended to her generous lips; she often pursed them, when she feigned being upset. When she smiled, which was frequently, her white teeth brightened her face, and her pink tongue, which she stuck out to me continually, was positively seductive.

118

There's a four-letter word for what I was thinking and feeling as we were looking each other over that night. It would be another two years before I learned it. It begins with an "l" and ends with a "t".

I found Marta's voice in speaking Italian modulated to brush me back with a feigned criticism and draw me closer for a personal compliment. We were both conscious of "being in public" on the street and needing to act like children for passers-by to see and hear.

Marta was exciting me like no American girl I knew. I was almost glad when Pop emerged and called my name. I was getting too hot!

Pop had been crying and was wiping tears from his eyes when he said to speak up but be gentle with his mother.

I entered the dark room exited and scared, not sure what to expect. There was a dim light a few feet away but only her shoes and dark, ankle-length skirt were illuminated.

"*Nonna*," I called, "It's Jerome, your grandson."

"*Figghiuzzu miu*, come closer, so I can see you."

I moved closer and could see the outline of a face then I heard a gasp and "Girolamu, my baby, is it you? Have you come to apologize and forgive your mother?"

Her Sicilian words were not easy to understand at first but I gradually picked up the thread of her meaning. She was confusing me with her son, Pop, who may have looked like me when he was my age.

As hard as I tried, I could not put a meaningful sentence together, and in great frustration I moved to her and fell at her feet crying. Something strange happened as I blurted out "Mama, I love you and miss you so much! I'm sorry if I ever hurt you or made you sad. Please forgive me."

*Cignu Russu* took my face in her hands and kissed my head, saying "*Figghiuzzu miu*, Mama's body and soul are almost healed and at peace. If only Michele would return to say good-bye, I could close my eyes and wait for *paradisu*. Please come back tomorrow."

"Yes, Mama, I will," I said without thinking. "*Sabbinirica*, Mama."

When I told Pop the first part of what had happened, he was also sure *Cignu Russu* was hallucinating, mistaking me for Pop as a child. I didn't go into the mention of "Michele," or my own hallucinatory experience. There was something about each of those moments I believed would upset Pop but I wasn't sure why. I thought to ask Aunt Helena who Michele was when Pop was not around: whether she'd tell me was another matter.

On Palm Sunday, Pop and I, with Michela and Marta, went to Mass at the *Church of the Madonna del Giubino*. Palms commemorating the entrance of Jesus into Jerusalem on a mule were everywhere in abundance.

At home, one of the local, younger priests came calling at eight AM to serve sacraments to those who were unable to go to church. This was a weekly routine for Father Sigismundi who took special care of the Tommaso family.

With the beginning of the holiest of weeks, Marta and I saw a lot of each other but we were never alone. We would walk ahead of Pop and Michela, and I taught Marta expressions in English. By Holy Thursday, we were speaking a language no one else in the family could understand. In this way, we flirted and made fun of others, even our parents.

Each night I would look in on *Cignu Russu*, to tell her I loved her. On Monday night Marta and I went in together and I could see how these females were two sides of the same coin, as Pop had told me about his mother's childhood. There was more than a little of "Nunzia, the nutcracker" in Marta and perhaps some of the swan but with a light tan down.

That night, *Cignu Russu* produced a very old photograph for us to look at. She said it dated from the summer of 1913 when she was thirty-nine and Girolamu was almost three. The whole family was in the studio shot and could be picked out easily. Even at thirty-nine, *Cignu Russu* was beautiful, standing to the left of her seven children, while Pippinu stood on the right with Girolamu in his arms.

No doubt she had bewitched the photographer who took great pains to capture her full figure with her hair splashed over each shoulder and running down the sides of each full breast to her small waist. The picture cried out for color, but nothing could prevent her physical beauty from shining through.

After we studied the picture and identified each child, *Cignu Russu* requested a picture of us together. Marta said there was a photography machine in one of the downtown stores where you could go into a booth, close a curtain and take several bust shots all for five *Lire*. The best part was that you saw the results right away. Marta promised *Cignu Russu* we would take some pictures for her the next day.

120

On Tuesday, Pop and I, Michela and Marta went shopping and stopped to take the pictures. Fifteen *Lire* later, we emerged with twelve two-inch square black and white photos. Marta and I each kept two and we gave *Cignu Russu* and the rest of the family the balance. On the back of each picture, we wrote our names then dated and signed them. On our copies, we also wrote "All my love," in English. Until I saw Marta again in 1969, those photos were my most prized possessions.

Our schedule called for us to fly home on Saturday. We had an early flight out of Palermo, so there was a tearful farewell at seven AM. We all kissed and hugged. Marta kissed me on each cheek as she whispered "I love you," in English and I did the same. I looked at our picture together for hours, daydreaming of what might be someday.

My height, just average
My weight, just average
And my I.Q.
Is like you'd estimate
Just average
But evidently
She does not agree
Consequently
If I seem at sea

It amazes me
It simply amazes me
What she sees in me
Dazzles me, dazes me
That I've learned to clip my wings
And soften my ways
These are ordinary things
Unworthy of praise
Yet she praises me
Just knowing I'd try for her
When so many would
If they could, die for her

I'm the one who's worldly wise
And nothing much phases me
But to see me in her eyes
It just amazes me

## Signura Maistra, vossia chi ci avi ccà?

I want to finish my account of my special birthday celebrations with Pop. The next one we enjoyed together was the best of all: November 11, 1966, when I was thirteen.

Pop said it was time for me to be spending my future birthdays with some friends. The only person he had seen me with was James and Pop did not like him.

James had recovered enough from his illness to take care of himself, but he went on a permanent disability pension. He was allowed to continue his piano studies which were judged to be therapeutic. James had been welcomed back by his family and tension eased because nobody wanted a recurrence of his illness. We took up the thread of our friendship in early fall.

Pop could not fathom what an "effeminate" young man was doing spending time with a new teenager, unless it was to take advantage. I told Pop continually that James looked out for my welfare and was very protective, period.

Lathem's best friend was to become a "Guru" to me, helping shape my social conscience, as well as my taste in music, theater and the rest of the arts. By the end of this year, we would begin to talk a lot and listen to music, or we went to Carnegie Hall for concerts, and to the The Met and The New York City Opera, for live ballet and opera.

James would reinforce my interest in Sinatra, and introduce me to Jazz music and masters of the piano, the instrument he continued to study. He would bring over a copy of Sinatra's album *Only the Lonely*, and would talk about the wonderful music and lyrics of "Blues in the Night," by Arlen and Mercer.

James explained how Nelson Riddle's arrangements showcased and complemented Sinatra's voice. He called Sinatra's singing on the album the best interpretation of American Art Songs he had ever heard. He always referred to The Great American Songbook as a collection of America's Art songs.

We would listen to Errol Garner and discuss his "Misty" with the same seriousness as we gave to Arthur Rubinstein's version of Rachmaninoff's *Variations on a Theme of Paganini*.

By now, I had learned that James had loved Lathem, whom, James said, returned his love. I accepted that statement and asked no questions. When Lathem was killed, James had a breakdown. His recovery had taken eighteen months. Then Mom passed away and James had a setback.

Finally, when I was thirteen, we both had come to terms with Mom's and Lathem's deaths, and we resumed a teacher-pupil relationship, as I finished my first year in middle school. Even though James was twenty-five, he always treated me with genuine concern and respect, as if I was a spiritual son born to him and Lathem. He fulfilled the role of "Big Brother" to me quite naturally.

But I digress. It was the actual day of my thirteenth birthday, when Pop said he had something extra-special planned. We took the subway into Manhattan but went to midtown instead of downtown. From Herald Square we walked several blocks east down 34th Street to number 207. It was a place called Nicola Paone Restaurant.

It turned out that Paone, an American, with Sicilian Heritage, ran the place and sometimes cooked certain special dishes. He was also a singer of Sicilian folk music and Pop's favorite entertainer. Pop had several of Paone's 78 RPM recordings which he played over and over on Lathem's old monaural phonograph. This was the same artist we had heard Christmas Eve at Don Silvio's house.

I asked what Pop liked about Paone.

"He gave many of us immigrants a voice, so that other people would understand how I feel about my homeland, my original language, and the songs that tell what it's been like to come here and try to succeed in America."

I was dumbstruck: not only was my father speaking to me in Italian, but he was having a serious conversation with me about himself.

Pop continued, "Paone is a very great performer. I was hoping he'd be here today and maybe sing something. Let's order lunch."

We ordered antipasto and the famous *Pasta Serenata* and *Veal Boom Boom* dishes Mr. Paone personally prepared, whenever he was in the restaurant. Their presence on today's menu gave Pop hope.

It was about three-thirty PM and most of the lunch crowd had left. Our table was the only one occupied in a section near the bar. Suddenly, there was a gentleman standing at the bar a short distance from our table. He was wearing a fitted, smart blue suit and caught Pop's attention.

My father had ordered a glass of Sicilian wine and said something which shocked me: "*Sabbinirica, Maestro Paone* – I drink to your health and long life."

The diminutive gentleman in the blue suit "bounced" over to our table in two quick strides. He introduced himself formally, and wished us both good health as well. Mr. Paone called for a glass of red wine and a coke for me.

His voice was robust and musical. It was impossible not to listen to him talk, so expressively, so seductively, in fluent Sicilian. He and Pop exchanged some words, each smiling warmly. I had hardly ever seen my father smile before.

Mr. Paone turned abruptly and left in a hurry returning in a few seconds with his *Chitarra*. Everyone else in the place stopped eating and talking and sat listening expectantly.

Pop told Mr. Paone that his favorite song was, *Signura Maestra*. Mr. Paone touched a few strings of his instrument, and then was off to the races, as he breathlessly portrayed a young boy asking his teacher, "What do you have there?," proceeding to go through the female anatomy from head to toe with popping sounds representing genitalia. It was one of those naughty songs from Mr. Paone's collection: *Songs My Mother Never Taught Me*.

He finished the song with a great flourish. This man, whom I estimated to be about Pop's age, maybe fifty-five, had just zipped through a song he'd composed, containing many verses and repetitions, in an extraordinary and flawless performance. I had never seen or heard live entertainment, outside of school, what with TV, records and movies.

By the way, the food was outstanding. As Pop was paying for our meal, Mr. Paone reappeared with a couple of his studio photographs. He signed them with panache: "To my *paisano*, Girolamu" and "To my *paisano*, Jerome," respectively, and dated them November 11, 1966. Heaven bless Nicola Paone.

That night at home, Pop and I listened to his 78RPM recording of *Signura Maestra*, with Pop interpreting the lyrics. We laughed our heads off and embraced. It was the most moving moment in our relationship. I sensed Pop was crying but he held me close and kissed my head, so I wouldn't see the tears.

That Christmas week (1966), after Mom's mass and before our annual feast with the Tommasos, James took me to see *The Nutcracker Ballet* at the Metropolitan Opera House. The Met had moved to Lincoln Center for the Performing Arts.

I was thirteen and I had experienced three more epiphanies: Pop's metamorphoses and mine, live music and live drama. Each encounter would permeate and enrich the rest of my life.

### GOIN' TA BETHLEHEM

It wuz OL' Mose's mule dat sweet Mary rode
Goin' ta Bethlehem.
It wuz OL' Mose's mule dat sweet Mary rode
Goin'ta Bethlehem.
It wuzn't no team o' Pharo's horses
It wuzn't none a dem
It wuz OL' Mose's mule dat sweet Mary rode

Goin'ta Bethlehem. (Repeat after each "Amen")
Amen! Amen! Amen!

It wuz the star o' David dat Joseph saw
Goin'ta Bethlehem.
It wuz the star o' David dat Joseph saw
Goin'ta Bethlehem.
It wuzn't no jew'l from Pharo's tresa
It wuzn't none a dem
It wuz da star o' David dat Joseph saw
Goin'ta Bethlehem. (Repeat after each "Amen")
Amen! Amen! Amen!

It wuz da Lord God Jesus in Mary's wumb
Goin'ta Bethlehem.
It wuz da Lord God Jesus in Mary's wumb
Goin'ta Bethlehem.
It wuzn't no chil' o' Pharo's Harlit
I wuzn't one a dem
It wuz da Lord God Jesus in Mary's wumb
Goin'ta Bethlehem. (Repeat after each "Amen")
Amen! Amen! Amen!

An' now each Christmas Day we all celebrate
Goin'ta Bethlehem.
An' now each Christmas Day we all celebrate
Goin'ta Bethlehem.
An, Mary an' Joseph an' de Lord Jesus an' we is born again
Dat's why each Christmas Day we all celebrate
Goin'ta Bethlehem. (Repeat after each (Amen")
Amen! Amen! Amen! Amen!

## Goin' ta Bethlehem

There is one event I want to describe from that Christmas of 1966, concerning a gift that Pop gave to Don Silvio and his wife Vita. Gifts for the host and hostess were never solicited nor expected: only grab bag toys and games for the children were an institutionalized event, complete with distribution by a jolly Santa himself.

On that Christmas Eve, Pop and I arrived in his work truck laden with an eight-foot by three-foot box containing a surprise gift. He had not allowed me to see the contents of the box. Although heavy, we managed to get it out of the basement and into the truck's cargo area.

Several men met us at the gate to Don Silvio's property and assisted in removing the box and taking it into the house. It was deposited next to the beautiful ten-foot Fur tree, alight with a rainbow of bulbs and glass ornaments which reflected the glow.

That night, as we paused before dessert was served, Pop got up and made a brief announcement. "My uncle Silvio and Aunt Vita welcomed me and my son Jerome back into the Tommaso family last year. My Sonia in *Paradisu*, Jerome and I will be forever grateful for that honor and act of love.

"While we will keep doing everything in our power to return that loyalty and love in any way we can, we wanted to give Don Silvio and Vita, as the spiritual parents of this entire family, something that would always be a reminder of that bond. The contents of this box, we hope, will represent that connection, especially because it was made with the love, care and skill I learned at my father Pippinu's knee."

The last comment drew Oohs and Ahs from everyone, and I saw how moved Don Silvio was by the reference to his beloved brother. As planned by Pop, with Don Silvio's assent, six male servers moved to the box, opened it and began removing the contents to display before the tree, according to a layout guide on paper read by one of them.

No one was prepared for the dazzling display of Girolamu's artistry in painted wood: a *Crèche*, or Nativity Set, on a scale of eighteen inch high standing figures with detailed faces. The expressions were very lively and packed with emotion. The colors of garments were vivid in blues, greens, reds, yellows; and the flesh tones subtle to clearly signify ethnicity and age, shepherds and Kings, temporal and divine presence.

After the figures were completely aligned, all lights but those of the tree were turned off. A special spotlight that Pop brought with us then flooded the *Presepio*, with enough light to throw the scene in high relief for all to see.

The reaction was at first hushed, as though we were all witnessing the birth of Jesus for the first time. Eventually, "bravos" rose to "magnificent" with an ovation worthy of a Florentine master. The scene was eerily like one I saw years later in Laguna, California at The Pageant of the Masters. There real people recreated a two-dimensional painting in three-dimensional life.

St. Francis of Assisi is credited with producing the first live pantomime-tableau of the birth of Christ around 1223 CE, in a cave near the monastery in today's commune of Greccio, about 58 Km SE of Spoleto and 80 Km NW of L'Aquila.

This effort helped to cultivate the worship of Christ. It was sanctioned by Pope Honorius III, and within a century every Roman church in Christendom was on its way to being graced with a *Presepio* at Christmas time.

This is one of those cases where life imitates art (Pageant) imitating life (Assisi) imitating legend (Christ). Some are amazing works of painting and sculptural art, although the local five and dime stores almost anywhere will sell little plastic versions at Christmas time that are crap and border on being sacrilegious.

After dessert, the whole scene was mounted on the eight-foot by three-foot box it came in which stood forty inches high. Seven groups of six people each were formed to pass by the *Presepio* in close proximity to appreciate the detail of the work. Later there was a definite buzz about who the figures resembled among the present company.

Mary looked like Mom and baby Jesus like me. Pop was Joseph. I saw he had two little mounds protruding from either side of his bald head: life imitating art or vice versa? Some people actually believe that Joseph was the first cuckold: God's cuckold!

Lathem and James were a shepherd and his lamb and the three Wise men were Don Silvio, Gold, unmistakable; and according to Pop, his father, Pippinu, Frankincense; and Michele Occhipinti, possibly Pop's biological father, Myrrh. I began to cry, losing my ability to discern other resemblances.

The interesting development of this exercise was the disagreement among the guests as to who was who, or if any statue resembled anyone at all. Pop told me later that all the Tommasos he knew were there, including his mother, brothers and sisters, aunts and uncles: plus several others with a touch of Tommaso blood he wanted to "immortalize."

The key, he said, was to examine the animals and the angels, often overlooked. I did notice a red swan somewhere. Pop, I'm sure was settling a few scores, although his negative feelings about Lathem and James always revulsed me.

This holiday surprise also solved the mystery of what Pop did in his spare time: all those years in Mr. Farante's cellar and in the locked room in our basement in Queens.

Over the next months, Pop would begin decorating our home with his little and large masterworks crafted in colored wood.

He also made many gifts of them to family members, when he started observing birthdays and anniversaries.

## War does not determine who is right – only who is left

*Bertrand Russell*

I realize I've left out some relevant information about how I dealt with the Vietnam War. It's not very dramatic, so I'll move through it quickly.

One of the benefits of joining the Tommaso family, and having Don Silvio as your Godfather, was making useful contacts within and outside the family. That first Christmas with the family after Mom died, I met a cousin who changed my life for the better.

Cousin Vito Genna was a veteran of the Korean War, who joined the New York State National Guard in 1954, when he was twenty. At this time, Vito was moving up the enlisted man's ladder looking for a forty-year career before retirement.

He had married a beautiful Irish-American red head eight years ago and they had three lovely daughters. Vito knew a little about my brother Lathem's death and was very sad over what had happened.

Vito told me the following Christmas (1966) that it wasn't too soon to think about my own situation, as the war in Vietnam was escalating and I'd turn eighteen in five years. (1971)

He said to me that New York State was developing a program to bring younger men into the National Guard system at the age of sixteen, to build up the guard's ranks. More importantly, this system would also provide a military style disciplinary experience for teenage boys at a critical stage in their lives.

The model was a combination of what the Boy Scouts and Military Academies had to offer, but the goal was to be prepared to serve New York State for anything from natural disasters to civil unrest. Vito said he would keep me posted on what developed.

# Will Power: The Birth of William the Conqueror

In September of 1967, I had a physical exam at school by Dr. Weiss. He was upset that no one had tested me for an underactive thyroid condition. Dr. Weiss said a male my age should be taller, weigh more and have more fully developed "genitalia," as well as a circumcised penis. He explained the latter terms to me in less inscrutable language. I was filled with dread. Dr. Weiss gave me a letter to bring home requesting my father to take me to see our family physician for another opinion.

That night I told Pop about the letter and what Dr. Weiss said. We didn't have a family doctor. Pop last saw a physician when he was twenty-eight (1938): a young doctor the family used named Calistrella.

I checked with Mrs. Milano upstairs and she said Dr. Calistrella was still the family's physician and had been for over thirty years. But the doctor had moved from Brooklyn to Manhattan where his practice was now. Her daughter, Rose, had seen him about four months ago.

I tried to remember when I last saw a doctor. If I was right, Mom used to take me to St. Luke's Hospital in Brooklyn for an annual checkup. But I hadn't been there since Mom died almost two years ago.

At dinner time I questioned Rose about Dr. Calistrella and she said, "Wow, he's a real ladies man." She proceeded to tell me nothing I wanted to hear, like he's in his fifties, but suave and beautifully dressed with a soft touch, and the manners of an aristocrat. His wife is an opera singer in Europe, and his patients include Uncle Silvio and all his business associates. The only bad thing about going there is his nurse, Loretta, who is a witch with a capital B and obviously is in love with Arturo.

"Who's Arturo?" I asked.

"Dr. Calistrella, silly boy.

"Oh, I see. Rose, I have a note from my school doctor to see our family doctor about my thyroid. But we don't have a family doctor."

"You want an appointment with Dr. Calistrella?"

"I guess so. Dr. Weiss at school wants to see a report on my visit. He said it's important."

"Let me check with mom. Somebody will have to take you."

In two weeks I got to see Dr. Calistrella. Mrs. Milano went with me to Kenmare Street in Manhattan. One of Don Silvio's drivers took us there and brought us home.

Arturo Calistrella, MD saw certain patients in this office after five PM, when he finished his rounds at Wickersham Hospital uptown. He was everything Rose said and more.

Not much taller than five-foot six-inches, Dr. Calistrella had a tan to envy and a smile that showed teeth as perfect as a movie star's. There was a trace of a European accent in his clearly enunciated speech. I inhaled a pleasant scent surrounding him, which some years later I identified as *Zizani*. His navy blue pin striped suit perfectly fit every contour of his small frame.

Dr. Calistrella did everything he could to make me comfortable. He also introduced me to Loretta, a fortyish, small-breasted brunette in a white nurse's uniform. She smiled and said they would take good care of me.

After reading Dr. Weiss', note and examining both sides of my back jaw and upper neck, Dr. Calistrella asked Loretta for my height and weight. He asked me to sit down and called Mrs. Milano over.

"Jerome, I suspect you may have an underactive thyroid, as Dr. Weiss suggested. We are going to draw some blood from you now. Then we will run some tests to confirm or deny our first impressions. I will need to see you back in one week, same time, and we will discuss the results. And yes, you should have a circumcision for health reasons. We will deal with that in due time. He shook my hand saying, "You are a fine young man, Jerome. See you next week. Loretta will take your blood sample and will give you an appointment card. Goodnight."

I kind of stood in awe of his smooth manner, smile and speech but a blood test, now! My hands started to sweat and my tongue went dry. Loretta came over saying, "Let's try your right arm." She pressed her right index finger around the center of my arm where it creased and said, "Good."

She tied a thin rubber hose around my upper arm and wiped the area that was "good" with an alcohol pad. Then she said, "Look up at that chart and study the letters. I'm going to ask you a question in a moment." I looked up, felt a tiny pinch in the middle of my arm, and studied the eye chart.

In a few seconds she said, "All done." She untied the rubber hose and pressed a small wad of bandage on my arm.

"Please hold that bandage in place," she said as she put some adhesive wrap around the bandage to keep it firmly in place.

"What about the chart?" I asked.

"Anything wrong with your eyes?" she replied. Then she smiled and winked, and handed Mrs. Milano an appointment card. "Good night, Jerome; good night Mrs. Milano."

We said good night and I thought she's no witch. I think I like her. I almost forgot about the circumcision-almost.

The upshot of the testing was that I, indeed, had a severely underactive pituitary gland.

"The therapy," Dr. Calistrella said, "will consist of a series of injections to your buttocks. Loretta will give you the shots once a week for a month, and then monthly for seventeen additional months: a total of twenty-one shots. By the spring of 1969, you should be taller, filled out and heavier."

Loretta squeezed my arm and winked at me saying, "And Wee Willy will grow, too!" Dr. Calistrella rolled his eyes and sighed, shaking his head. I blushed purple-red.

I was disturbed by the bad news/good news proclamation. How could I look forward to eighteen months of real injections, with only "you should be" on the other side of the coin? In any event, Don Silvio took care of all costs associated with my visits to Dr. Calistrella. Within a month, I got past any fear of shots.

Loretta would pull my boxer shorts down and lovingly rub alcohol on one side of my butt. Then she gave me the shot for eight seconds, holding my left arm as she withdrew. Loretta softly rubbed the spot again, and then applied a small round band aid. She gently picked up my shorts and my pants.

I had the queerest sensation when her hands and fingers touched me. Wee Willy even jerked once or twice. I think I was getting a crush on Loretta.

Obviously, my hormones had been awakened by these shots. I felt like one of those super heroes who morphs into a new persona to take action. Of course, this transition was slow and incremental. But with each new shot I developed "growing pains" and Wee Willy was lengthening.

Then came the circumcision. No more of that for now. I can't describe the pain when you're fourteen!

Overall, I endured three difficult examinations in Dr. Calistrella's office. Each came after a blood test result was evaluated.

After each six-month shot the doctor examined my genitals, and Willy was quick to respond to digital stimulation. The first time, Dr. Calistrella examined my gonads and Willy jerked to six inches.

The second time, the doctor called Loretta to see the reaction and measure: it was eight inches. On the day of the last visit, my height was sixty-eight inches; my weight was one hundred-forty-five pounds; and my penis, in a tumescent state was measured at ten and one-half inches, arching up like a scepter.

Before I left the office, Loretta asked me if I had someone I knew and trusted to talk about sex and sexual activity. She asked whether my father and I had ever discussed the subject. I said no, but immediately thought of James and said I knew someone else I trusted. She gave me a box that contained what she called pro-phylactic devices. On the street and at school I heard them referred to as "scum bags."

She said I should learn how to use them to prevent both disease and the unplanned fathering of children.

"Jerome, the way you're built now, you will be sexually active more and more. One or two of these should be with you at all times."

She kissed me on both cheeks and said "Take care of yourself and we'll see you in three months." I felt like Mom had just given me the warning.

I had already been testing my new equipment for the last six months. I was masturbating every other day with recent *Playboy* centerfolds I swiped from my barber's magazine rack. I dreamt of sex with girls and had wet dreams. Starting with my fifteenth birthday I decided to make some moves in the real world.

I was a senior in Middle school and not very popular. Having grown so much over the last year did not help with the girls. I was not repulsive but no pretty girl would look at me twice.

My mild manner and general respect for girls drew certain females to me continually. They were usually less attractive than I. These girls had more hair in the wrong places over hefty bodies that boasted broad shoulders, fat ankles and bellies that exceeded their breasts in size.

At Christmas time they would line up and give me gifts of ties and socks, and I would thank them with a cheek-kiss you give to sisters. This situation worsened when I started to sprout in early 1968.

Most of the girls I liked at school were southern Italian and

Jewish. I discovered that several of my favorites had signed up for the Romance Languages Club at school. Students of French, Italian and Spanish would meet twice a week. There would be discussions about mutual interests; the planning of summer trips to Europe to refine language skills; and presentations by selected members on the importance of their languages in the modern world.

I enrolled early. I was already a second year student of Italian, my only A-grade class. At our first meeting Rachel Zipel, a cute, smart French Language member, was elected President of the Club. Along with Rachel, two of my other favorites had joined: Jenney Scianna and Roseann Passalacqua. Both of them were in my Italian class, and I had more than a nodding acquaintance with them. They were both pretty and fluent in Italian, and had immigrated to America from Italy three years ago. I set my sights on them first and hoped for a shot at Rachel later.

Mom had taught me some French at home over the two years before she died. I had also picked up some from Lathem and more from James. My approach with Rachel would be to represent myself as someone interested in learning some French for the first time. At least I could fake it for a while.

I had been encouraged when I learned that only two other males had joined the club. I was quickly convinced that Michael Lerner and Cleve Edison (French) were card-carrying lavender lovers. It was a terrible thing to think. But one of the practical things I had learned from James was how to pick out homosexuals in a crowd.

It soon appeared I was proven wrong, when I found out that Cleve had bagged Theresa Miranda (Spanish) one night.

But it turned out to be a disastrous one-off, like his bid to claim bisexuality.

As a warm up exercise I decided to test one of the "big" girls I knew who was going to give me a birthday present. None of these girls was in the language club.

When my fifteenth birthday approached, the Club decided it was a good excuse for a Thursday-night party. My birthday fell on the Friday and school was closed for Veteran's Day.

One of the "hefty girls," devoted Erda Friss, caught me at lunch period on Wednesday with another gift. This time it was three white on white initialed handkerchiefs. The initials "JT" were in navy blue and I was impressed. I was particularly "horny" that day and went for broke.

I said I wanted to give Erda something, too, something personal. What would she like besides my usual cheek-kiss? She looked embarrassed but overcame any qualms and whispered, "I want to play spin the bottle with you, alone."

I said I wish I knew of a place where we could be alone and spin the bottle for "show and tell." She literally snorted and whispered, "Yes, and I know where." Well dear reader, I consider myself a gentleman and never reveal intimacies with a woman.

What I will say is that after several kisses, including the French variety, I gave Erda a preview of Willy by pressing her arm against the burgeoning flesh. She didn't resist, so I asked if she wanted to peek? I told Erda she was the first teen (I didn't want to lie about Loretta) to see the new Willy in the flesh.

That night I told Pop my classmates and I needed a place for my party. "Why don't you have it here in the basement?" he said. I almost fell over from the shock.

"You'd let me bring my schoolmates here for a party?"

"Why not," he replied.

My mind was racing to find a way to use the party as a springboard for my next conquest. I realized my hope of getting Erda to tell her friends about the size of Willy was likely but pointless, as none of them appealed to me. This time I'd be looking to hook up with a pretty member of the Club, probably Rachel: because she was also smart and Jewish.

I had good reason. It turned out that Erda was German and Catholic. So the subject of confession came up. Erda was unwilling to tell Father Siegfried at St. Leonard's Church that she handled Willy. Having seen Willy would be bad enough. I was hoping Rachel would be more circumspect about such matters.

All eight girls coming to the party and I took public transportation to our house. The gay blades were not interested, but two other older girls asked if they could bring their boyfriends. I said yes because the odds were still good and three males looks better than one. The boyfriends were also older and one had a car. The others arranged to be picked up by midnight.

Rose Milano had done me the favor of purchasing party stuff that afternoon and decorating the basement. I invited Rose and her mom to join us but Rose said she didn't do "kiddie" parties. I kissed her on the cheek and thanked her. I was feeling my "oats" and raring to dance with a girl in my arms.

I had been on my best behavior all night. The unattached eight had stayed aloof from the two couples. This gave me free rein to organize games, and tell jokes I had memorized all week.

I had the old monaural phonograph playing all the latest 45 RPM hits. The Beatles were still the rage, so I had their latest LP. The girls danced in groups and I would join in, or peel one or two away when I could slow dance a little.

When the four large pizzas were delivered by Mamma's Ristorante, I served everyone and a few of the girls helped. We all listened to some nice tunes while we ate. I provided a variety of cold sodas, at the beginning of the party, when I announced that there would no alcoholic beverages.

The two couples complained and wound up leaving early to "get something good to drink." When they left, I was ready to make my move.

It seems to me that all the strategy I am about to unfold will sound like it sprang from the mature mind of a precocious over-sexed teenager. True confessions: I found a book in an old piece of furniture that had been in the basement of our house before we moved in. It seemed like *Kismet*, or serendipity, two words I did not know then but which were nonetheless appropriate.

*How to Gently Bend a Woman to Your Will*, by Cosgrove P. Courtland, in a third edition from 1943, seemed like the answer to my needs. I actually flushed red when I saw the word "Will" in the title. Mr. Courtland was a "Gilded Age" *bon vivant* whose experience kept guiding him to revise his book for the children of the "Jazz Age" and the Depression Era in America.

My Courtlandesque strategy was simple but required restraint and patience. I would spend time with Rachel building up her ego about her looks, her brains, her mastery of French. Then I would tell her that although I was mastering Italian, I was a Francophile at heart. That's where *La Belle et La Bete* would come in handy.

From there to an invitation to go with me to Koletty's for ice cream one afternoon, and ask if she'd consider tutoring me a bit, in case I chose to switch my language affiliation. Then a luncheon date at Gottlieb's Jewish Deli on a Saturday.

All through lunch talk about *Les Miserables,* the 1934 film based on Hugo's novel about the struggles of *Jean Valjean*. He was played by Frederick March and Charles Laughton played *Javert.* Another WOR-TV oldie I was deeply moved by. The next Saturday, ask her to the movies and sit where we can hold hands and neck.

Then let things cool down. Be cordial when you see her but find excuses for not calling her. At this point, choose a less attractive girl outside the group, and do with number two what you did before with number one. This should get Rachel confused when she discovers I'm seeing number two.

When I'm alone with Rachel, ask her why she's giving me the silent treatment. Don't let her get too upset before telling her I have a confession to make. I apologize for dropping her and taking up with another, but say there's a very good reason why.

This is where I have to be most persuasive. I must convince her that my feelings for her were getting out of control. I had become desperate to kiss her, embrace her and hold her tightly against me. I knew she was not that kind of girl, and so, I turned elsewhere to prevent her from hating me for wanting her so badly.

This tactic had a sixty-forty chance of working, so said Mr. Courtland. It helps if number two is not from the same ethnic group as Rachel. The best upshot is for number one to lust for you, in her own way, of course.

You must then find the time and place where you can enact a romantic scene, which builds passionately, fueled by hormonal tension, to a physical encounter. The objective is not to bag Rachel the first time, but to give her a warm, visceral experience with Willy; then let nature take its course.

Well, to make a long story blossom, I succeeded in introducing Willy to Rachel. One Saturday afternoon when my house was empty, leaving the cleaning service to do their job, and Pop was working, I brought Rachel over and we went down to the basement. After a warm up of kissing and caressing, I told her I had to show why I was so unhappy.

I pointed to the obvious swelling between my legs and then dropped my pants: she was surprised; when I dropped my boxer shorts she took in a deep breath and stood for a moment with her mouth open, looking expectant and scared. I lied, saying she was the first to see what a strange and unwelcome thing had happened to me. She asked if it was painful.

"Oh no, I said it's the urgency to do something with it that frustrates me."

Rachel looked at me then looked at Willy again. "Have you ever done it with anyone?" she asked. I sighed loudly relishing the fact that I could tell the truth on this one.

"I have never had sex with a girl before, Rachel. I'm so confused and frustrated. I need your help." She said she would help and she did. I think she was surprised when she saw William's trimmed top.

And that dear reader is where I must leave you. Although, in summary, I will quote an old expression used to define the fastest way to communicate any message before the internet: "Telephone, Telegraph, Tell a Woman." My phone rang morning and night, and I was sought out by a bevy of young women, even an enlightened Italian Catholic, anxious to befriend the young man who possessed William the Conqueror.

Nonetheless, Rachel and I remained close over the next few years: through her marriage and divorce and into a new intimacy we both welcomed. I was puzzled as to why I found her so attractive. Unlike Marta she was slender, small-breasted and fair but she was so well spoken, bright and sophisticated. My passion for her was slow burning, whereas my flesh-based passion for Marta was white-hot. Ah, well.

## "I Ain't Got no Quarrel with the VietCong" M. Ali

Now, back to the National Guard. Well, three years later (1969), cousin Vito called Pop and told him what had happened. Vito said New York State was ready to announce the Junior New York State Guardsman program for sixteen year old boys. I could sign up in November, 1969 and become a full Guardsman by November, 1971.

Vito told Pop the Guard's ranks were already swelling with young men looking to avoid the draft. The best thing about early enrollment was that a spot would be reserved in the regular Guard when you turned eighteen.

Pop was skeptical because cousin Vito mentioned that there would be a six-month active duty obligation as there was with Lathem. Vito pleaded with Pop, telling him this was the only way to keep me from the war, whatever the risks involved with six month's active service at Ft. Dix, New Jersey.

Thankfully, Pop said he would have me call cousin Vito to discuss this further. Pop knew that I needed his consent to do anything like this, so long as I was under the age of twenty-one.

Cousin Vito invited me over to his home in Brooklyn for dinner one night. Pop insisted that Rose Milano go with me by train. Vito said it was fine. His wife, Liz, met us at the door. She was more beautiful than I remembered her from last Christmas. Her three daughters screamed and danced around us. The middle one, Deirdre, fixed her eyes on me and asked me if Rose Milano was my wife. I blushed and said, "No, I'm not married." Deirdre smiled, said "Good!" and skipped away.

After a wonderful meal of corned beef and cabbage, Vito and I sat in his den, while Rose helped Liz clean up. Once in a while, Deirdre stuck her head in to say hello. "My daughter has taken quite a shine to you. I've never seen her do that before," Vito said.

The upshot of our conversation was that cousin Vito convinced me of the wisdom of taking his advice. I was sure I could persuade Pop to go along. Vito also asked me about Lathem.

I told him everything I remembered about the official reports and what Morton Fox had told me at Lathem's wake. Cousin Vito assured me that when I served my six months active duty at Fort Dix, he could assist me in locating someone who might help me learn the truth.

As Rose and I said good night to cousin Vito and his family, Deirdre came up to me and said she wanted to kiss me good night. I blushed again but Liz's affirmative nod made me kneel down to Deirdre. She latched her arms around me and kissed me hard on the mouth. Then she looked at Rose and then me saying, "Remember don't get married until I'm sixteen! I'll be waiting." We all laughed except Deirdre. She walked away and muttered "Remember."

## MOSTLY MARTHA

Jane has the lips; Mary has the arms,
And it's hard to resist Lola and her charms.
Sue wants to be everything to me.
Yet in dreams I always see ...

Mostly Martha, Mostly Martha
Makes me melt like butter on toast
Mostly Martha, Mostly Martha
What has she got? She's got the most.

She's the she meant for me;
That's for certain, that's for sure.
In her spell I can tell
She's a habit I can't cure.
Other girls I have met, I can get and then forget
But I know I will live to regret (repeat chorus)
Grace has the face; Trudy has the style.
Lulu Belle has the swell "Come and Get it" smile.
Eve makes me purr when I dance with her.
She's a doll, but I prefer ...

Mostly Martha, Mostly Martha
Makes me melt like butter on toast.
Mostly Martha, Mostly Martha
What has she got? I only know that she's got the most, the
                              [most.

## DOMANI

Maybe you'll fall in love with me Domani
Maybe tomorrow night the sun will shine
I'll change my name from Johnny to Giovanni
If you will say Domani, you'll be mine

Come to me, Senorina from Italy
Hear my plea and I'll hire the hall
All your Uncles and Aunts
And your Ma and Pa and your Paisani
They all agree that we should wed Domani

You are so super-duper bravissimo
Don't say no or my poor heart you'll break
'Cause your Uncles and Aunts

And your Ma and Pa and your Paisani
They all agree that we should wed, Domani

## Beam Number Four

I was about to cover my second trip to Calatafimi, Sicily when I got sidetracked. After two and one-half years of growth (1967-1969), I had added another two inches – to my height (5'10") and now weighed one hundred fifty-three pounds.

A workout routine became part of my daily schedule, and I had filled out and was muscular. No more "99 pound weakling" who had sand kicked in his face. It's true, Charles Atlas, born Angelo Siciliano, would have been proud of me.

Sadly, the purpose of this trip, hastily put together, was to see *Cignu Russu* who was judged to be on her death bed. Pop called to say we'd be there in forty-eight hours, and that his mother should be told we were on our way. It was July 1969 and, once again, Don Silvio cleared the way for us.

The flights were nerve wracking and we wept from time to time, praying that my grandmother should be alive when we got there. I had recently been fitted with glasses to correct a stigmatism in my left eye. When I was in dim light, they helped me focus. I ordered them as bifocals, so I could read without changing glasses. They took some getting used to.

Thankfully, phone calls from the airports to Calatafimi confirmed that *Cignu Russu* was alive and heartened that we were close. The taxi ride was wild and scary but Alberto Biaggio, an experienced driver (he said) got us to Calatafimi quickly and safely. Of course, that meant we did not stop for any red traffic lights and averaged 110 kilometers per hour the whole trip.

We rushed into the house hugging and kissing Angelina who greeted us. I wondered about Marta. Pop and I went into the bedroom together. Giuseppina and Helena were there as was Marta, sitting on the bed and propping up my grandmother so she could see us. Marta put a pair of eyeglasses on *Cignu Russu* to help her vision. She was very emotional and belied her ninety-five years.

When she looked at us she began to moan then gasp for air. She raised her arms and looked directly at me, saying clearly, "Michele, you have come back to me." Her fingers begged me forward into her thin arms.

"Oh, Michele, now you will take me to *Paradisu*." With her last bit of strength she wrapped her arms around my neck and expired. Marta screamed and pulled her arms from my neck yelling "Do something! Do something!"

Pop grabbed me and threw me to the floor, as a chorus of women began to moan; then the loud keening began. A local priest, who had already given her the last rites and went out for a smoke, rushed back into the room and did what he could do to revive her. But she was already dead.

I had lost my glasses when Pop threw me across the room and I hit my head on some furniture. As I tried to regain full consciousness, Marta knelt down beside me and took my head in her hands, pressing it against her breast, asking if I was alright. Her long curly hair, redolent of coconut oil, draped over my face.

I thought I had gone to *Paradisu* but I fought the burning urge to embrace her completely. "I think Jerome is ok," she said to no one in particular; and no one noticed. Marta found my glasses and put them on my nose. She kissed my forehead gently, then helped me to my feet, squeezing my hands and holding them tightly.

The whole scene was surreal, with everyone crying and holding each other. Only Pop glared at me. How could I know I robbed him of the one embrace he had lived for all these years: he saw that I did not initiate the embrace, and the others also saw that as well.

When an ambulance was called for, and everyone said their last goodbye to the corpse, I watched my Pop closely. Slowly he regained his composure and came to me to hold me. "I'm sorry, Pop."

"It's not your fault. She had these hallucinations for over thirty-five years. At least she seems to have died happy. I hope this is not a bad week for wakes and funerals. I'll check with the priest about a Wednesday burial, and if that's good we'll have her laid out Monday and Tuesday in a closed coffin. I hope I don't have to ask your Godfather for help."

"Pop, you'll tell me about this Michele?"

"I promise I will after the arrangements are made."

I stepped outside the bedroom and went to each of my relatives and embraced them without saying a word. Interestingly, I was now taller than all of them, as none wore shoes with heels of more than an inch in thickness. My eyes nervously searched the room for Marta to no avail. I held off asking for Marta, hoping not to call attention to my infatuation with her. I decided to step out on the street until the ambulance arrived.

After a minute, Marta appeared. Neither of us had gotten the opportunity to really look at each other. She was about to say something when I instinctively put an index finger to my lips. I took a step back and stared at her. If I had thought that she was a beautiful child, I now was struck by her physical maturity which proclaimed womanhood. My mouth moved to articulate a word but only air came through and then "Marta, you have become a beautiful woman at fourteen."

"And you, Jerome, have become a beautiful man in two years. Are you sixteen yet?"

"No, I'll be sixteen on the feast day of the horned." She was going to laugh but instead spoke earnestly, "You never have to fear me giving you horns, Jerome. I only wish we could marry now."

"Marry now at fourteen, Marta?"

"My teacher told us that young girls from proper families in old Verona married at ages thirteen and fourteen, like Juliet."

"Does your mother want you to marry very young?"

"Some days yes, when I flirt with all the boys at school: some days no, when I flirt with all the boys at school. But if I had you, Jerome ... if I had you, I would stop flirting forever."

"Marta, when I look in my mirror, I don't see a nice face, a face any girl or woman could love. I wasn't blessed so at birth. You should have seen my brother, Lathem: blonde hair, blue eyes and a beautiful face with a quick mind." I saw her confusion.

"He was my half-brother, same mother, different father.

"My mother was a beautiful woman, Marta: I worshipped her. But you are beautiful beyond all beauty."

I stopped and looked into her eyes, saying "I know I'm young but you are the fulfillment of all my desires. If and when I know that I'm also the fulfillment of your desires, I'll ask you to marry me."

She said, "I've been waiting for you to ask."

"I want to marry you," I replied. "But we must wait until I'm eighteen, and even then I'll need Pop's permission because I'll still be under twenty-one. It won't be easy."

"I'll do my part," she said. Marta looked around then faced me and pursed her lips in a soft kiss. I did the same. This feeling had to be what love is like, but I was too naïve to understand it was the first of many such moments which define the stages of love beyond infatuation.

Living arrangements were a bit complicated, as a young couple had been top-floor tenants for nearly three years. It was decided that Aunt Helena, now seventy-four, would share her bedroom, which had two single beds, with Marta temporarily. That allowed Pop and me to share the second bedroom in single beds on the second floor.

Aunt Giuseppina, now eighty-nine and Cousin Angelina, nearly seventy, still made it up those stairs to the second floor. Michela had the third floor to herself.

We lived with this arrangement for the two weeks we stayed. It was wonderful being among all these loving women. Another epiphany struck: except for Pop and James, I preferred the company of women of any age to male companionship. I felt safe and secure, as I always did in Mom's embrace.

The weather was exceptionally hot, so we waked *Cignu Russu* just one day before the funeral. Very few people remembered her and those that did would not come to her wake anyway. Lacking space for her at *Madonna del Giubino*'s cemetery, Don Silvio obtained a plot behind the nearby Church of *Maria Maddalena*. Pop paid for the headstone. It had the following inscription:

**Annunziata Helena** (*Cignu Russu*) **Greco Tommaso**
Madre Amata
10 Aprile 1874 – 11 Iuglio 1969

**Girolamu Occhipinti Tommaso**
9 Settembre 1910 –
Amato Figlio
Riuniti in Paradiso per Sempre

We were all stunned as we saw the headstone. Pop looked at me and said "This is where my body belongs: next to my mother. Promise me you will bring it here when I die. Then fill in the date."

"I promise, Pop, you can count on me."

I never asked about the inclusion of "Occhipinti" in his name and he did not tell me about Michele until years later.

Except for one excursion to the Garibaldi monument on the *Pianto Romano* hill Pop wanted to make, Marta and I spent as much time as we could in the water. Pop did not insist that we all sit around and mourn for *Cignu Russu* in black what with temperatures approaching one hundred degrees. His time in America away from the family dulled the importance of such traditions. Of course he had made an exception when Mom died.

Pop and I had purchased bathing suits and broad-brimmed hats the day before at a local department store. Marta had a new bathing suit she'd gotten for her birthday. Michela, who had a very good shape, wore black shorts under a long black skirt and a sleeveless tank top under a half cape also black. She capped her outfit with a large black hat with a floppy brim.

Pop financed taxi service to and from *Castellammare del Golfo* due north of Calatafimi. There we could recreate without upsetting local citizens of Calatafimi. He, Michela, Marta and I all climbed down primitive access stairs to the rocks above the coastal water.

Michela brought two small beach chairs, and some magazines, so that she and Pop could relax and enjoy the sun on a large flat rock about ten feet above the water. The spot also gave them maximum sight lines to try and keep an eye on me and Marta. I was very pleased to see them conversing freely and smiling. Pop was either exhausted or relaxed or both. At one point, I saw them laughing just before Marta swept me to the rocks.

Marta's suit was a close-fitting black affair. Several white butterflies adorned the front. The whole effect when encapsulating Marta's olive-brown, curvaceous body was very sensuous.

I knew I was blushing just looking at this beautiful young woman. I especially noted how flat her stomach was. Of course, until we hit the water she wore a lovely black shoulder wrap for propriety.

The water that day was almost warm and a delight to swim in, but Marta wanted to talk first with her back to the parents, as we treaded water. She told me that in a minute we would swim out some distance to let us be observed. Then we would head for the rocks and go in among them but only for two minutes. We would reemerge to be seen again and then back to the rocks.

At that point, I should follow her carefully as we made our way to a small, secluded piece of beach that appeared only at low tide and only for a half hour then. We were going to catch the beach almost midway through the tidal movement which gave us about twenty minutes to do something before we'd have to leave and show ourselves again. What we were going to do, Marta said, she would inform me of during our two minutes among the rocks.

Marta's bathing suit, July 1969. Author's Private Collection.

I knew I already had a full-blown erection just looking at her and listening to her talk. Marta had taken control and I was along for the ride.

When we were in the two-minute drill, Marta grabbed me and embraced me tightly, but I put my right hand to her mouth and said "This is our first real kiss, Marta, let's give ourselves completely to each other through the kiss."

I looked into her eyes and closing mine put our lips together. Her soft breasts against my chest and Willy's hardness in her groin made us both stop a second; we caught our breath, and she said "I must be very careful because my mother will inspect me later: all must be done with the tongue and mouth. Do you understand?" I nodded affirmatively.

For some strange reason a thought popped into my head: "It's What You Do With What You Got." How far away the wise old owl was that sang that song. Context is really everything. She kissed me again and I had the urge to suckle her breasts.

## Forest Park Picnic

The closing months of 1969 put a final cap on a tempestuous year with bittersweet events. Both situations involved my Godfather, Don Silvio. The first was Labor Day eve, August 31, 1969, when the Tommaso clan was treated to what turned out to be Don Silvio's last family picnic at Forest Park in Queens. The annual picnic was observed on Sunday, so all families could enjoy the Monday off with their own families and friends.

Don Silvio arranged to cover the one concern on most minds: attendance at mass and abstention from food from the previous midnight before receiving the Blessed Sacrament that morning.

Monsignor Paluzzo, a good friend of Don Silvio, was the first person at the cordoned off section of the park that morning. Their friendship went back many years, leading up to the Priest's recent vigorous sponsorship of Silvio to become a Grand Knight of the New York State Council of the Knights of Columbus.

The Monsignor counted out the forty-five chairs, already delivered and set up, for the impromptu mass which he would celebrate at seven-thirty AM. All invited attendees, men, women and children, were expected to be in those seats by seven fifteen.

He was available for "courtesy confessions" between six-thirty and seven fifteen AM, so long as abstention was in order. The mass would conclude at eight-twenty AM and arrangements to prepare breakfast would begin.

To stave off hunger pangs, orange juice, coffee and small "Danish" pastry would be served immediately by a staff of ten servers, circulating to deposit their provisions, and plastic utensils, onto colorful plastic tablecloths covering the ancient wooden picnic tables.

The acquisition of a specific spot in the park was sealed by reservation a year in advance, with appropriate fees paid up front by Don Silvio to friends in the Department of Parks. This space included enough tables and bench seats for all, plus a minimum of five *Gufulata* stoves on which most of the final cooking would be done.

The last necessity was accommodated when Don Silvio's construction company truck pulled up just within the circle of our space to drop off a "Temporary Restrooms" free standing structure on wheels. There were three stalls each for women and men plus soap, sinks and paper towels. The men's enclosure also contained three exposed upright stalls.

At nine AM, cooks and servers went into action, using an electric generator to fire up an elongated frying surface to prepare fresh eggs and hash brown potatoes to order. The surface also sizzled with pounds of thickly sliced premium bacon and ham. Bagels and bialys, fresh from ovens in a corner bakery on Delancey Street in Manhattan, were available as is or toasted on a buttered frying surface.

The line of hungry guests moved quickly along a parallel route where orders were barked and fulfilled, while guests picked up firm paper dishes on which their orders were put. Refills on orange juice and coffee were made by servers continually until ten thirty AM: then clean up began and servers brought in new large plastic garbage cans to collect all refuse for removal.

All this conspicuous consumption was accompanied by reel-to-reel tapes of music piped into the area on a quartette of Boze speakers. The best of Italian-American singers were represented, ranging from Bennett, Como, Damone, Darin, Laine, Martin and Sinatra to Toni Arden, Joni James, Marlene Verplanck, June Valli, Morgana King and Connie Francis.

Activities for the old (Bocce Ball) and young (softball game) were planned and executed with precision. All necessary equipment was provided.

The older men who had no interest in either activity, were welcome to sit around philosophizing as they chewed on, and occasionally smoked, the inevitable De Nobili "guinea stinkers."

To quench thirst on what was going to be a warm fall day, bottles of soda bobbed about in heavy, waterproof cylindrical cartons loaded with floating chunks of ice. The dark fragrant brew from the ever ready coffee pot was available all day (wine and beer were available at noon).

Vita Tommaso and her cadre of daughters (-in-law), Mary Milano and daughter Rose busied themselves with the preparation of the lunch meal. Actually, one hundred meatballs had been fried the day before, along with sausage, pork ribs, chunks of pork and veal and two dozen beef *bracioles*. Everything had been packed and refrigerated and delivered to the picnic site at eleven-thirty AM.

Twelve pounds of #8 Ronzoni spaghetti was on hand and twenty-four loaves of freshly baked *Pistaluna* bread. A fresh tomato, meat gravy with lots of basil and garlic had also been prepared the day before. It, too, was delivered at eleven-thirty AM in four twelve-quart sealed pots.

Five men who delivered all this food then went to work firing up the *Gufulata* stoves. Two large cooking pots would eventually sit on each stove: one for the meat gravy and one for the spaghetti. Lunch would be served promptly at one-thirty PM.

The luncheon meal would be accompanied by selections of Country and Western music, a particular favorite of Don Silvio. The Sons of the Pioneers, Rex Allan, Gene Autry, Roy Rogers, Patsy Kline, Hank Williams, Eddie Arnold and that great Sicilian Cowboy, Frankie Laine, would bring a touch of Americana to an Italian-American meal."Tumbling Tumbleweeds" was his favorite song.

Adults and children were encouraged to have a nice *siesta* after lunch. Blankets and pillows were made available for adults and sleeping bags for children. All music ceased to allow drowsiness to take effect. Soon the mid-afternoon buzz of insects was broken by snoring and snorts, leaving the onlookers, mostly women, to laugh and gossip to their heart's content.

At five PM, the deliverymen returned with the food for the evening meal. There were fifty, three-quarter pound boneless rib steaks, and three quarts of *salmurigghiu*, the concoction of fresh tomatoes, olive oil, garlic, basil and pepper to adorn each stake for spectacular flavor. A prepared salad of fresh greens, tomatoes, mushrooms and goat cheese was included, along with more loaves of freshly baked bread.

The *Gufulata*s had been cleaned up after lunch and were now fired with clean charcoal. Three *Gufulata*s were designated for types of steak desired: one for Very-Rare and Rare; one for Medium-Rare and Medium; one for Medium-Well and Well-Done. The remaining stoves were used for baking and frying potatoes.

Monsignor Paluzzo returned for the evening meal at six-thirty, and led everyone in a prayer of thanks to God and Don Silvio for the bounty of food and familial love which marked the whole day. The musical entertainment was solidly Sicilian-Italian-American, as tapes of songs performed by Nicola Paone, Louis Prima, Jimmie

149

Roselli, Jerry Vale, Julius LaRosa, Toni Arden, June Valli, Morgana King and Connie Francis enlivened the meal.

A final delivery was made at eight-fifteen. All the freshly prepared desserts arrived with carafes of steaming coffee. In addition to the usual ricotta-based confections, pumpkin and pecan pies marked the change of seasons.

At this juncture, staff brought in some large outdoor lights and revved up the electric generator, so we could enjoy the last part of the meal in light. By ten PM everyone was saying goodbye and personally thanking Don Silvio and Vita for another memorable Tommaso family picnic.

Recalling this event as I do now, some thirty years later, it is so bitter sweet because only a few of us who were there keep the memory alive. Don Silvio was not Robin Hood or some other hero out of folklore. He was a human being, flawed as all of us are, but with a sense of family honor and love that informed everything he did, known and unknown. He surely was the last of a dying breed.

## End of an Era: Beam Number Five

The second and most sorrowful event of that fall season fell on September 28, 1969. It was the peaceful passing of Don Silvio in his sleep and in his own bed. Only Dr. Calistrella knew how precarious Don Silvio's heart condition was and he was sworn to silence. It was a "valve issue" we were told. "Unpredictable," the doctor stated, as Don Silvio wished it known. Dr. Calistrella, eyes burning red, added "I will never know a human being as wise, kind and loving as Don Silvio." He spoke for all of us whose lives had been positively touched by my Godfather.

This was indeed a cataclysmic event in my life, but I wondered about the fallout to the family at large. No one had sensed that Pinu could fill his father's gas tank let alone his shoes. But Pinu seemed to relish the changing of the guard and he assumed the mantel with swagger.

The occasion of Don Silvio's death was greeted by certain communities within New York State as second in its devastating effect only to that of FDR's passing. If he had enemies they feared him while he lived and they were unknown to the general public. Everyone, including his enemies, adorned his regal uniform with an array of verbal medals that spoke eloquently of his leadership, compassion, wisdom and sense of justice.

While Don Silvio did not lie in state as some would have wanted, his body in an open casket did lie in the largest room the Greenpoint Chapels had. Also, his was the only wake in the place, allowing large groups to come inside to waiting areas.

From these holding spaces, small groups would be funneled in to pass the casket and exit quickly. Family and specified others were moved to another room until the flow of public traffic was halted for one hour. After another hour, the process would be repeated.

This continued all day from nine AM to nine PM. for three days and nights. Some people waited as many as three hours to walk by the casket. The Funeral Mass was aptly *Puccinian* in every respect. The burial was worthy of Wagner's *Gotterdammerung*.

I was sitting with Pop and Rose Milano who had begun to show an interest in my company. At this point, I was torn between grieving for my Godfather and looking, hungrily, at a picture I had taken of Marta in that bathing suit before we left Calatafimi in July.

The two competing occupations did overlap because Aunt Giuseppina and her women were dependent on Don Silvio's generosity. I wanted to make a mental note to ask someone about that situation, but Rose kept breathing down my neck and touching my leg when she could.

"Jerome, we need to talk, please. Come with me, please."

I excused myself and woke Pop up doing so. I said I'd be back for the next family viewing in thirty minutes. Rose motioned me to a door in the back of the room: she opened it slowly and pushed me through before slipping in.

We were in another small but empty room. Rose put her hand to her mouth signaling I should be quiet. We went through another door she found that had steps leading down somewhere. I followed her lead until we were in a kind of subterranean space with furniture and fixtures.

"What is all this?" I asked.

"This is where we have sex for the first time.

"Is that why you dragged me down here?"

"No, I'm suffering from a disease that only you can help me cure."

I voiced genuine concern for Rose's health: "What disease and how can I help?"

"Oh, silly boy, I'm not dying, I'm 'horny' and need sex desperately!"

"'Horny?'" like in *cornuto*?"

"Well, not exactly. You see women who stray in a marriage give their husbands "horns," if they have someone else's child which the husband believes is his. When I say I'm horny, it's because I lust for sex. I'm not looking to make horns: that's what young men do when they impregnate married women. Get it?"

"So you brought me here because you're lusting for sex with me: since when? You just noticed I've grown up in the last couple of years?"

"To tell the truth, my mother showed me some of your underwear briefs recently. She pointed out that your pouches remain large, even after washing and drying, stretched out. But the clincher came when mom was downstairs last week and caught a glimpse of you coming out of the shower."

"What did she see?"

"She said two things: first, *'Egli è dotato come un oscuro stallone arabo!'*; secondly, *'La cosa gli pende come un grosso salame!'* What do you think of that, Jerome?"

"Guilty as charged."

"So we have a deal, then?"

"I make no deals until I see my lawyer. Ok, we'll talk about it later. Right now we have to get back upstairs and quick."

We returned to the waiting room just as the family was moving back to the viewing room for the next hour. I spotted cousin Vito and escaped Rose's clutches for a little while.

Vito was still very upset over our loss of Don Silvio. He thought of my Godfather as a caring father, much like most of Don Silvio's family, friends and acquaintances. Then he said something strange.

"It's really hard to see someone you love and idolize as having flaws. Your Godfather was a great man, Jerome, but like most politicians you have to sell your soul sometimes to get what you want. I'm afraid he was no different." He saw a puzzled look on my face and continued.

"I've been really close to this family for fifteen years, and I studied every decision Don Silvio made that I learned about. He was the smartest politician that never ran for election. He didn't need to be elected, once he reached a point in his career where he was able to call most of the shots.

"Don Silvio was smart: a lot smarter than anybody that ever

gave him orders. But he played by the party rules and did what was expected of him to rise in the party. I had no trouble with any of that stuff.

"One day, I was talking to one of the old men down at the Democratic Club in little Italy. I had run an errand for Don Silvio and stayed to have lunch. The old timer didn't know that Don Silvio was my mother's first cousin, or that I even knew him.

"As we got into the lives these men led, the old man told me that to become a full member of the Family, a man had to commit murder, sooner or later. It was not optional. He said in a whisper with a gesture of turning a key in a lock 'Era la chiave che aprì la porta.'"

Vito had tears in his eyes. This veteran who had seen combat in Korea and once told me there was nothing harder than killing a man, even your sworn enemy, could not reconcile two sides of a man's nature that seemed completely antithetical. I sensed his pain and felt my own.

"Vito, I don't believe it. I read that every rule has an exception. I'd rather believe Don Silvio was the exception." Those were big words for an oversexed naïve teenager. It made me feel better for myself and cousin Vito.

I always wondered why Vito chose to tell me that story: I was turning sixteen in November, and I would join the new Guard program. We did have a special bond. More than I imagined. Somehow, I think he felt I could be trusted with his observation and would never utter it to another living person. I never did.

I lived with that illusion about Don Silvio, and many others, all my life. Once again, I thought about the film, *The Man Who Shot Liberty Valance.* If I were to write Don Silvio's obituary, I would note this: "When the legend becomes fact, print the legend." The news media in and around New York State did just that.

# In Memoriam

Sonia Lisak (Yarmolinsky) Tommaso:
November 30, 1920 – December 20, 1965 (age 45)
Lathem Yarmolinsky, Jr.:
March 5, 1943 – August 20, 1963 (age 20)
Tonio Tommaso:
January 17, 1894 – December 28, 1965 (age 71)
Annunziata Helena (*Cignu Russu*) Greco Tomasso
April 10, 1874 – July 11, 1969 (age 95)
Silvio (Cesar) Tommaso:
October 10, 1893 – September 28, 1969 (age 76)
John F. Kennedy:
May 29, 1917 – November 22, 1963 (age 46)
Martin L. King:
January 15, 1929 – April 4, 1968 (age 39)
Robert F. Kennedy:
November 20, 1925 – June 6, 1968 (age 43)
United States Armed Forces in Vietnam, Cambodia and Laos:
November 1, 1955 – April 30, 1975
<u>58,300 Killed; 153,303 Wounded; 1641 Missing in action</u>
Enemy Armed Forces and civilians: North Vietnam,
Cambodia and Laos: over <u>two million</u> dead, wounded
and missing.

# THE MILLER'S SON

I shall marry the miller's son
Pin my hat on a nice piece of property.
Friday nights, for a bit of fun,
We'll go dancing.
Meanwhile ...
It's a wink and a wiggle
And a giggle on the grass
And I'll trip the Light Fandango,
A pinch and a diddle
In the middle of what passes by.
It's a very short road
From the pinch and the punch
To the paunch and the pouch
And the pension.
It's a very short road
To the ten-thousandth lunch
And the belch and the grouch
And the sigh.
In the meanwhile,
There are mouths to kissed
Before mouths to be fed,
And a lot in between
In the meanwhile.
And a girl ought to celebrate what passes by.
Or I shall marry the businessman,
Five fat babies and lots of security.
Friday nights, if we think we can,
We'll go dancing.
Meanwhile...
It's a push and a fumble
And a tumble in the sheets
And I'll foot the Highland Fancy,
A dip in the butter
And a flutter with what meets my eye.


It's a very short fetch
From the push and the whoop
To the squint and the stoop
And the mumble.
It's not much of a stretch

To the cribs or the croup
And the bosoms that droop and go dry.
In the meanwhile,
There are mouths to be kissed
Before mouths to be fed,

And there's many a tryst
And there's many a bed
To be sampled and seen
In the meanwhile.
And a girl has to celebrate what passes by.
Or I shall marry the Prince of Whales.
Pearls and servants and dressing for festivals.
Friday night with him all in tails,
We'll have dancing.
    Meanwhile...
It's a rip in the bustle
And a rustle in the hay
And I'll pitch the Quick Fantastic,
With flings of confetti
And my petticoats away up high.
It's a very short way
From the fling that's for fun
To the thigh pressing
under the table.
It's a very short day
Til you're stuck with just one
Or it has to be done
On the sly.
In the meanwhile,
There are mouths to be kissed
Before mouths to be fed,
And there's many a tryst
And there's many a bed,
There's a lot I'll have missed
But I'll not have been dead
When I die!
And a person should celebrate everything
Passing by.
And I shall marry the miller's son.

# The 1970s
## Decade of Liberation

The new decade ushered in years of maturity, coupled with humility, and some exciting developments like the discovery of Stephen Sondheim and my own sexual prowess with women. However, there was some rough going early on that nearly devastated the Tommaso family in America.

As I approached my eighteenth birthday, Pop said he was going to take me to a new place for lunch in Little Italy, lower Manhattan, that was going to open in April, 1972. This restaurant, which the family had invested in, was to be called Umberto's Clam House. The recommendation had come from Pippinu "Pinu" Tommaso, Don Silvio's son who had taken over his father's operations when my Godfather passed away, asleep in his own bed, in 1969.

## Beam Number Six

Pinu was in his late forties, Pop said, and always had the habit of backing out of doors with two husky bodyguards behind him. He had shifty brown eyes that constantly sized up all that lay before him: zooming in here, calibrating distance there, so as not to overlook anything out of place or unusual. Pinu had a sharp instinct for survival, and vowed that he would die in bed like his father.

As it happened, Pinu did die in bed, but it wasn't in his bed and he was still in his forties when it happened. He died in the bed at a small West Village hotel: his throat slit open by a male prostitute I'll call Doris.

The account that follows is an edited version of all that was learned about Pinu's murder. My sources were Pop, who furnished purloined copies of the Medical Examiner's Report and Police investigative summary reports the family had been given in secret; newspaper clippings, conversations with Tommaso family members, including Mary Milano, Vita Tommaso's sister, who had heard a lot about Pinu over the years.

I certainly took poetic license to fill in peoples' thoughts as they related to the murder and its aftermath. I actually enjoyed providing the motive for, and detail of, the murder itself. This is a fictional journalistic account of the events as I saw them, invented them and summarized them.

Apparently, Pinu was reneging on the usual price he paid Doris for his services, something he had done before. Doris had protested but was warned to "Take it and like it!" or he and his family would be brutally murdered. That time, Doris considered murdering Pinu, believing he could pull it off because his identity was known only to Pinu.

The way their trysts worked was to have Pinu come to the same hotel every week with his bodyguards. After the bodyguards assured the room was safe, they went down to the lobby to drink, smoke and play cards for two hours.

Out of an adjoining room Doris, who had walked up from the lobby in drag, wearing a raincoat, wig, hat and glasses, would knock on the door of Pinu's room and then Pinu would open his adjoining door allowing Doris to enter. Doris had removed his woman's clothes and left them in the adjoining room he had come from. Pinu would personally "frisk" Doris to be sure she had nothing harmful in her possession.

When their business was done, Doris would go into the adjoining room and clean up. Then he would get into the woman's clothes again, pulling the hat down over his glasses. Opening the door to his room, he looked to be sure no one was coming, and then started down the stairs.

He was always a few minutes ahead of the bodyguards and would pass them in the lobby on his way out to the street. Pinu had instructed his men not to look at or stop his prostitute, as she left the hotel. This was a routine followed over many weeks and worked like a well-rehearsed play.

This particular night, Doris was really pissed at Pinu for cheating on his fee. Rather than saying something like "I'm a little short this week," Pinu would threaten to "cut Doris' balls off," if he didn't take it and like it. Doris thought for a moment and decided to commit murder.

Pinu had undressed and was positioned dog-like on the bed with his butt higher and his head lower. A substantial amount of petroleum jelly was rubbed into his anal area by Doris who had put on plastic gloves.

"Do you want the dildo to suck on while I'm working the rear?" Doris asked.

"Yeah, let me have it."

"Is your *Ramses* bag on, sweetie?"

"Yeah, yeah, it's on."

Doris opened a long black case at Pinu's side and pulled out a ten inch lifelike dildo. As he was handing it to Pinu, he slid something out from its center at the root, where he had planted it, dropping it at his side unseen by Pinu. It was a slender straight razor.

Doris had slipped a *Ramses* bag onto his own penis, to insure nothing could be left for the medical examiner or police to find. Doris then whispered, "Whose turn is it to get fucked?"

Pinu rasped back, "Cut the crap and get on with it!"

"Alright, sweetie, here I come," whispered Doris.

After mounting Pinu's buttocks and finding his wide anus, Doris pushed his hardening penis in and began to stroke. Pinu had put the dildo in his mouth and was sucking it. Pinu started moaning with satisfaction and then jerked as he was reaching an orgasm. Doris picked up the razor discretely and unlatched the six-inch, precision-sharp blade. He grabbed and pulled Pinu's hair up and back, as he slid the blade deeply across Pinu's throat.

Without wasting a moment, Doris knowingly slashed deeply across the back of Pinu's neck, severing large blood vessels simultaneously, causing immediate exsanguination and loss of consciousness, then death. A lot of blood poured across the bed.

Doris smiled, saying, "I don't know if you're kosher, honey, but you've been prepared to meet ancient dietary laws. I hope your boyfriends are hungry."

With that, Doris pulled off his empty *Ramses'* bag, flushed it down the toilet, removed the plastic gloves, went next door to clean himself and get dressed as a woman. He paused only long enough to empty Pinu's wallet of twenty-one hundred dollars and removed two diamond rings he was sure he could sell in Mexico.

In less than ten minutes he was looking out the door to his room. Seeing no one, he pulled his hat over his glasses and walked slowly down to the lobby and out as Pinu's bodyguards watched. Assuming this was an early night, they slowly trudged up the flight of stairs to Pinu's room.

Doris went around the building to a room where an incinerator sat. He quickly pulled off the female clothes to reveal a thin, dark suit underneath. He burned the plastic gloves and everything of the woman's clothes. He found a pair of mens' loafers in a dark corner where he had left them upon entering the building. Then he ran down a side street and one block over to The Duplex, 61 Christopher Street at Seventh Avenue.

This old cabaret haunt featured an in-drag performance each night. There, Doris blended in with the crowd (he was not on staff but performed Berliner songs by Weill for drinks from time to time). Doris made sure everyone he knew saw him. He alleged to have been waiting for a spot to do a number for over an hour. A smoky, loud atmosphere prevailed with faces lost in the hurly-burly of the crowd's movements.

Needless to say, Pinu's bodyguards were shocked and confused when they entered the room. One of them sat on the bed and began to cry. The other did not lose his equilibrium and made a quick call to one of the Family's highly regarded captains and he was given precise instructions.

A laundry truck was to quietly pick up the body, transfer it to a plastic bag, and drive it to a small general hospital in Brooklyn. The hotel management was "friendly" and was paid well to clean up the rooms and remain silent. There were no records associating Pinu with the hotel.

Pinu Tommaso was forty-eight years old, married with two daughters, also married, and three grandchildren. His demise left a big gap in the Family's ability to carry on with all operations.

In the days that followed, much jockeying for position and brokering for spoils was being done. The end result was that Vita, Don Silvio's widow and Pinu's mother, as well as Pinu's widow, and children, were to come under the care of the Galliardo Family, something they all dreaded.

The Galliardo's would provide protection, privacy and a stipend for all to get by on until Pinu's estate could be settled. This move essentially removed Pinu's immediate family, including a brother, three sisters and their children from the center of power. Nobody liked this arrangement, least of all Pinu's bodyguards who were demoted but kept on since Pinu's family trusted them.

We never heard what story was concocted to explain the death to the family. Likely, a scenario of infidelity with an unknown woman was used and the bodyguards exonerated.

A few days later a closed coffin was on view for two nights only at Greenpoint Chapels in Brooklyn. A quick funeral, with only immediate family in attendance, ended in St. John's Cemetery. The former bodyguards were fuming because the Galliardo Family was dragging their feet trying to find Pinu's murderer.

"Pazzo Peppe" Galliardo, the head of his Family at forty-two, was one of the few people who found out about Pinu's sexual proclivities some years ago, and he decided that there was no need to do anything now. Besides, he thought that if he had any trouble with the Tommaso family, the factual information about Penu's "queer life" could come in handy.

The New York City Police Department official report included a likely scenario that was eerily on target. A person was identified whose activity that night fit in the pieced-together story.

By then, Doris had gotten out of New York quickly and gone to San Diego with sixteen hundred dollars left of Pinu's money and the two rings. From there, he slipped into Mexico. The trail went cold after that.

We may never know what became of Doris or whether he had gotten away with murder. For one person, Peppe Galliardo, it had been a godsend. He had been restrained while Don Silvio was alive. Then he began to plot ways to overthrow Pinu; then some "Queer son-of-a-bitch" comes along and saved him the trouble.

Of course, things got worse when in April of 1972, Galliardo was at Umberto's Clam House late one night celebrating his forty-third birthday, and he and his party were hit by two gunmen. "Pazzo Peppe" was dead and the fortunes of the Tommasos sank.

However, cool heads prevailed and the Tommaso family was bloodlessly and completely out of the Family business. Thankfully, all of the local real estate owned by Don Silvio and Pinu remained in the hands of his immediate family.

Don Silvio's widow and all the children became legitimate landlords: Vita, her remaining son and three daughters and Pinu's widow. They managed quite well and blessed Don Silvio's wisdom in providing for them all.

While I had no interest in who whacked Galliardo, I always thought it would be appropriate if it had been Pinu's bodyguards.

### A Midsummer Night's Dream with Two Nurses

Over the next two years I became a member of the Junior New York State National Guard, and spent two weeks each summer of 1970-71 up at Camp Drum, New York, near the Canadian border.

After I reached eighteen I became a member of the regular Guard. I went to drills every Monday night at the 42nd Street Manhattan armory, working with a medical unit. I never got home before midnight.

During the two summer weeks, my unit ran the hospital at Camp Drum. I had an eight hour tour of duty, 8:00AM to 4:00 PM, except Sundays. I didn't know who to thank, but whenever I saw my cousin Vito, I thanked him.

Cousin Vito and his family spent the same two weeks at Drum. They had a cottage in an out-of-the-way space. He urged me to spend time with Liz and the girls when I was off duty. But one visit to their cottage convinced me it would be the last. Liz was so sweet and welcoming but Deirdre concerned me.

She had grown into a lovely eleven year old girl who acted like a sixteen year old. I felt awkward being in her company. After making small talk with Liz, and having a cup of coffee, I said I had to get back to the hospital. Deirdre was disappointed but I said I'd come another time when I could stay longer; I never did go back.

I volunteered to stay extra hours at the hospital. Besides, there were two lovely nurses in their twenties on duty there and we struck up a relationship. They shared a cottage off site and drove to the hospital every day.

By the end of the first week, I was spending long hours at their cottage learning a lot about sex from professionals. Apparently, RN stood for "real nice" and "regal nude": "round nipples," "ream now," "rectal nightmare," "roasted nuts," "ram noodle"; you get my drift. The time flew by and I wanted to make a reservation for next summer but couldn't.

If things were looking good for me and the National Guard, I received even better news at the end of 1971. For Guardsmen like me, a decision had been made to offer an option to break up our six months' active duty into two consecutive years of three months of training for each summer, June 1 through August 31.

This enabled full-time college students to complete their course work for undergraduate and graduate programs in four and two years, respectively. I thought the program was great. For those two years, our two weeks of summer camp at Fort Drum were suspended but not the weekly drills.

In 1974, my summer camp and weekly drills would resume for six years, unless I "reuped" and looked to build a second career with the New York National Guard for at least twenty years. If I chose to call it quits after six years, I would receive my honorable discharge from military service. Cousin Vito kept advising me to stay in until at least the Vietnam War was over.

My ultimate decision was to stay in the Guard and become an indispensable administrative adjutant to the highest ranking officer I could find. Cousin Vito approved this plan and ultimately hooked me up with a very nice Major who aspired to higher rank.

## Beam Number Seven

It was during my first tour of active duty, June through August 1972, at Fort Dix, New Jersey that I learned what had happened to Lathem.

Cousin Vito advised me to complete basic training (the first eight weeks) then get settled in for the four weeks of practical weapons systems training, before making contact with his Army friend at Dix. This non-commissioned officer was in a position to introduce me to a Colonel who had access to Lathem's records.

I had prepared a detailed letter about the case with citations from the file released to us in 1963. The letter worked its way through the military pecking order as Vito told me it would. Finally, the Colonel's office gave me an appointment with his adjutant for personal screening, as Vito also predicted.

I was calm and most respectful with the adjutant, pointing out how Lathem's death destroyed my mother and upended our lives. I made mention of something Lathem had allegedly screamed just before he was hit. The adjutant told me he would write a report of our meeting for the Colonel and I would be notified by mail as to his decision.

A week went by and I was worried because I was about to finish my training regimen and head home. The next evening I was visited by the NCO Vito had initially referred me to who said the Colonel wanted to see me. A meeting was scheduled for Saturday, which was very unusual, but I didn't care if I lost a weekend pass as long as I could settle this matter.

What made it doubly weird was that I was to meet the Colonel at his private home in another part of Dix. The NCO was to pick me up and drop me at the Colonel's house.

That morning, the Colonel invited me into his home as the

NCO pulled away. We sat in his office where he slumped behind a large Mahogany desk. He offered me some water and began to speak in a serious and respectful tone without any formality.

"Private Tommaso I would like to express my personal sense of loss not just for your brother, Private Lathem Tommaso, but also for Silvio Tommaso who I understand was your Godfather and Great Uncle. He was a dear friend of my family's and very instrumental in the success of my military career."

I quickly recalibrated the situation and felt much more at ease in the Colonel's company. "Thank you for your heartfelt sorrow, Colonel."

"Private Tommaso what I am about to tell you is classified for various reasons. I will address your concerns as to what actually happened that night. I will be brief and to the point but I must be explicit, reflecting what we were told, under oath, by those soldiers around Private Lathem Tommaso.

"Your brother was in a unit that was diversified as to race, ethnic and religious background of soldiers. It seems he became friendly with two or three black recruits and a Private Morton Fox, a young white male. The nature of his involvement with the young black men appears to have been sexual.

"He was referred to as their 'Bitch,' as heard by other unit members. He and Private Fox seemed to be just friends with mutual interests.

"On the night of the exercise, he was apparently being verbally harassed by the black men for refusing to have sex with them. As they were on the ground in a 'low crawl' movement, the verbal assault took on single words or short phrases like 'Bitch,' 'Cocksucker' and 'Ass suckin' homo' and 'Mother fuckin' queer.'

"Apparently, after the latter expression, Lathem found an opening in the barbed wire above him and struggled to his feet, screaming 'I'm not queer, Mom, I'm not queer! Help me Mom. I'm not queer!' At that point the first shells cut him down.

"There were some disciplinary measures taken but the black men testified that Private Lathem, not they, solicited the sex, after seeing them masturbate in the latrine. There were no witnesses to contradict that allegation. I'm sorry, Private Tommaso. That's all there is."

I was sobbing and blowing my nose. Strangely, what the Colonel told me was not shocking. In my heart of hearts I knew Lathem was a homosexual. I wondered if James ever had an inkling about what went on at the base? It was so sad and tragic what Lathem endured and then to die that way.

I thanked the Colonel for his time and the information. He reminded me that our meeting never took place, but that he was glad he could do something to comfort the Tommaso family to whom he was indebted. He made a quick call to the NCO who arrived five minutes later.

Two weeks later, I signed some papers, loaded my duffle bag and waited for the bus to the terminal on Forty-Second Street, Manhattan. From there I caught the subway and "el" to Queens.

Rose Milano had offered to pick me up and, as much as I wanted to see her, I said no. I needed time to think about the mess that had become my life. She did pick me up at the train station in Queens.

September first of 1972 and You Are There! Where? I was feeling sorry for myself having knowledge about Lathem's death I could not share.

Marta, who wrote to me three times a week, could not believe I hadn't gone to Calatafimi last summer to intervene when she was forced to become engaged. Aldo Sanfidele was a twenty-eight year old man who had a small dry cleaning business in town.

She had patiently saved her virginity for me since the summer of 1969. I received pictures from her. She looked better than half the women who were Playboy centerfolds and she was dressed. Her mother, Michela, must have kept her under lock and key. Of course, with Don Silvio and Pinu gone there were no threats of reprisals. However, there was also no money coming from the States.

The recent passing of Giuseppina (no one from the States went) shuffled the apartments again, as Angelina and Helena now shared the first floor, Michela and Marta were on the second floor and the third floor was rented like the top floor, so there would be two incomes.

The women went through two potential tenants before getting a middle-aged blind man and his daughter. Not being able to see Marta was a blessing to the family, as two sets of newlyweds nearly broke up over the husbands' obvious lust for Marta, now seventeen.

I felt very guilty because after Don Silvio's burial in early November 1969, Rose Milano seduced me on the night of my sixteenth birthday, after the parents were asleep. She was eighteen and a freshman at the City University.

In her mind, sex was natural and necessary but a huge distraction from schoolwork. She made me an offer I thought was reasonable and convenient: we would become sex slaves to each other, so we could focus on our studies, never worrying where the next sexual encounter was to be found when desired.

It was practical, it was safe. She had been on the pill for three years, having lost her virginity at sixteen. I could stop using "rubbers."

Remember, I just turned sixteen and was a sophomore in high school. What we were doing was technically illegal: no? Rose said it was all in the family and no one else would ever know. So on February 1, 1970, we made a vow to each other to be faithful, at least until we both graduated.

What would I say to Marta when I saw her again? She was going to be sixteen next spring. What could I possibly offer her? Mom probably would have told me she'd give me permission to marry at eighteen. Marta would be close to seventeen then.

We could be married in Calatafimi and return to the States to live. I would be facing four years of college in order to be a good breadwinner. What would Marta do? She might get pregnant right away. Then what? Who would support us? What would happen to our marriage?

Next day I told Pop what I was thinking. He used a new Sicilian expletive under his breath ending with "*imbecilli.*"

Now, don't get me wrong, Rose Milano was not very pretty but beyond that she was all woman, "zaftig," I would say. One day, I scrutinized Mary Milano and found her to be "zaftig" as well. Since Mary was only forty-one, I figured Rose still had some good mileage left before the upper-arm fat started to hang.

So while the woman I loved and lusted for was about to marry in Calatafimi, Rose Milano and I began a four-year affair.

## Mediocrity Is not a Mortal Sin

I had graduated from High School in June, 1971, and was advised to apply to the City University undergraduate college. My grades were at the B, C+ level, but I did fairly well on the mandatory state exams (thanks to Rose) and received an academic diploma.

The other reality was the "Open Enrollment" policy at the

City University, which catered to much less qualified students, in the name of ethnic or racial equality. The controversy did not affect me directly, and I took advantage of a situation that helped me, or so I thought.

I breezed through four years with an English major, compiling a 3.5 cumulative index (CI). Based on that performance, I was encouraged to apply to the graduate school of the same college, which I did.

By the time I received an M.A. in English (June, 1977), "Open Enrollment" was history. However, its effect on future academic scrutiny, and the concomitant dismissal of it that followed, lived on for over a decade, despite my 3.8 graduate CI.

Today, a week before classes are to begin, I am going to see Dr. Chester Aloysius Cassidy, head of the English Department at the local Catholic University. His secretary called me at home to arrange a meeting to discuss my application to teach at the university. We were to meet in his campus office promptly at Two PM. I was early and he was late. From there it descended into several lower rings of Dante's *Inferno*.

Dr. Cassidy was a tall, gaunt man with thinning gray hair crawling from atop his red and white scalp down over his small ears and almost fusing with the thick white brows covering his watery blue eyes. He wore a suit that may have been green once but there were many shiny patches around knees and elbows that cast an indistinct sheen. His shirt may also have been white once but appeared tinted blue. The tie was a vivid Kelly Green, no doubt saved for special occasions but not today.

Dr. Cassidy had the habit of talking to me as though we were in a confessional, all "Do you not see that, my son?" "Do you have any doubts left, my son?" and "There you have it in God's nutshell, my son."

He would glance at some papers in front of him, then look up at me and lock his eyes on mine. "Let me be brief, lad. Everything I've read about you, and heard from some of your professors at the City University I called, has led me to one conclusion: you are a classic *mediocretan*" (emphasis on the fourth syllable – his).

"I coined that word some years ago to help me separate the academic wheat from the chaff among prospective teachers for higher education, Mr. Tomm-ass-o" (emphasis on a long second syllable – his).

He waited for a minute to let that statement sink in.

"Now, a *mediocretan* is one who may have the ability to master a subject, but is in no way capable of conveying the essence of a subject, in a multidisciplinary manner that is effective, efficient and exciting. The mastery of this broader universe, Mr. Tomm-ass-o, is what you are incapable of achieving."

"Dr. Cassidy," I said, "do you know the film *The Wizard of Oz*?"

"I know of it, my son."

"Well, the second syllable in my surname is pronounced the same way as the Wizard's domain: Tomm-asz-o, if you please."

"Certainly, my son," he continued. A sly smile tried to form on Dr. Cassidy's dry mouth. "Lad, may I ask you, do you read a great deal; that is books of fiction and non-fiction? Could you name me the top five books on the *New York Times'* best-seller lists? Do you read the *Times*? Do you know what it is, my son?" He paused for a reply.

"I have a large collection of classic books from the Heritage Club: over ten-year's worth."

"That's admirable, my son. But have you read any of them?"

(I was prepared with my standard reply: "Well, I've read some of all of them and much of a few and most of several and all of a couple." I decided to quit while I was ahead).

"I thought as much, my son. A collection of the world's best books, yet not one original idea in your head, and very few pinched from the greatest minds of the past.

"It is one thing to actually be mediocre, but quite another matter when your self-assessment confirms it. That can be shattering."

"Most people are mediocre: the faceless rank and file of any organization, state or nation. Is it any wonder then that most people lead desperate lives filled with hopeless illusions?"

"But, my son, all is not lost. I can wholeheartedly recommend two career paths for you which can lead to a productive life, although, likely, one which lacks distinction but guarantees complete anonymity.

"Become a civil servant, as soon as you can. Eschewing that inclination, our rising Community College system offers many opportunities, and a haven, to *mediocretans* like you.

"A few former colleagues of mine are still teaching at several in Queens and Nassau. I would be happy to provide you with a letter of introduction, which, coupled with your generally morose demeanor, could assist you, if you insist on trying to educate anyone. At least at these institutions you'll only have to stay a few steps ahead of your pupils, something even I acknowledge you may be able to do.

"My son, you must face the facts that you appear to have an insatiable curiosity worthy of a Renaissance man, while your intellectual acumen is anemic at best. You are singularly cursed with the capacity to see greatness in others, while knowing yourself to be wanting in any capacity for meaningful creativity.

"Your ambitions never know fruition: they merely wither and die. Mr. Tomm-ass-o, any horse can start a race, but only a thoroughbred will finish first. You'll let me know about the letter?"

He paused again, waiting for me to say something. I felt a tear meandering down my right cheek.

Dr. Cassidy's tone softened a bit as he asked: "Are you a Roman Catholic, my son?

"Yes, sir, I am."

"Would I be far off if I said you were a stranger to confession and absolution in Holy Mother Church?"

I replied, "No, sir" (I almost said "No, Father").

"I thought not, my son. Alright, I want to share something with you that could turn your life around. After all, you're only twenty-four years old.

"Well, each and every morning, lad, I eat a Jew! Not just any Jew but the big Boyo, Jesus himself, my son."

He looked at me to see the effect of his bizarre statement. His grin indicated he was satisfied. I was sure my jaw had dropped.

"Did you know that Jesus was a Jew, my son?"

My vacant looked confirmed my indecision.

"Well, lad, it is not really your fault. You see, Holy Mother Church, in her infinite wisdom, has been keeping a low profile on that issue for nearly two thousand years. It wouldn't do for everyone to think that the Christ-Killers of Jerusalem were his kin, if you get my drift. Oh, Pope John exonerated them a few years ago, but it's the "Jews for Jesus" movement that needs watching.

At this point my eyes were beginning to cross and I could feel my face twitching just below them.

"It's the miracle of transubstantiation, my son. My three siblings and I ate the Jew every day in Hell's Kitchen. And guess what? We've become more like Jews in the process. Each of us has excelled in our fields of endeavor.

169

"Let me explain: for various reasons, like the rejection of Jews throughout their diaspora and the holocausts big and small to try and destroy them in ancient and recent history, Jews have evolved into the greatest intellectuals over the centuries. It's for survival, lad.

"And while thought and the pen are still formidable weapons, Jews have also learned to wield the sword of justice, and very successfully at that.

"My point, lad is that if you returned to your religious family and started eating Jesus every day, even you could begin to excel from the nourishment his body and blood provide."

I suddenly recalled some section of *The Golden Bough* which touched upon communal cannibalism to perpetuate the spirit of a revered, dead leader. But I could not recall enough information to raise the issue of its possible appropriation by Holy Mother Church's "transubstantiation" idea, *mediocretan* that I was.

Dr. Cassidy rolled up his left shirt cuff to reveal a hairy, otherwise bare and slender wrist. "Oh, look at the time. I have to make my 4:45 to New Haven. Remember Mr. Tomm-ass-o, become a civil servant! Eat a Jew every day and may God bless you, my son. Goodbye."

I was shaking in my shoes. The old bastard nailed me, nailed me! I was nothing but a sad *mediocretan* trying to rise above my low lot in life. He saw through me like a series of PET scans.

Suddenly, the sound of a Heavenly Host riveted me where I stood. Hallelujah, they sang, Hallelujah! Let the self-loathing begin. As I shouted "Hallelujah," and was falling to my knees, the door burst open to reveal Dr. Cassidy's ancient secretary, Gladys, who exclaimed, "What the f ..." as I hit the floor and inadvertently broke wind – for five ... very long . . . seconds. Gladys saw, heard, smelled, screamed and slammed the door shut running as though she had witnessed an act of sacrilegious sexual perversion!

I was losing control of my senses. Then a thought struck me. What is my mantra? "It's What You Do With What You Got." I repeated it three or four times, and I began to feel better.

As the great American philosopher F. Loesser once wrote: "Remember, mediocrity is not a mortal sin."

# A LITTLE PRIEST (SOMEWHAT ABBREVIATED)

. . . For what's the sound of the world out there?

What Mr. Todd, What Mr. Todd, What is that sound?

Those crunching noises pervading the air?

Yes, Mr. Todd, Yes, Mr. Todd, Yes, all around —

It's man devouring man, my dear,
And who are we
To deny in here?
Ah, these are desperate times, Mrs. Lovett,
and desperate measures must be taken.

(placing an imaginary pie in front of him)
Here we are now, hot out of the oven.

What is that?

It's priest. Have a little priest.

Is it really good?

Sir, it's too good At least.
Then again, they don't commit sins of the flesh,
So it's pretty fresh.

(looking at it) Awful lot of fat.

Only where it sat.

Haven't you got poet
Or something like that?

No, you see the trouble with poet
Is how do you know it's deceased?
Try the priest.

(tasting it) Heavenly. Not as hearty as Bishop, perhaps,but
not as bland as curate either.
And good for business — always leaves you wanting more.
Trouble is we only get it on Sundays ...
The history of the world, my love ...

Save a lot of graves,
Do a lot of relatives favors ...

Is those below serving those up above.

Everybody shaves,
So there should be plenty of flavors ...

How gratifying for once to know ...
That those above will serve those down below! ...

Try the financier.
Peak of his career.

That looks pretty rank.

Well, he drank.
It's a bank cashier....

The history of the world, my sweet ...

Oh, Mr. Todd, Ooh, Mr. Todd, What does it tell?

Is who gets eaten and who gets to eat. ...
But fortunately, it's also clear ...
That everybody
Goes down well with beer. ...

Since marine doesn't appeal to you, how about rear admiral?

Too salty. I prefer general.

With or without his privates?

Have charity toward the world, my pet—

Yes, Yes, I know my love—
We'll take the customers that we can get.
High-born and low, my love.

We'll not discriminate great from small.
No, we'll serve anyone—
Meaning anyone—
And to anyone at all!

# Li Frati Mangiaracina

That night I told Pop what had happened with Dr. Cassidy. I told him I had been "spooked" by the cannibalistic talk of the professor. My memory had nudged me near passages I had read in graduate school from *The Golden Bough*. They dealt with the behavior of certain tribes in parts of Africa who consumed the flesh of defeated enemies to appropriate their skills and courage. There was also a reference to bodies of dead Chieftains being consumed for the good of the tribe they had led.

Pop said he was acquainted with cases of cannibalism in Sicily. He proceeded to tell the following story which he said was true. It concerned *Li Frati Mangiaracina,* a family of vintners and master chefs who served a local Mafioso in the village of T.

The father had named his five sons, *Pinot, Grigio, Trebbiano, Moscato* and *Catarratto*. Their greatest specialty was preparing important Mafioso hits to be consumed during a feast of three days: three lunches and three dinners.

The local Mafioso credo was: Kill our enemy; cook our enemy; eat our enemy; shit our enemy out; return our enemy to his family as his dead body turned into our feces.

After all hair, warts and other external growths had been removed, every part of the body was used for the six meals.

The body was cut into smaller more manageable parts and each was cooked in various ways including braised, smoked, roasted, grilled, boiled, fried, sautéed or added to soup stock. The latter method was especially suitable for boiling thick digits which could be sucked on like boiled chicken necks.

Legs of Man would be divided between flesh from above or below the knees. Man Shanks would be divided between left and right arms. Man Stews, as well as *scaloppine* and *saltimbocca* treatments with *porcini* mushrooms and garlic, over a variety of *polentas*, were also in order.

For six meals, selected members of the victorious family dined on these culinary curiosities, all basted in natural juices. Thereby, a potent enemy was killed and then ceremoniously consumed, removing the evidence. But then the *piece de resistance:* the defecation ceremony.

Each dining member collected his excrement directly tied to

the special meals and transferred it to large sacks. The collected sacks were emptied into a large piece of cheap pottery, and the victim's genitals and eyeless head (eyes were a delicacy but the head was needed for identification) was placed atop the pile.

That night, the closed and sealed pot was left at the local post office addressed to the victim's family. The following message was attached: "You're son was a pot of shit in life and returns to one in death. Break open the pot in your garden. The contents, beside his head, and impotent genitals represent his body consumed in ritual meals, then released as excrement. You are welcome to use his manure to plant vegetables in your garden. In this way you may feed off your son's body as we have. Flowers might do as well, so that every spring a part of your son will be born again. If you have other sons who want to break our law you know what to expect."

"That's awful, Pop," I said, when he finished.

"Not really, Jerome. You don't know half of what goes on in daily life around the world. Did you ever hear of a movie called *Mondo Cane:* that's one movie that told the truth about life around the world. One of the few movies I went to see with your mother: rest her soul."

I was about to cast some doubt on Pop's remark, when I recalled what Hamlet said to his friend Horatio: "There are more things in heaven and earth, Horatio, than are dreamt of in your philosophy."

As I lay in bed that night, Dr. Cassidy's last words came to mind and I resolved to take action. Within three weeks I was hired by a New York State agency to fill an entry level generalist position on Church Street in Manhattan. At that time I wrote to Dr. Cassidy for the promised letter of recommendation, indicating my interest in offering classes at Queensboro Community College (QCC).

Within a month, I received a letter from the head of the QCC English Department offering me, on a contingency basis, the opportunity to join the Continuing Education Department. The contingency was submission of my undergraduate and graduate transcripts from the City University.

I was now a "civil servant" in the first blush of official *mediocretancy*! Soon, I would be a part-time Community College Instructor, anticipating the joys, as Dr. Cassidy put it "of working in a 'Dead Letter Office.'"

As a continuing atheist, I nixed Dr. Cassidy's other idea. Many of my colleagues at work and others I socialized with are Jews.

174

Remembering Rachel, I decided to stick to the real thing.

## Beam Number Eight

Long after Lathem had died and James went in and out of psychiatric care, I was in Graduate School. James and I had not seen much of each other the last three years because his mother, Dolly, had developed an inoperable brain tumor.

James devoted himself to his mother's care to keep her at home and make her as comfortable as possible. For nearly two years, James put everything else aside, including his piano study. He continued to play only when his mother asked to hear something but that was infrequently.

Dolly finally passed away and James was inconsolable. Her death seemed to sap his vitality and his will to live. I attended the wake alone. Pop never came around to accepting James as Lathem's closest friend, and he had no respect for James' father and brother who had rejected Mom years before. James acknowledged me but we did not speak. I stayed fifteen minutes and left sorry I had gone. But I did it for Mom and Lathem and what I owed to James.

James moved into Greenwich Village supporting himself playing piano at a "Gay" bar. He kept in touch with no one. A few months later, one of the daily New York Newspapers carried a small article on page ten proclaiming James' murder by a drifter who had been apprehended while wearing several pieces of James' jewelry. I saw the article at my office on my lunch break. The murderer had cut James' throat. I ran to the bathroom to throw up.

A few days later, I dreamed that James was an actor appearing in *Antony and Cleopatra,* playing both roles simultaneously. From the shoulders up he was Antony, "the triple pillar of the world." From the armpits down to his belly button he was Cleopatra, with her "tawny front," turning Antony into a "strumpet's fool." From his groin to his feet he was Antony again, ". . . become the bellows and the fan/To cool a gypsy's lust."

At the end of the play, Antony lay dead before Cleopatra who now wore a blonde wig. Removing the wig, he said:

"Give me my robe, put on my crown, I have
Immortal longing's in me . . . Husband I come . . ."
But his hands were so big and muscular that instead of an asp,

he brought a fat rattle snake to his hairy breast:

"Dost thou not see my baby at my breast,
That sucks the nurse to sleep?"

As the snake moved to implant its venom, I saw its face and it was me! Oh, it was hideous! I woke up in a start, sobbing, my heart pounding.

James' family did not have a wake, and funeral plans were not disclosed, nor was the name of the cemetery where James' remains were buried. He was thirty-three years old.

I grieved for James because he was to me a kindred spirit: a bright and sweet friend and teacher who, like Lathem, suffered for something he could not change. Whatever personal demons he lived with never disrupted our friendship. He treated me like a son and a brother. After Pop, he was the only man I trusted with my life. His memorial is alive in my mind with every new hearing of music we both loved deeply. I think about him continually.

# I AM UNWORTHY OF YOUR LOVE

[John Hinckley sits on the couch in the basement rec room of his parent's house, picking out a song on his guitar, staring at a picture of Jodie Foster.]

HINCKLEY

I am nothing,
You are wind and water and sky,
Jodie.
Tell me, Jodie how I
Can earn you're love.

I would swim oceans.
I would move mountains,
I would do anything for you.
What do you want me to do?

I am unworthy of your love,
Jodie, Jodie.
Let me prove worthy of your love,
Set me free.
How can I turn your love to me?

[As he continues strumming, Lynette "Squeaky" Fromme appears across from him staring at a newspaper clipping of Charlie Manson. She sings to Hinckley's accompaniment, without acknowledging him.]

FROMME

I am nothing,
You are wind and devil and god,
Charlie,
Take my blood and my body
For your love.

Let me feel fire,
Let me drink poison,
Tell me to tear my heart in two,
If that's what you want me to do.

I am unworthy of your love,

Charlie, darlin'.
I have done nothing for your love.
Let me be worthy of your love,
Set you free ---

HINCKLEY

I would come take you from your
life ---
You would be queen to me not
Wife ---
Baby, I'd die for you ---
Even though ---

FROMME

I would come take you from
your cell ---
I would crawl belly-deep
through hell ---
Baby, I'd die for you ---
Even though ---

BOTH

I will always know:
I am unworthy of your love,
Jodie (Charlie) darlin'
Let me prove worthy of your love.
I'll find a way to earn your love
Wait and see.
Then you will turn your love
To me,
Your love to me...

# The 1980s
## Decade of the French Connection

## The Chameleon Elect

Many people believe the 1980s was the decade of divine retribution for the excessive promiscuity of the previous decade, especially within the Gay and Lesbian community. I do not! But I digress. I was talking about divine retribution, but I would like to segue into discussing a different kind of retribution. Retribution of a decidedly mundane nature was a policy used by the Reagan Administration against all Federal employees, the hated "civil servants," who were responsible for everything wrong with America: dark-skinned "welfare moochers," Roe vs Wade and the latest pimple on the Presidential dog's ass..

Is it any wonder then it was rumored that a conspiracy was afoot to raise money to get the release of John Hinckley so he could finish the job! I'm not big on conspiracy theories. Thankfully, President Reagan recovered from Hinckley's attempted assassination.

You will note that I have included the lyrics to a song from Stephen Sondheim's *Assassins* in this section. The song deals with abnormal obsessions with another person which can lead to heinous crimes of murder (Manson) or attempted murder (Hinckley). Remember the pregnant Sharon Tate and other innocent victims of the Manson family's inhumanity.

Ronald Reagan lived to demonstrate that, among other accomplishments, a politician can move 180 degrees from one principled position to the exact opposite principled position with impunity and believe the country, not he, had changed.

So, rather than complain about these matters, I have included in the following section the complete text of Ronald Reagan's radio speech given shortly before election day of 1948, so you may read and draw your own conclusions.

\*\*\*

This is Ronald Reagan speaking to you from Hollywood. You know me as a motion picture actor but tonight I'm just a citizen pretty concerned about the national election next month and more than a little impatient with those promises the Republicans made before they got control of Congress a couple of years ago.

I remember listening to the radio on election night in 1946. Joseph Martin, the Republican Speaker of the House, said very solemnly, and I quote,

"We Republicans intend to work for a real increase in income for everybody by encouraging more production and lower prices without impairing wages or working conditions," unquote.

Remember that promise: a real increase in income for everybody. But what actually happened?

The profits of the corporations have doubled, while worker's wages have increased by only one-quarter. In other words, profits have gone up four times as much as wages, and the small increase workers did receive was more than eaten up by rising prices, which have also bored into their savings.

For example, here is an Associated Press Dispatch I read the other day about Smith L. Carpenter, a craftsman in Union Springs, New York. It seems that Mr. Carpenter retired some years ago thinking he had enough money saved up that he could live out his last years without having to worry. But he didn't figure on this Republican Inflation, which ate up all of his savings, and so he's gone back to work. The reason this is news, is that Mr. Carpenter is 91 years old.

Now, take as a contrast the Standard Oil Company of New Jersey, which reported a net profit of $210 million after taxes for the first half of 1948; an increase of 70% in one year. In other words, high prices have not been caused by higher wages, but by bigger and bigger profits.

The Republican promises sounded pretty good in 1946, but what has happened since then, since the 80th Congress took over?

Prices have climbed to the highest level in history, although the death of the OPA was supposed to bring prices down through "the natural process of free competition."

Labor has been handcuffed with the vicious Taft-Hartley law.

Social Security benefits have been snatched away from almost a million workers by the Gearhart bill.

Fair employment practices, which had worked so well during war time have been abandoned.

Veterans' pleas for low cost homes have been ignored, and many people are still living in made-over chicken coops and garages.

Tax-reduction bills have been passed to benefit the higher-income brackets alone.

The average worker saved only $1.73 a week.

In the false name of economy, millions of children have been deprived of milk once provided through the federal school lunch program.

This was the payoff of the Republican's promises.

And this is why we must have new faces in the Congress of the United States: Democratic faces. . . .

## The Children of Paradise

Just before the 1980s rolled in, I received a call from Rachel Zipel Minsky. I hadn't talked with her in three years, since she became Mrs. Minsky. She had invited a couple of school friends to her wedding and that was the last time we spoke.

"Jerome, I'm so glad I tracked you down. I'd love to see you. Are you still single?"

"Oh, yes, I'm still single. Is everything alright, Rachel?"

"Jerome, to be brief, I'm divorced and taken my maiden name back and moved to Queens, which is closer to where I teach Secondary school. There are too many details to go into now. When may I see you?"

"Well, I happen to be free this Friday night."

"Jerome, I'd love to see you Friday night."

Since her car was newer, and probably ran better than mine, I asked Rachel to come over to the house. Pop would be home but he usually put in a few hours on his next painted wood project. We always had a pizza delivered and relaxed. At this time we had the house to ourselves, looking for a prospective tenant.

While Mrs. Milano moved in with her sister in 1970, Rose stayed upstairs until she graduated college with an advanced degree. Our affair had begun petering out after four years. At her graduation where she received her Master's Degree in Romance Lanuages, she surprised us. Rose announced her engagement to a Professor of Romance Languages at the City University. Someone she had never even mentioned before.

I was relieved and ready to get back into the social whirl of dating. Rachel's call came at a good time.

After Rachel arrived, we exchanged kisses and a few complementary words to each other. She was still slender and cute but some strain was showing through her eyes. We said hello/goodbye to Pop and went to my favorite Chinese restaurant on Queens Boulevard.

It was a lovely evening. The food, the company and the talk were excellent. Rachel was anxious to tell me about a film she recently saw in Manhattan at a French Film Festival. *Les Enfants du Paradise* is a film made during the Second World War in France. It's about the theater and life.

She was bursting to tell me more, but she wanted me to see it with her while it was still playing. Rachel said we could go tomorrow afternoon.

I invited her to stay over with me tonight, and see the film tomorrow, going in by train. She accepted enthusiastically and I began to wonder what was up?

Nevertheless, as we made love that night, I used protection, and she said she was on the pill. Then we spoke about her disappointing experience with marriage. Because of her former husband, she said she was down on men and felt unable to trust any. She remembered me as someone she had trusted in the past.

Rachel recalled wistfully how she gave her virginity to me, willingly, when she was eighteen. I said nothing but remembered the event as beautiful, bordering on sacred for me. To tell the truth, I had imagined that we were married that day and on our honeymoon when we made love. Somehow that legitimized what we did, removing the stigma of "sleeping around." I never told Rose Milano anything about her until much later.

Her career as a teacher was fine, but she needed something more in her life. At twenty-four she was a skeptic about love and marriage.

I told her about my long relationship with Rose, which was essentially based on lust and sexual gratification. I also told her about my long distance relationship with Marta, now married with three daughters. Rachel asked me if I ever wanted children. I told her I was much too selfish to want children. She said that was honest: the world already had too many unwanted children. She, however, thought that becoming a single mother might suit her somewhere down the road.

"You're seriously thinking of taking on that responsibility by yourself?"

"Jerome, let's be honest, father's generally take on a very small role after a child is born. That's been my experience with my parents and other members of my family. All my married girlfriends who became mothers have told me similar stories. Is it all that different in your family?"

"Not in my immediate family. My father become a parent to me only after my mother died: I was already twelve. I can't argue with you on that issue. Who knows what kind of father I'd be? But I don't intend to find out."

Rachel said it was not an issue at this time. But she was looking ahead. Her parents, she believed, would be supportive, if the deal did not include another husband. It also helped that she was a teacher and had nearly three months a year off.

I told her that I was even contemplating a vasectomy for my own protection. Having sexual relations with women on the pill did not always prevent pregnancies. After all, the man was taking the woman's word she was on the pill.

Rachel smiled and asked if I will show my sexual partners my vasectomy scar and surgical report before having sex with them. *Touche'*! Nonetheless, it appeared prudent to prevent all possibility of paternity, to coin an alliterative phrase.

Rachel said that many men were getting "V-jobs" but hedging their bets by first donating to sperm banks. All the reports she'd read on the latest technology indicated that sperm from young healthy donors could be frozen for years. The sperm would be available for future use, if they changed their minds about becoming a parent. She had lots of literature, if I was interested.

I found the discussion to be stimulating and we made love again with protection. Rachel was a wonderful partner but I wasn't taking any chances until I found out what she was after. In a little while she became pensive then turned on a bedside lamp to look me in the eye.

"Jerome, I think I've been in love with you since I willingly gave you my virginity, almost six years ago. You were the one I trusted and really wanted to marry. Anyway, here we are now neither of us wanting marriage and I still love you. Am I deluding myself if I hope that one day you'd consider fathering my child?"

I was overwhelmed by what she said and I actually began to cry. "Rachel, I can't believe you could feel that way about me. Listen to me, please. After my fifteenth birthday party Rachel I went out of my way to make you. I set you up because I wanted to have sex with you. You were honest and really cared, when I said I had a problem. You helped me and I was grateful but then I felt guilty. My selfishness gave me no cover. There was no conquest.

"I was troubled by what I had done to you. That's when I realized I had an impulse that was strange to me. I believed I cared for you but I couldn't understand what it was you saw in me.

"And I had these thoughts completely ignorant of what my features must have suggested to you, a Jewish girl. It took a colleague of mine to tell me that I looked like an Arab, someone you probably would hate. I didn't have a clue."

"I guess you are still clueless, Jerome. Some of my cousins in Israel look a lot more like Palestinians than you do; although I was a bit puzzled by your circumcised penis."

"If I had known you set me up, I never would have spoken to you again. But when we reconnected, I turned to you because of the experience we had shared. I wanted to have real sex and I trusted and liked you.

"When we got together, I was scared but you made it easy for me and it was beautiful not dirty. I realized then that I loved you but I already knew that if I brought a gentile home my parents would not be happy. For all my independence, I bowed to tradition and married a very nice Jewish man I didn't love. True confessions: I made him miserable for almost two years. Then I told him the truth and asked him for a divorce. He said he loved me but couldn't live as we had been in constant misery.

"I didn't want alimony just the divorce. Our lawyers worked it out and we parted amicably. My parents gave me hell, until I told them the truth. They forgave me. Finally, I told them I would never marry again. They were OK with that, too.

"My teaching career was going well and I started graduate school working for an MA in French. I'll have the degree next June. I moved from Brooklyn to Queens to be closer to graduate school and work.

"Last summer I spent a month in France with a couple of girlfriends. It was my second trip there and it was wonderful. I got to speak and read French among French people in many different places. Someday, I'd like to live there, maybe in Provence. You've been to Europe, right?"

"Well I've been to Sicily three times. I told you about Marta.

But I haven't been back there since she married about twelve years ago. I spend two weeks at Camp Drum with the National Guard every summer. Much of my vacation is taken in days for long weekends and for the week between Christmas and the New Year."

"Rachel, I'm very flattered that you'd consider having a child with me. No, flattered is the wrong word. I'm honored that a women I deeply respect would even think of doing such a thing with me. Only my mother held me in such regard. I never expected another woman to feel the same way. Of course, there's Marta.

"Why don't we just agree that for now I'll donate my sperm for the future. I'm still not sure about the vasectomy but I can do one with or without the other. I certainly love your company and our sexual relations have been great. I also think you'd be a terrific mother. If I were ever to seriously consider doing it, you'd be the only one."

The next day, we wept for most of the three hours of the film because it was so beautiful a work of art, depicting, the program said, "a world obsessed with theater and crime in 1820s Paris." I had never seen extended pantomime before and nothing like the artistry of Jean-Louis Barrault as *Baptiste*. There was the beauty of the mature Arletty as *Garance*, desired by all men and giving her body to some, with contempt, but trusting none with her heart.

Perhaps most interesting of all was the successful depiction by Jaques Pre'vert and Marcel Carne', the film's creators, ". . . of a vanished epoch, a 'lost paradise' of Proustian proportions."

In addition, an essay in the program notes explained that each character and their actions symbolized aspects of French behavior during the Nazi occupation when the film was made.

By the time we had an early dinner at The Carnegie Deli, we had agreed to see each other two weekends a month. Within several weeks, I decided to get a vasectomy but not before donating a significant amount of sperm to a bank for my own use. Rachel was happy with that, and I was very happy with Rachel.

We became very close, best friends. Rachel's intelligence shown through all our conversations, whether related to problem solving or art or even politics. We both loved the theater and were liberal Democrats trying to survive in the 1980s. Then we began spending every weekend together. I was never happier.

On her thirtieth birthday, June 15th, as we were enjoying a prime porterhouse for two at Peter Luger's Restaurant in Brooklyn,

VHS and DVD cover art. Personal Collection of author.

she popped the question.

"Jerome, with all my selfish heart, I want to have a child with you. It's been six years since we first talked about it and I'm ready now. I don't want you to feel cornered. We have a wonderful friendship and great sex, probably because we're not married. I would be devastated if you refused but I would accept it and move on. If you thought you were selfish, move over, I have become the queen of selfish."

"Rachel, I've spent six years sharing life with you, although part time. It's been a kind of fairy tale because of our willingness to

186

share yet be selfish in equal measure. I've had a desire to get closer to you in some meaningful way, without marriage. Maybe this is it."

She began to cry and took my left hand pressing hard. I reached over and put my right palm under her chin.

"I think you're more beautiful tonight than I can remember, and I love you more than I can believe. Let me explain.

"You know all about Marta and the torch I've carried for her. How deeply I thought I loved her. But all my precious memories of friendship and love are with you. How can this fantasy even compete with that reality?

"She wanted me at her wedding twelve years ago, to witness what I was losing. But before I left Sicily, she told me over and over how she still loved me and always would. We never had sex or a serious conversation about life. I thought she meant to hamstring me for not saving her from a fate she didn't want. Maybe she did. Maybe she understood how best to punish me for destroying her fantasy of true love.

"But what do we have in common besides some screwed up bloodline and a teenage lust that was never satisfied. She's had three children since then, and she still signs all her letters to me "All my love, Marta," in English.

"You want to talk about selfish. What do you call this fantasy love affair she and I have shared for almost fifteen years, while you've been steadfast and faithful to me throughout these same years: I'm the king of selfish, Rachel.

"Look, I have no reason to believe she's ever been unfaithful to Aldo. They've had three girls together and I'm sure Marta's a great mother. From all the pictures she's sent me, they are a lovely family. Where does that leave me? Loving a phantasm that's been constructed in my brain? Or loving you, in the flesh and through our minds? I see that all my fantasies about Marta have no basis in memory: they never change or grow.

"Thank you for bearing with me, Rachel. I would be truly thrilled to father a child with you. You have no idea what your trust means to me. I have no choice but to love you."

Rachel burst into tears and people all turned around to see what the matter was. Even our waiter came running over. Rachel got her composure back, raised her right hand while holding my left hand tightly and said. "I'm alright. It's just that we're" – she paused and looked directly at me, saying "expecting."

"Mazel Tov! Mazel Tov! Mazel Tov!"

Sylvia G (for *Garance*) Zipel was born July 2, 1985: long and with a head full of fuzzy patches of red hair, weighing seven pounds six ounces. Mother and child are doing very well.

Thankfully, Sylvia (I suggested it, thinking of my Godfather; Rachel loved it immediately) had her mother's complexion. I was surprised to learn that red hair ran in Rachel's family, too. The child was clearly destined to be gorgeous.

Rachel and I agreed that I would not tell Pop until he had the opportunity to meet mother and child. Until then, it would be our secret. Strangely, there were no such concerns among the Zipel family. The grandparents, having only one child, Rachel, were ecstatic about Sylvia and welcomed me into the inner circle of single parenthood as Uncle Jeremiah. Rachel had smoothed the way for me.

## The Remembrance of Things Past

Pop was now seventy-five, long retired and busier than ever. His production of high quality, hand painted woodworks continued. Shortly after my thirty-second birthday, I found an ad in my Sunday Times posted by a gentleman in Manhattan who owned Renaissance Replicas.

This was a high end business for reproductions of 15th and 16th century European painted and sculptured masterpieces: mostly Italian. The owner of "R&R" was one Antonio Spinosato, a master carver and painter. I gave the ad to Pop.

Well, one day Pop paid Mr. Spinosato a visit. They got to talking about master carving and the old country and Antonio said he was from Montevago, Sicily. Pop almost fell down and then told Antonio about Calatafimi. They were practically *paisani*, and the rest of the morning flew as two artisans talked shop and sipped some red wine.

Mr. Spinosato's success came by virtue of the fact that his father had been able to purchase in 1932 the building Antonio lived in and which contained the storefront space used for his business. Not having to pay rent in the high rent district of the east seventies was the formula for success.

Besides, Antonio had one tenant on the top floor who paid twelve hundred dollars a month for five small rooms and a bath which served as his studio. There was no pressure on Antonio to produce much: only to produce high quality pieces.

Before he left, Pop gave Antonio photos of his past and current work. Mr. Spinosato was very impressed but wanted to see this stuff up close. Pop invited him over on a Sunday afternoon for dinner, so Antonio could eyeball and touch Pop's work.

That Sunday Pop asked me to stay home and help him cook. I had a better idea. Since Antonio was a widower and only sixty-six, I suggested we invite Mary Milano over to cook and join us for dinner. Mary was still a good looking woman at fifty-four and I always liked her cooking.

This dinner also provided me with the opportunity to bring Rachel and Sylvia over. Pop knew Rachel as my friend but had not seen her since she started showing early in her pregnancy.

Mary Milano said yes and told me her father had family over in Montevago, some cousins she had never met. She asked if it was possible to invite Rose and her husband, Professor Bonaldo Vincitello, since she cooked dinner for them every Sunday. I said of course.

This was going to be quite a day for the Tommasos. I called Rose Vincitello and told her about Rachel being a single mother and not to make an issue out of it. My wish was her command, as she had never told her husband about me.

Rachel had cold feet but I clinched it when I told that for me it would be a family day unlike any I had ever known. And it was.

Mr. Spinosato was good company and he praised Mary Milano effusively for her cooking and beauty. Rose, now thirty-five and wanting to have children, took to Sylvia like an Aunt, and Rachel and Dr. Vincitello engaged in a spirited discussion of the use of old French verbs by distinguished writers like Hugo, De Maupassant, Flaubert and Proust.

I kept the wine flowing and redirecting conversation to Pop's work. Mr. Spinosato found everything Pop showed him to be remarkably excellent. He was so impressed that he made Pop an offer: reproduce the small triptych alter scene in the photograph Mr. Spinosato provided. If he was satisfied, he would work out a deal to pay very well for Pop to reproduce masterpieces for clients of Renaissance Replicas.

Needless to say that Pop was thrilled and a little scared. This was something he had longed to do from the time his father, Pippinu, had talked to him as a young novice about the great Michelangelo. Pippinu's skill for restoration work could be translated by Pop into reproducing great works of art and be paid well for the work.

After dinner and dessert, as Mr. Spinosato rose to say good night, I told Mary Milano that Pop and I would clean up so she, Rose and Bonaldo could leave early. I added that Pop and I had business to discuss.

She offered Mr. Spinosato a lift to the train station, but he thanked her saying he had come by car. He did kiss her on both cheeks and reminded her to get the names of those cousins in Montevago. Giving her a business card, he asked her to call him at any time. He would enjoy hearing from her, he said.

With only our little family left and Sylvia asleep, I sat Pop down and said the three of us needed to talk. "Sure," Pop said in his best English, "What's up?"

I told him I appreciated his speaking what little English he could in front of Rachel, but that we needed to speak Italian and I would translate for her. He said "OK."

I asked Pop if he wanted to become a grandfather. He gave me a sly look and asked me how since I wasn't married. With some trepidation, I calmly told him all about Rachel and me, and said I was sorry that while she was pregnant I had told him she was on a sabbatical in France. The beautiful child with the fuzzy patches of red hair was his grandchild.

I summarized all my questions and Pop's replies for Rachel. He looked at Rachel and walked over to sleeping Sylvia. As he came back I saw tears running down his cheeks.

He wanted to know if we planned to get married. I told him we had no plans to marry. Pop thought that was unfair to the child, and would limit our access to the baby. I told him how understanding and generous Rachel's parents were. In addition, Rachel's grandparents on both sides of the family were dead. Pop would be the only grandparent and he could be introduced as Giuseppe, Jeremiah's father.

Rachel rolled her eyes at that remark, then threw her arms around me and kissed me sweetly. Pop was confused. I reiterated everything slowly, finishing with the fact that Sylvia would remain our secret from the Tommasos and any strangers we encountered. Beyond that, whether at the Zipel's home or here in our own house, we could show our affection for Sylvia. I also confirmed that she was named for my Godfather. Pop wept some more.

It took some doing to walk that tightrope but we managed. Rose was the only person who probably put two and two together, but she was not sharing that with anyone. Periodically, I reminded her about Bonaldo's ignorance of our affair.

Mr. Spinosato loved Pop's reproduction of the triptych and bought it on the spot. He gave Pop a large catalogue of pieces already sold, and some orders for rare pieces he still needed to fill. Noting which pieces were most desired and the preferred order of their creation, Mr. Spinosato gave Pop the catalogue. Pop did this work at home, after Mr. Spinosato supplied the wood, paint and any other necessities.

# The 1990s
## Decade of Social Eruption and Baptiste's Choice

### Sax in the White House

> "I'd do anything for you
> Anything you'd want me to
> All I want is kissing you and
> Music, music, music. . . ."

I supported Bill Clinton in two elections but I could not condone his extramarital sexual activity. Frankly, it was none of my business or anybody else's, until he got BJs in the White House from you know who. He denied having sex with Monica under oath. This was a fundamental, inexcusable mistake on his part. If getting BJs does not constitute sex for him perhaps he better understood, as a former Rhode's Scholar, that Ms.L had actually performed *fellatio* on the President: a kind of oral sex.

However, this gross indiscretion by President Clinton led to an impeachment. A dark day in American history when Republican's thought more about avenging President Nixon's resignation in disgrace, tied to undermining the Constitution, and less about potentially bringing down the Clinton Administration for oral sex in the White House.

And it took a Special Prosecutor (our name for him in Brooklyn and Queens was *Starr-mingia)* to post all the lurid details on the internet and have an enraged father complain: "Now I have to explain what oral sex is to my nine year old son." I would have bet at the time that the little gentleman already knew the drill and probably could have given his dad a few pointers. We have not yet managed as a nation to rid ourselves of that damned puritanical streak our English forefathers brought with them to America.

My final thought on the matter. None of this would have happened if Monica had played a real flute and accompanied Bill on his sax, making music instead of whoopee, in the White House. Do you think "whoopee" would have been more acceptable as in "I did not make whoopee with that woman in the White House?" It's certainly vague enough, and it has a nice alliterative ring to it.

I felt your pain, Mr. President, but as the old song says: "Pick yourself up, dust yourself off and start all over again." Here are some sacred words to live by: "It's What You Do With What You've Got."

Who knows, the public has forgiven or forgotten many other sinners. Did you know that Charles Manson is still alive and living very well in prison? Now that's blind, impotent justice for you.

And your wife Hillary has stood by you through it all, and taken a lot of heat from women and men. You know, Mr. President, you could get back into the White House someday as the first, First Gentleman. Just give newly-elected Senator Hillary R. Clinton a chance to don the mantle of the "Comeback Kid."

## No It's Not Shakespeare's Seven Ages of Man

It was in the middle of this decade that Pop regaled me with his definition of the four stages of man, when he reached his eighty-fifth birthday. I tried to translate his Italian, sprinkled as it was with Sicilian speculations, but found it rough going. When I thought to turn it into rhymed doggerel, taking a few liberties with precise meaning, it fell into place. Pop never read it because he never mastered enough English to read a weather report. Anyway, the following caveats are offered: Your experience may vary, and Pop, if he ever knew what *Viagra* was, never said a word to me.

## The Four Stages of Man by Girolamu Tommaso

Stage One: ages 16 to 65
A sirloin rump, an easy dump, a ferocious hump; libido: torpedo
Stage Two: ages 66 to 70
You shake the snake and inflame its eye, and wait patiently for a spurt that doesn't hurt. Over time, you watch it go limp and dry.
Libido: recedo
Stage Three: ages 71 to 79
A chicken scrap, a bloody crap, a fitful nap; libido: dormedo
Stage Four: ages 80 to 85
A watery gruel, an impacted stool, an impotent tool; libido: desedo.

193

# Baptiste: Garance or Nathalie?

Life had been going along well for me, Pop, Rachel and Sylvia as the 1990s were drawing to a close. I was now spending the better part of every weekend with Rachel and Sylvia. They would come by us every other weekend, so Pop could see them. The basement was now devoted to everything which would engage and entertain Sylvia: video/audio tapes, laser discs, books and educational, interactive toys.

On alternate weekends, I would go to Rachel's apartment on Friday nights. The next day Sylvia would stay with her Zipel grandparents, if Rachel and I were seeing a matinee performance on Broadway. Otherwise, Sylvia would join us if the fare was appropriate for her. Then she'd spend Sunday with the Zipels.

I was very fortunate to work near Number Two World Trade Center where a half-price tickets booth opened at eleven AM weekdays. Of course, having a boss who went to the theater every week was fortunate. It was much easier for me to get the tickets on his behalf, while I was getting mine. The best part was that on Fridays you could purchase seats for both that evening as well as the Saturday matinee. You could do the same thing on Tuesdays.

In the course of a year, our little family would see dozens of plays and musicals: anything by Sondheim, new or revived, and August Wilson's plays, chronicling the black experience in America for every decade (that's the plan) of the century. We even took Sylvia to see Sondheim's *Passion,* and found she somehow understood what Fosca was feeling. That scared the hell out of me. She and Rachel sorted it all out.

Regarding Sondheim, let me say that my earlier quote (Christmas 1965) about Sinatra's unique place as a singer of American songs applies to Sondheim's unique place as a musical dramatist. Substitute "musical dramatist" for "singer" and voila!

I still received some passionate letters from Marta whose English had become better with each year. I did not dare to respond to her emotion. It was unseemly, I thought, for her to carry on this way.

Pop and I had not gone back to Calatafimi when Aunt Giuseppina and Cousin Angelina died. But when Pop's sister Helena passed away, two years ago, we went back for a week. Pop wanted to visit his mother's grave site again. We insisted on staying at a B&B, rather than have Marta's family shuffle to accommodate us. I felt safer.

We had all our meals with Marta's family and always enjoyed seeing Michela. Aldo had put on a lot of weight but Marta looked amazingly well at forty-two. In fact, she was much trimmer than in the recent pictures she sent Pop of their twenty-fifth wedding anniversary celebration last year. None of her daughters had her natural beauty but they were well educated and bright.

Marta kept smiling all the time, showing off those white teeth which lit up her beautiful face. She was wearing her hair as I remembered it, long and curly, different from the pictures Pop had shown me. I was getting nervous.

I was very uncomfortable in Marta's house, feeling guilty for my old lust and passion for another man's wife. At all cost, I made sure Marta and I were never alone together.

When we said goodbye, Marta gave me some homemade cookies to take with us. She whispered that they were very special, as we kissed goodbye. Michela emotionally embraced Pop and me, as we entered the taxi.

When I opened the cookie box at the airport to have with some coffee, I noticed an envelope taped to the inside cover of the box. I removed it without Pop noticing and put the envelope in my pocket. When we were in the air and Pop had fallen asleep, I took out and opened the envelope.

There were two pages inside, along with a lock of her hair and a swatch of her old bathing suit with a white butterfly. She said the hair and the butterfly were to help me remember how much we loved each other almost thirty years ago. She had never stopped loving me, despite Aldo and her children, whom she loved in her own way. We were fated to be closer together one day, although she did not know how or when.

She closed by saying that in her heart she had always been true to me and would remain so. Could I please send her a token to show her I felt the same way?

In my mind I now had a real dilemma on my hands. How do I assuage Marta, if, in fact, that's the thing to do? Do I let Rachel know what Marta wants? I decided to talk to Pop and get the benefit of his thinking. He was surprisingly empathetic and gave me some good advice.

"Jerome, you owe your loyalty to Rachel," he said. "She's the mother of your child, and she has been better than a wife to you. End the masquerade, so you can be a real father to Sylvia.

"You and Marta are not children anymore. But you should know something about my mother that scares me."

Pop finally told me all about Michele Occhipinti.

"He was my mother's lover before and after I was born. They had been lovers as teenagers and made vows to each other. When he went to study in Rome he had second thoughts about my mother. He felt so much guilt that he turned to the priesthood to solve his problem.

"But my mother could not accept his rejection. However, once he began the process to become a priest, she decided she wanted to marry and as soon as possible. Pippinu Tommaso was a good catch.

"When Occhipinti returned as a priest, my mother had six healthy children, having lost her first: a daughter who was still-born. Eventually they became friendly again. By the time all the children were in school, Occhipinti yielded and they resumed their love affair.

"Even though they exercised great care, my mother became pregnant with me when she was thirty-six. She was certain she had conceived with Occhipinti. She told him to find an excuse for going to Palermo for two weeks: just get out of Calatafimi.

"Now she had to deal with Pippinu because she had stopped having regular sexual relations with him for nearly three months.

"My mother knew how to seduce a man. Pippinu was flattered by her renewed attention. She told him she had prayed to the Holy Mother for one more child. This would give them a "lucky" seventh. She hoped that she would not show much for at least a couple of months. This would blur the time of conception.

"She told Pippinu that this was the fertile time of the month for her. They had intercourse four times the first week and three times each of the next two weeks. Pippinu was nearing exhaustion.

"My mother waited three weeks before telling Pippinu her period was late, although she was already pregnant for two months. He was overjoyed and blessed her belly with a sign of the cross every day for good luck.

"*Cignu Russu* was relieved when the midwife said no more children after I was born. *Signura* Ravello was puzzled about my full development for a supposed premature child. She shrugged it off to the 'Will of God.'"

Pop still felt like he was in limbo concerning who his father was. However, my grandmother's explanation put that question to rest for me. The other matter that grated on Pop was the fact of his mother giving Pippinu the dreaded *cornutu*. He remembered Pippinu's ranting about man's double dilemma when he was a child: war and horns.

## Beam Number Nine

I accepted Pop's unexpected revelations as a cautionary tale. I was trying to figure out for a couple of months how to tell Marta it would never work for us. Then I got a call in the middle of the night from Marta: Aldo had collapsed and died of a massive heart attack at fifty-six. Could I please come to her in her hour of need. It was Sunday morning. Oh, shit!

Marta's call put me into another circle of hell; as the old saying goes: "From the frying pan into the fire." I felt like a candle being burned at both ends with time running out. I told Marta I would do my best to make the funeral but I would come as soon as possible.

Again, I turned to Pop for advice next morning. He told me he would not go and neither should I.

"It's a trap, Jerome. If you go she will draw you into her web. I don't see any way you end up that's good for you, Rachel and Sylvia. They are your family now. Don't abandon them."

Pop was right but I was still a selfish SOB. At this moment, all I wanted was Marta. I had no time to look at all angles, so I resolved to go and see what would happen.

This was still Sicily. Widows didn't leave the burial site to run off with their lovers. Marta was no exception, she just happened to be a devoted wife and mother otherwise living out a thirty-odd year old fantasy about me. But look who's talking.

I called Rachel at nine AM. She had plans to take Sylvia to the Metropolitan Museum at eleven. There was no point in running over to her apartment, so I asked her if we could talk for a few minutes. She agreed.

After explaining what had happened, I asked her for her input.

"You're putting me in a tough spot, Jerome. We had agreed to be friends and lovers and parents. I have never pressed you on your role with Sylvia, giving you free reign to get on with your own life. But you seem to be telling me that now you and Marta can have each other and maybe get married in a year. It sounds like you're both locked into this fantasy that ignores other loved ones that have a legitimate claim on your love and devotion.

"Is she prepared to walk away from her mother and daughters and any future children the daughters may have? Can she leave Sicily for good? Or are you thinking of relocating to Calatafimi?"

I replied, "I can't think past getting on a plane and going to her in her grief. She loved her husband in her own way, as she does her children. Rachel I have to go and find out how we truly feel about one another.

"You know I value your council and I'll keep your words alive in my brain for guidance."

"Just one last thing, Jerome: remember I love you and Sylvia loves you. We'll be here when you return. Please be careful. *Au Revoir*, Jerome."

Is it possible to see a dark, forbidding forest in front of you in the dead of night, yet continue to run toward it because you've got to see what lies on the other side? That's how I felt but I paid for those expensive airline tickets anyway. I could only take one week of emergency leave off from work. That meant I had a few days at best to learn my fate.

When I called Marta the next day, Michela answered the phone. She said that Marta and her daughters were making arrangements with a local funeral home for the wake. Aldo had a large family and many friends. He would be laid out longer than usual but the funeral would have to be Saturday.

I told Michela I was coming and would arrive Wednesday morning in Palermo and take a cab down to Calatafimi. She asked me why I was going through such expense to be there. I told her the truth: Marta wants me there.

Michela paused a moment. Then she asked me if it was wise to listen to her daughter. I asked if she meant that Marta was so grieved that she might be saying things she didn't mean.

"No, Jerome. She seems to be perfectly fine. I wonder if there's any grief to hide."

I assured Michela that she knew more about that than I did.

"Jerome, I know Marta better than I know myself. She's got something on her mind. Be very careful or she'll lead you down a thorny path with no shoes to your grave."

"I'll see you all then Wednesday morning, Michela. Goodbye."

I wondered how much Michela knew about me and Marta. Did Marta confide in her about us? Who else could she turn to? It was going to be very tense, I felt: tense and exciting. I couldn't wait to get there.

My one black suit needed to be pressed. Who was going to notice it? Marta would notice. I packed my best charcoal gray tie and three sky-blue shirts. I managed a quick visit to my barber for a trim and I was ready for Sicily.

For all the days I'd be there, the world would be draped in black. Sicilians knew how to do black: for a day, a week, a month, a lifetime. Marta looked great in black. I gave her three months before colors started to enter her wardrobe. There would be complaints but Marta would say something like: "You hypocrite! You need black to hide your body not to proclaim your sorrow for losing the man you cursed up and down the street while he was alive."

I arrived minutes before the family was leaving for the wake. As I thought, it was a sea of black dresses, skirts, sweaters, shoes: the uglier the better. It was theater: a charade of mourning, an outward show hiding the mixed feelings inside. I realized I was the only male Tommaso present. Marta's three sons-in-law were working and would come tonight.

Michela greeted me warmly, telling me the daughters were taking it badly, in contrast to Marta who always preferred to smile rather than frown. I paid my respect to each daughter but Marta was missing. In a minute she came into the room saw me and began to weep uncontrollably.

I helped her into a chair and she sat me down next to her, taking my hands and not letting go for fifteen minutes. She said "Thank you for coming. Now I can breathe again."

When the room started to fill with Aldo's family and friends, I took a seat in the back next to Michela. It was all so depressing. I wanted to grab Marta and take her away where we could be alone and make love. Even I found that impulse disgraceful but I couldn't shake it all day.

The wake droned on: Wednesday, Thursday and Friday. All the same faces, voices; weeping, moaning, keening: "Aldo, Aldo, Aldo, too young to die." There were moments when I almost envied Aldo's indifference to sight and sound.

The routine was stultifying. I could barely stay awake even after a good night's sleep. Marta and I hardly exchanged a few words, even though we had all our meals together. The daughters were relentless: when one stopped sobbing another would start as in a round. Michela and I would exchange knowing glances about this display.

The funeral at the *Madonna del Giubino Church* and the burial in the church's cemetery was solemn and moving. It was a much needed tonic after the airless room filled with sonnambulants looking less alive than Aldo. About twenty-five of us went to a local restaurant for a midday meal. That's when Marta came to get me.

She sat me down to her right with Michela to my right. On Marta's left were her three daughters and their husbands. Aldo's parents were seated to the right of Michela. Marta took a spoon and tapped an empty glass in front of her. She was going to speak. I know I blanched but my dark skin prevented total embarrassment.

"My dear family and friends, I would like to formally introduce you to someone I have known longer than any of you but my beloved mother, Michela. He is the only male Tommaso here today. He came from America earlier this week to be with me in my hour of need: my cousin Jerome Tommaso whom I dearly love."

After a few painful seconds of silence, Michela started clapping and everyone followed suite, although the daughters' applause was obviously tepid. I felt bound to say something, so I stood up.

"I would like to personally express my sympathy and condolences to the entire Sanfidele family. I do so, on behalf of my father, Girolamu Tommaso, as well. He is eighty-nine years old and could not make the trip.

"Marta and I met in 1966 for the first time. It was my first trip to Sicily, and my first chance to meet all the Tommasos in Calatafimi. We have remained friends all these years.

"Now, I would like to offer this prayer for the soul of Aldo Sanfidele. May his soul be at this very minute before the throne of God and may Jesus lead him into Paradise to his eternal reward." I shuddered but I made the sign of the cross. "Thank you."

Judging by the spontaneous applause, I hit a home run. I'm sure I blushed again. I was such a hypocrite but a happy one. Marta took my left hand and squeezed it, as she wept looking at me. Michela took my right hand and kissed it. I kissed hers back.

I had a flight out of Palermo at ten AM. Marta insisted on driving me, despite pleas from her daughters and sons-in-law. Michela came along to chaperone us. I said my good byes to the family, picked up my luggage and put it in the car.

"*Andiamo,*" Marta called from the driver's seat. Michela was sitting in the rear. It was a late model Ford Escort sedan. Marta hit the gas and we were off.

We had about a forty-five minute drive but Marta wasted no time before she said most emphatically, "Jerome I love you, I adore you. After more than thirty years my greatest wish will be granted: you will marry me. Yes?"

I looked at Michela who smiled and shrugged her shoulders.

The fantasy I shared with Marta overwhelmed me: "Yes, Marta I will marry you." I took the moment to give Marta a small package that contained the token of my love she had requested. I told her to open it later when she was alone. It was a flat, red glass heart the size of a silver dollar: inscribed on the obverse "All My Love, Jerome" and on the reverse "For Marta, Forever."

The remainder of the trip was spent discussing all the problems and roadblocks to our marrying. They were many in number. Finally, Marta told me that nothing else really mattered if we wanted it. It was a question of the timing: six months, a year. She asked if I could wait that long. I assured her that I could. Then I thought of Rachel and Sylvia.

I took the last fifteen minutes of the trip to explain about my other family. I emphasized that Rachel asked me to make her a mother but that we never married. Sylvia believed I was an Uncle Jeremiah. Marta was amazed that such relationships were tolerated and openly entered into. Ultimately, it did not matter to Marta, as she was willing to embrace my family in order to love me.

When we got to the airport we stopped at a curb near the departing flights entrance. Marta told Michela to close her eyes for a minute. Michela sighed and closed her eyes.

Then Marta slid closer to me and put her arms around my neck and put her mouth close to mine. I inhaled her sweet breath and we kissed and kissed for a minute. Marta whispered: "The next time I see you we will sleep together and make love all night. I promise, Jerome."

I got out of the car gingerly and grabbed my luggage to put in front of me, as I said goodbye to Michela and gave Marta one last kiss. I walked slowly through the doors of the airport until my erection had finally dissipated.

## AS YOU DESIRE ME

As you desire me, so shall I come to you,
Howe'er you wander, so shall I be,
Be it forever, or be it just a day,
As you desire me, come what may.
I doubt not but you will do what you will with me,
I give my life to you 'cause you're my destiny.
And now, come take me, my very soul is yours.
As you desire me, I come to you.

When I got home that Sunday, I called Rachel and asked her to come over. She said she'd bring Sylvia so we could have a frank discussion about us as well as Marta. I dreaded doing that but agreed anyway. Before they came, I filled Pop in on the trip.

Pop said I was truly an idiot. Did I not understand that Marta and all the rest of the family in Calatafimi would never leave their home. This was not 1905. Even earthquakes, like the one in 1968 which ruined Vita right next door didn't chase anyone away.

He assured me that middle class status which Marta had would keep her in Sicily. Marta owned a nice, spacious house and the family business was successful. She would also stay because her daughters were not leaving.

"Then the grand children will come, cementing her to Calatafimi; all this sacrifice, Jerome, just to satisfy your lust. That will pass soon enough but you'll still be in Calatafimi with those three "Sanfidele 'cows' ruling the roost."

Well Pop could really be persuasive when he got hot over something. I knew he was right about one thing: I would have to move to Calatafimi and adjust to living a lifestyle I disliked immensely. Real life problems were such a pain in the ass.

Somehow my psyche was still under the influence of the Hollywood Solution, which meant I marry Marta and we live happily ever after as the movie ends. After all, I gave Rachel exactly what she wanted. As Pinocchio sings, "I've Got No Strings." Could I possibly walk out on Rachel and Sylvia now and feel free?

As the King of Siam sings, "Is a puzzlement."

When Rachel arrived with Sylvia she seemed cool and distant. Sylvia was happy to see me and said so. I started to tear up and what came out was "I love you both very much."

"We love you too, Father," said Sylvia smiling and taking my hands.

"Rachel I thought we agreed . . ." Rachel cut me off.

"You left me no choice, Jerome, I was out of leverage. I played my last card because neither of us wants to give you up. Like it or not we are a family. If you're planning to marry anyone here I am, the queen of selfish."

I instinctively took her hands and kissed them. Then I took her and Sylvia into my arms and broke down, sobbing. They began to cry and we stood there weeping, and I remembered Sondheim's *Company* and a song he wrote:

> You're always sorry,
> You're always grateful
> You're always wondering what might have been.
> Then she walks in. . . .
> You're sorry-grateful,
> Regretful-happy.
> Why look for answers where none occur?
> You always are what you always were.
> Which has nothing to do with,
> All to do with her. . . .

We each had questions for the others and our discussion was frank, honest and to the point. Sylvia had inklings from the time she was six that I was her father. However, she wasn't sure if it was just something she wished were true, or the kind of presentment someone with her intelligence could conclude to be very likely.

When she turned seven, Sylvia developed a burning desire to know who her biological father was. Unbeknownst to me, Rachel told Sylvia that she would be given the information when she turned sixteen. Rachel had not yet fully reckoned Sylvia's status as a gifted child, and did not want to rush to that judgment.

Within a year she regretted her concession. It now looked like Sylvia would be out of high school before her sixteenth birthday. Rachel had made good on her promise even before Sylvia's sixteenth birthday came because she wanted to bring matters to a head now.

They both loved me and wanted us to be a real family. Sylvia suggested I marry her mother and adopt her, giving them both the Tommaso surname. I was overwhelmed. What they said made perfect sense. Why was I still reluctant?

Finally, Rachel said they had no legitimate hold on me. They didn't want me to give in to them, if my heart wasn't in it. Rachel made it clear that I had kept my part of the bargain, and that Sylvia was more than any mother could have hoped for. They'd had each other for almost sixteen years, and could continue to live that way. Sylvia's future promised to be one glowing with great achievement and personal fulfillment.

Sylvia is an extremely precocious adolescent who will enter Bryn Maw before the age of sixteen. She already speaks, reads and writes English, Yiddish, French and Italian with authority. She will tackle Latin and Greek, as she wants to become a humanities scholar with a concentration in Classic Antiquity and the Renaissance.

While Tommaso genes are in her makeup, I believe Rachel has given her a rich Jewish heritage and the tutelage of a master educator. But when I think of Mom and her intellect, I give thanks to the Lisak genes for some of Sylvia's brilliance.

I started playing Uncle Jeramiah's VHS copy of *So Dear to My Heart* for Sylvia when she was two. Three months later, she was singing along with the wise old owl: "It's What You Do With What You Got." This philosophy and the owl (Bryn Maw's mascot) stood her in good stead as she "Got a Lot" and Rachel guided her choices of "what to do with" it.

When she was nearly four, I played Sylvia my laser disc version of *The Thief of Bagdad* which she enjoyed enormously. She fell hard for Sabu. "He's the smartest and most beautiful boy in the world," she exclaimed. The affair between the King and the Princess left her cold. She just wanted to join Sabu as a sailor and go "sailing out to sea."

For Sylvia's fourth birthday, we all spent a long weekend in Washington, D.C. to show her the places and symbols of our national heritage. We were also able to attend the production of Sondheim's *Into the Woods* at the Kennedy Center. Sylvia loved it and we had an enjoyable evening discussing it. The experience made Sylvia a Sondheim fan for life. We saw other productions of his shows whenever we could.

When she was six, I played her my new laser disc version of *La Belle et La Bete*. Sylvia really flipped over this one, as she could understand most of the dialogue before reading the subtitles, just like Lathem. It was weird to me that my mother and Rachel had taught their first born child to master French.

At ten, I was hoping a first glance at *The Children of Paradise* would whet her appetite for more. She never budged as each long half played out. She cried for *Baptiste's* ultimate loss of *Garance* but already understood that he belonged to another woman and they had a child together. By the age of fourteen, and many viewings of *The Children of Paradise* later, Sylvia was explaining the film to me and her mother.

All these memories of Sylvia's growing up came back to me that night. I had invested a good deal of myself in her, as my mother had done for Lathem and me. Of course, I understood that what I had done with Sylvia was the easy stuff, especially because of her brightness.

Rachel and her parents did the hard stuff relating to rearing a child: dealing with feeding, changing diapers, illness and about a hundred other things most men from Pop's generation absented themselves from.

Most men from my generation are different, helping with chores that were once the sole responsibility of women. The 1970s seemed to start a revolution, what with women declaring their independence and demanding more from live-ins and husbands.

Somehow I missed all that because Mom was the only real parent I had. She indulged Lathem and me, never asking very much of us. Strangely, I still wound up more like Pop than like Mom. I am exceedingly selfish and willing to slip into my fantasy life when harsh reality rears its ugly head: like now.

I can't get Marta out of my mind. She looks great and still has that animal magnetism about her; and the things she said: "The next time I see you we will sleep together and make love all night. I promise, Jerome."

Was this one of those cases where only the wisdom of Solomon could solve the dilemma? What would Don Silvio do in this matter? I think his view was always do the best for the greatest number and live with the consequences befalling the few. Now if I apply that thinking to my situation what do I have?

## May 18, 2001
## A new Millennium: Sing: I am (Bushed) by the Supremes

### Beam Number Ten

Pop was working on one of Mr. Spinosato's antique reproductions fifteen years later when he suffered a stroke on May 6, 2001. He was paralyzed on his right side, and even though he was left-handed, he could not do any sensitive work with his left hand which developed a tremor.

While he was recovering in a nursing home, Pop said he prayed for death every day. In his condition, he had nothing more to live for. He was happiest when Rachel and I would bring Sylvia to see him. I translated between them, although Sylvia at nearly fifteen could hold her own speaking Italian. We told her that it would please Pop if she addressed him as *Nonno,* since he loved her as her grandfather and she did.

Cousin Vito came several times to see Pop as did Mr. Spinosato who had had a brief fling with Mary Milano. Most of the Tommasos that knew Pop were dead. A few reverted to an old sense of hostility that grew back after Don Silvio's passing.

One day when we were alone, Pop seemed confused but then told me a story about my mother that dated back to the first months after I was born. He said he had come home early that day and found no one in the kitchen or Lathem's bedroom. The door to his bedroom was slightly open and he quietly approached to see who might be in there.

He silently pushed the door open another few inches and saw something that mesmerized and appalled him. Mom was seated in a vanity chair next to their bed. Both breasts were exposed. I was in her arms nursing at her left breast. Her right arm was extended with her hand in a beckoning position. Her eyes were staring at something. Her mouth was open but no sound came out.

Pop had to open the door a few more inches to see what Mom's eyes were fixed on. What Pop beheld was Lathem standing a few feet from Mom with his left arm reaching out to her. Pop lost his breath but then walked calmly out of the apartment closing the door silently behind him.

Before he got to the next landing, he bellowed out *Buttana! Mi facisti curnutu!* He repeated it several times as he dashed out into the street, completely hysterical. He ran to a Tommaso cousin's home for solace. Rose Genna, a close cousin to Don Silvio welcomed him. Her son, Vito helped return Pop to Mom three days later: no questions asked. Pop had not seen these relatives in over twenty years, nor would he see them again until years later. But someone was watching out for Pop.

Why Pop recalled that particular moment and chose to tell me about it remains a mystery. I checked with the nurse on duty about his medication. One of the drugs he was taking could, as a side effect, dredge up horrific memories. Perhaps in some deep dark corner of his psyche, Pop still harbored a belief that mom had given him horns.

I felt compelled to look into arrangements for taking Pop's body to Calatafimi, as his prognosis was not good, and he did not want to live. I was told his body would have to be shipped within seven days of embalming, especially if there was to be a wake before a ceremony at the burial site. Alitalia told me what I needed to know in order to make the arrangements. I needed a certification of death signed by a physician.

A few days later on May 13, 2001, Pop called me early in the morning saying there was something important he had to tell me but not over the phone. He asked me to come by as soon as I could. I skipped Sunday breakfast with Rachel to get to the nursing home quickly, but fifteen minutes before I arrived, Pop suffered a coronary embolism and died in his nurse's arms.

Pop was on view for one day only, and a small circle of family and friends attended the wake. I arranged for a special viewing for Rachel, Sylvia and the Zipels to avoid explanations. All day I tried to puzzle out what Pop had to say to me but drew a blank. Of course, cousin Vito and Liz came. After they left, I ran around setting things up for the trip to Calatafimi.

The day after Pop's death, I called Marta at noon her time to give her the news. I first took a moment to tell Marta I loved her and wanted to marry her now. Seven months had passed since Aldo's death and it was time. If I was going to Calatafimi for a funeral, I was prepared to stay for a wedding.

# Fantasy Number One: I Marry Marta.

My decision to stay in the Guard and become an indispensable administrative aide to the highest ranking officer I could find was a good one. Cousin Vito hooked me up with a very nice Major with whom I worked for twenty-five years as he rose to Brigadier General.

Eventually, I was credited with thirty years of part-time service in the New York State National Guard, earning a modest pension. That came long after cousin Vito retired, as a decorated veteran with forty years of full-time service and a very good pension. Thankfully, he was still alive and in good health to enjoy it.

Only Deirdre, the *scucciamenta* made some of his days stressful. She went through boyfriends like a runny nose goes through tissues. Finally, at thirty-five she married and had four children in five years. Vito had to add a wing to his ranch house because his two other daughters had left and then returned to the coop.

I did visit them every so often, and Deirdre was always there to roast my nuts. But when we said goodbye, she would always kiss me on both cheeks and whisper in my ear "I still love you, Jerome. You broke my heart." I guess some people carry their most persistent illusions to their graves. I should talk: what about Marta, what about me?

My own financial health was a little thin. The regular New York State agency, in which I invested twenty-eight years of full-time employment, qualified me for a good pension at age fifty-five. So my cash flow was staggered: a modest Guard pension payable at age forty-eight; a good State pension payable in seven years; and substantial Social Security benefits payable in sixteen years.

Oh, yes, there was the house I was selling for $240,000. Closing was set for June 10, 2001. This was the two-family house in Queens given to Pop by Don Silvio's estate in 1969. Pop and I lived there until he died.

I was selling to our tenants of ten years, the Stagione family, which had grown from newlyweds into parents of two boys and a girl. It was a little tight for them the last three years, so we gave them access to the basement for birthdays, etc. Jack Stagione did a lot of work around the place when Pop was no longer able to. They became family very quickly.

I was glad I was in a position to sell the house at a good price, although well below market estimates of value due to the expected rental income. Pop had no mortgage and the Stagione's were good people. I thought about what my Godfather would have done in my place. It was his kind of deal. I think he would have been proud of me. The proceeds from that sale were my nest egg, as I prepared for my future with Marta.

There were some unresolved issues between us. I wanted to return to the States within a year, Marta was non-committal. She had three daughters between ages twenty-three and twenty-seven. Marta's daughters had been university trained and formed a corporation with their husbands, after Aldo died, to control his dry cleaning business and expand it. The potential growth picture was rosy, and each daughter planned her family growth accordingly. Marta would want to be around when grandchildren came along.

My mother's grave was in Queens not Calatafimi; I still felt compelled by her wishes for eternal rest. All Marta's relatives were buried in the exclusive cemetery grounds of *Madonna del Giubino's Church*, thanks to the forethought and generosity of Don Silvio Tommaso. Marta's own family would be the last of the line to be so accommodated.

Perhaps splitting time between Calatafimi and New York City was in order.

Having one child of my own, I realized I needed to be sensitive to family issues with Marta. Thankfully, the Tommaso house was owned free and clear by Marta and her mother. But what will happen when I'm on the scene benefitting from the Sanfidele estate by marrying the widow?

Aunts Giuseppina and Helena, as well as cousin Angelina, had gone to their eternal rest. Michela was the only other occupant of the house.

All my correspondence with Marta and monthly phone calls to her resulted in a holding action. She's not quite ready. All of Aldo's affairs are not yet in order. She needs time.

The day after Pop's death, I called Marta at noon her time to give her the news. I first took a moment to tell Marta I loved her and wanted to marry her now. Seven months had passed since Aldo's death and it was time. If I was going to Calatafimi for a funeral, I was prepared to stay for a wedding.

"What funeral?" she asked sounding alarmed.

"My father's: I'll have his body there in a week for the burial."

She suddenly got hysterical and became incoherent. Michela got on the phone and said there are problems. She asked for my number and promised to call me back at three PM her time to explain everything.

I waited for the call until nine AM when I had to leave to finalize the funeral arrangements. None came. Two times in between I called Marta's number but the phone just rang. I left.

## Fantasy Number Two: I Marry Rachel

After sending my "Dear Joan" letter to Marta, I called Rachel to tell her it's done. Now we'll make plans for the wedding and adoption. I insisted on a civil ceremony and Rachel agreed. Rachel would like to retain her maiden name by hyphenating it with mine: Zipel-Tommaso. I liked it, Sylvia G. Zipel-Tommaso liked it; a done deal. We plan to file all the necessary papers after we bury Pop.

Where are we going to live? Rachel's apartment is small but Sylvia's moving to Pennsylvania to live on campus so one bedroom will do. But we would need a sofa bed at the minimum or a two bedroom apartment for her return or visits. I was considering selling my house, now that Pop has passed on, to our tenants, the Stagione family. Otherwise, we can keep the house and live in the first floor apartment and give the tenant full use of the basement.

All these matters will have to wait until I return from burying Pop in Calatafimi. Rachel and Sylvia want to come with me. But we have to bury Pop by May 22$^{nd}$ or run into problems with Italian Public Health authorities. Rachel's got classes until the end of June and Sylvia has final exams next week. She graduates in early June. I promise them nothing will happen to change our plans.

Pardon my interruption of these fantasies, while I get back to the reality of burying my father.

The Limo-Hearse I'm leasing meets me at the airport. As an affiliate of the funeral home in Calatafimi, they charge me half the going rate. Pop's casket is loaded into the back of the Limo-Hearse and I sit next to the driver.

Nino is the amiable gentleman driving. We have a pleasant, if generic conversation about soccer, a sport I know little about. He thinks Italy will make it to the World Cup this year. I wish them luck. We arrive safely at the funeral home in forty minutes.

I'm surprised to find no one from the family at the funeral home. When I enquire about the Sanfidele family I get shrugs of implied ignorance. The viewing is for the evening hours of six to nine PM. The funeral and burial will take place at the *Church of Maria Maddalena* tomorrow. I'll use the afternoon to arrange for the headstone to incorporate Pop's date of death.

**Annunziata Helena (*Cignu Russu*) Greco Tommaso**
Madre Amata
10 aprile 1874 – 11 luglio 1969

**Girolamu Occhipinti Tommaso**
09 settembre 1910 – 13 maggio 2001
Amato Figlio
Riuniti in Paradiso per Sempre

## O PARADISO

O Paradiso, dall' onde uscito
Fiorente suol, splendido sol,
In voi rapito son!
Tu m'appartieni!
O nuovo mondo,
Alla mia patria, ti posso offrir!
Nostro è questo terreno fecondo,
Che l'Europa può tutta arricchir!
Spettacolo divin!
In te rapito io son!
O nuovo mondo,
Tu m'appartieni a me!
A me!

O paradise, emerging from the sea,
Flowering earth, brilliant sun,
You entrance me!
You belong to me!
Oh new world,
I can offer you to my homeland!
This fertile earth is ours,
Which can enrich all Europe!
Wondrous scene!
You ravish me!
Oh new world,
You belong to me!
To me!

I called by Marta but again there was no answer. I had my cab take me to the house. I rang every floor, nothing. Then I heard shuffling in the entrance way behind the door. A voice like Michela's asked "Who is it?" I told her it was me and the door was unlocked and opened. Michela stood there in a robe looking old and as if she had been crying. She asked me to come in. I paid the cab driver and followed Michela to the first floor apartment.

What Michela proceeded to tell me took my breath away, and finally caused me to laugh out loud like a lunatic. Marta was in Palermo getting married to Duke Alfonso Augusto Zaragoza, age forty-six, from Spain!

Michela said it was a whirlwind affair steeped in courtly romance. A month ago, Alfonso spotted Marta from his yacht sun bathing topless on a large rock in the *Golfo di Castellammare*. She sat on a white beach chair with a high back and wings which folded inward, limiting her frontal exposure to the Gulf.

The Duke's boat could not get closer, so he got into a small motorized dingy and came in within thirty feet. He shouted "Hello" and woke her up. She didn't cover herself until the Duke invited her to join him if she could swim to the dingy. He spoke Italian beautifully.

Marta stood up to give Alfonso a good look at her olive brown shape and bare breasts. Then she pulled her suit's straps onto her shoulders, stepped to the edge of the rock and dove into the water. Within seconds, the Duke pulled her aboard the dingy and they motored to the yacht. Michela noted that the Duke was about my height and weight with curly black hair and a dark complexion. She also mentioned that Arabic influence was very strong in Mallorca, the Duke's home, now an autonomous region of Spain.

After a week of conspicuous consumption of chilled champagne and caviar (my words, not Michela's, as I coined another alliterative phrase), the Duke, widowed six months ago, proposed marriage to Marta. Michela was told Marta mulled the offer over for five seconds before she said "Yes!" in Italian, Spanish, English and French.

And so today, at the Cathedral in Palermo, Duke Alfonso Augusto Zaragoza and Marta Tommaso Sanfidele were tying the knot, surrounded by the Sanfidele family and the Duke's crew in full uniform. A second wedding ceremony will take place next week at the magnificent Gothic *Catedral de Santa Maria de Palma de Mallorca*.

The newlyweds will honeymoon in Mallorca where the Duke has a small chateau. The Sanfidele family was invited to stay over at one of the local four star hotels. The Duke's yacht will take all members of the immediate family from Mondello to Mallorca the following day. Limos will convey the family from Palermo to Mondello where the yacht is harbored.

When I stopped laughing at this improbable Hollywood script, I asked doubtfully "E' vero?" Michela solemnly nodded affirmatively. I asked her why she wasn't with the others. She said there were two reasons: she despised the Sanfidele family, dead or alive, and she wanted to pay her respect at my father's wake, funeral and burial.

We were the only two people with Pop that night and the next day. Michela had something on her mind and wanted to talk.

During the hours of the wake we were alone, except when two older women came in. They were strangers but it was their custom to honor the dead whenever they could. We acknowledged them and they said a prayer at the coffin. They expressed their grief over our loss. Finally, taking cards the funeral home provided with some information about the deceased, they left. Both of them were actually crying.

I asked Michela if her comment about the Sanfidele family included Aldo. She had mixed feelings about Aldo because he helped solve one of her greatest problems but then tried to kill Marta's spirit in the early years of their marriage. He slew the dragon, she said, only to become more dangerous himself.

When Marta was sixteen, Aldo Sanfidele, a virtual stranger, came to the house and asked for her hand in marriage. He offered her a good life and home in which to raise a family. Aldo was a prosperous businessman with two dry cleaning outlets in Calatafimi. He had never been married before, spending his youth working hard for his parents and getting educated. At twenty-seven he was a good catch. The only problem Michela saw was selling him to Marta.

Aldo was short and very muscular but in the early stages of becoming stout. His thinning brown hair was evidence of a "vanishing prairie." Aldo's speech was sometimes punctuated with stuttering which ceased as mysteriously as it had started. He was burly but in a cuddly way, once you got to know him. Aldo prized education above all else as the key to success. This belief did not extend to women.

He appealed to Michela to take seriously the dangers Marta faced in the streets of Calatafimi. Aldo saw the youthful "Scum of the neighborhoods" who lusted after young women, many no longer escorted or chaperoned. He offered Marta safety and well-being in a healthy family life. Dealing forcefully with the scum in the streets was his specialty. Marta need never fear walking around Calatafimi. Aldo had been a wrestling and weight lifting champion at University.

Except for the fact that he was dead, Michela could have sworn that Don Silvio had sent Aldo to her. He appeared to be the man to solve her problem with Marta's beauty and runaway hormones in a town full of lewd and lascivious men. Michela went to work on Marta.

It took almost a year, and the incidents with the two newly wed couples who briefly became tenants, to convert Marta. Each new husband, on occasions several months apart, had tried to rape Marta, so consumed were they with her beauty and steaming sexuality. The police had to be called to restrain each of the wives who wielded knives and cleavers as they menaced their spouses' genitals.

Aldo was apprised of these incidents by Michela, so he would not forget Marta, and double down on his efforts to marry her.

The pressure on Marta was enormous. Her pleas to me in America for rescue were unsatisfied. So, at seventeen Marta wed twenty-eight year old Aldo Sanfidele. Her dowry was a rent-free apartment on the fourth floor of the home Michela shared.

Twenty-seven years and three children later, the bargain was gastric acid in the mouths of Marta and Michela. Then Aldo died.

I put my arm around Michela who was weeping as she spoke.

## Beam Number Eleven

"Aldo didn't marry Marta to educate her or give her free spirit any room to breathe. She was a sexual object to him: a beautiful cow to breed with over and over. Aldo wanted sons and she gave him girls. He blamed her and the curse of the 'Tommaso she-bastards' for their daughters. Can you imagine, a university man as ignorant of life as Aldo?"

I was moved by Michela's story. "How did she manage all the years after her last child – and only three at that?"

"Marta is an intelligent woman but her position was not strong when she got married. After her first child came in September, Aldo expressed disappointment with his daughter. Since business was good Aldo rented a spacious first-floor apartment nearby. They moved but Marta was crushed. She secretly took pills to prevent pregnancy and avoided as many intimate moments with Aldo as she dared.

"Eventually Marta conceived again and carried the child into her twentieth year. A second daughter was born. Neither of the girls looked much like Aldo but each had something of their mother in the face and eyes and skin complexion. However, the girls share in these features did not result in beauty but in a dark plainness. Even worse, was the slimness of their bodies: again, Aldo was very displeased.

"After the third girl came fourteen months later, Aldo was furious and Marta almost had a nervous breakdown. She had breast fed each of her girls, her breasts becoming huge, and told Aldo she did not want more children. Aldo demanded a son. So Marta made a pact with Lucifer to bring Aldo to his knees.

"Marta became pregnant again in May of the following year. She was nearly seven months pregnant when on the eleventh of November a pair of goat horns, stained with blood, were nailed to the front door of their apartment house. Aldo found them as he was the first one out going to work at six AM. The name Sanfidele was on a note congratulating him for receiving the *curnuti*. It was signed 'Intimate friends of Marta.'

"Aldo went completely wild: screaming, beating his chest, cursing Marta for her infidelity. He confronted Marta who swore truthfully that she was faithful. Enraged, he hit her and she fell. The police were called and Aldo was arrested after a horrible struggle. Marta was lying on the ground almost ignored by everyone. An ambulance arrived and rushed her to the hospital as she started to bleed: she eventually miscarried. It was a boy as she had hoped. She obtained a copy of the medical records from a physician who had been a friend of Don Silvio and who had actually delivered Marta in 1955. This Dr. Giambalvo also furnished Marta with photos taken of the dead child taken from her body before it was sent to a local funeral home to be prepared for burial.

"The record stated that she had miscarried a male child about seven months into her pregnancy due to the trauma of being hit

and violently thrown to the ground (by her crazed husband Aldo)."
Marta provided this evidence and her own statement to her attorney. It was to be used in the event anything happened to her at the hands of her husband, Aldo Sanfidele.

"She wouldn't see Aldo when he came to the hospital.

"Aldo had investigated the "horns" as best he could but found nothing to incriminate Marta or anyone else.

"When Marta finally came home, she spoke to Aldo as calmly and quietly as she could."

"Aldo, you murdered my son. I and God will never forgive you for that. If you are willing to be a father to our daughters, listen carefully to what I say. We will raise them to be well educated and independent. You will give all your energy and money to that task because from this moment you will never touch me again. We will live for our children not for each other.

"If you dare to touch me again make sure you kill me as you did my son. In any case, my attorney will provide the police with a complete record of your assault on me, seven months pregnant, and the ruthless murder of Aldo Sanfidele, Jr."

Michela said these last words with terrible emotion, as if she were the great Eleonora Duse in her prime."

I began to sense Don Silvio's invisible hand in the matter.

"Aldo accepted his fate," Michela continued, "and for twenty years he gave his life to his daughters. Although he and Marta were estranged, she recovered and regained her old self, living a life free from being a spouse. She learned to smile again and light up her beautiful face.

"Marta raised her girls to be bright, courageous and willful; and she gave herself to you, or her memory of you. She wrote to you like a woman who can't bear to be separated from her lover. She counted the hours, days, months and years until your return, like *Madama Butterfly*. Marta told me everything. She never once told you how she suffered; how she sacrificed; how she wept.

"We both prayed for Aldo to die. So you see, Jerome, there is a God after all. Or does Satan sometimes answer our prayers? I blame myself for this mess but what else could I do?

"Don't blame yourself Michela: none of us has the wisdom to make all the right choices and decisions in life. Not even Don Silvio. We must look ahead, understanding that we can't change the past but only come to terms with it."

The clarity of my words about someone else's problems reminded me of my inability to see my own until now. However, I did have one last question to ask Michela.

## Beam Number Twelve

"I know this is none of my business, Michela, but I need to ask you: will you tell me what Marta's father looked like when you became pregnant with her?"

Michela looked at me warily and asked "Are you sure you want to know, Jerome?" I nodded yes.

"Well, he looked like a Tommaso. I told Marta that when you came back in 1969 and Marta was fourteen."

"And did you tell her I looked like her father?"

Michela frowned. "The night before we all went to *Castellammare del Golfo*, I told her you resembled him. She wanted to know his name but I refused to tell her. Marta was beside herself and couldn't sleep. After you left, I urged her to leave you alone, and two years later I saw that she needed to marry or she would repeat our family history with a stranger."

"But who is her father?"

Michela snarled "You had your question and answer: no more!"

I was feeling cocky and wise like Sam Spade in my deductions and I had a wild hunch. "Did Marta know that you were Alfonso's mother, too?"

Michela fixed her dark brown eyes on me. "You're crazy, Jerome; you don't know what you're saying!"

Now I was angry: "You'd let Marta marry her own twin brother?" "How dare you let that happen?"

She sighed and lowered her eyes. "She's not Alfonso's sister, Jerome: I never met Alfonso's father." She looked up at me and whispered: "Marta's your sister."

I lost my breath and labored to catch it. Michela went on.

"Your father and I met in Queens when I went to America for a short visit in the summer of 1954. I was staying at Vito Genna's house for three weeks meeting the Tommaso family.

I was young and attractive and my mother vowed I'd die a virgin. But I refused to marry a stranger, a week after a hasty betrothal. The trip to America was to get pressure from the family,

218

including Don Silvio, to cooperate with my mother.

"One night your father came by Vito's house at dinner time. He entered the house like a fugitive on the run. He and Vito's wife, Rose, were cousins who had not seen each other in more than twenty years. Girolamu was estranged from the whole Tommaso family at that time.

"Vito was a generous man who held no grudge against your father. He was happy to help a family member when he could. Vito also knew this generosity had to remain a secret lest Don Silvio and the rest of the family react negatively. He took that risk for Rose's sake.

"Girolamu said your mother had thrown him out of the apartment for acting like a madman and frightening the children: and you only a few months old. He needed to let a few days pass before going back. Rose asked her son Vito to find Girolamu a place to spend a few nights in Brooklyn or Queens.

"Young Vito, recently returned from the war in Korea, set your father up in a small motel near LaGuardia Airport for Thursday through Saturday nights. Girolamu was told to order food at the nearby pizzeria for his meals. A man named Paolo ran it (for Don Silvio). Paolo spoke fluent Italian. But your father was not to identify himself: only to say home was in Calaltafimi. Paolo would ask no questions.

"Young Vito also gave your father a toothbrush, toothpaste, shampoo, soap and some cash. He told Girolamu he would call him mornings and evenings to make sure he was alright. Vito would pick him up on Sunday morning, assisting him with a call to Sonia, his wife, to apologise and beg for forgiveness to return to his family.

"I felt very badly for your father. On Friday morning, after Vito called him, I called to talk to him myself. He sounded so miserable. I said I wished I could visit him. He said he would like that. Rose suggested we make him a good meal and bring it to him by taxi service.

"Rose was a very sly woman. She did things for the Tommasos that even her husband did not know about. She and her son were very loyal to Don Silvio.

"When we arrived we delivered the food and Rose excused herself to do some local shopping (she spent three hours in Paulo's Pizzeria eating and reading a newspaper). Rose knew how hard a life Girolamu had been living. She asked me to be nice to him. I was ready to be more than nice.

"I never intended to betray our afternoon of love but Rose swore an oath of secrecy, promising no one would ever know. I didn't dream something would come of it. Five weeks later I was not upset over my late period. I accepted my mother's harsh and cruel words and Don Silvio's frustrations. I never told them the name of the father. But they never abandoned me."

I had caught my breath but was still reeling over this revelation: my life resembled a runaway Lewis Carroll fantasy but "Blunderland" was more the place.

Michela said she was sorry. However, now that I knew the truth, she said I was free to love my own little family. I began to tense up and tremble a bit. There was still an unanswered question.

"Michela, exactly when did you tell Marta her father's name?" She gave me a cold look but said nothing. I was now convinced she told Marta the same story about her fling with Pop, after the Duke entered Marta's life. Marta's hysteria on the phone must have been due to her realization that our father had died. True or false, it gave Marta a way out. She apparently grabbed it. It's my turn, now.

Michela suggested I change my plane ticket to leave sooner if I could. Neither of us wanted to face the triumphant Sanfideles but only I could leave.

I grabbed my things, called for a cab and kissed Michela goodbye. "Tell Marta that I'm very happy for her. I'll even call her Dutchess. Michela, will you tell her I know who her father was and put it to rest?" She said she would.

"Marta will be sad and happy at the same time, but she will think of you as a brother now."

I got to the airport quickly but nothing was available until the next morning. I booked a room at a nearby motel. At midnight I called Rachel and gave her most of the news. We both cried and said "I love you" to each other. I sent a father's love to Sylvia via Rachel.

The next day I made my escape from Sicily. I don't know when or if I'll ever return. We buried the last Tommaso in Sicily, as far as I was concerned. How about Pop and his *curnutu* fixation: hypocrisy or just part of the human condition? I guess I'm really more like him than not.

The first thing I'm going to do after hugging and kissing my wife-to-be and our daughter is visit Mom's and Lathem's grave site. Someday I will join them there, but for now I have a loving family of my own, three jobs (Public Servant, National Guardsman, College Lecturer) and a house without a mortgage plus with a great tenant. And, to boot, I'm still in Pop's "First Stage of Man." Now that's a pretty good American Dream.

I'm looking forward to a future of peace and prosperity. I'll give President George W. a chance to prove he's worthy of the office the Supreme Court gave him. If there is a God, I do hope He or She blesses America, Sonia, Rachel, Sylvia, Michela and Marta in that order. Of course, I must acknowledge that somewhere in the back of my mind, I'll be waiting for the next beam to fall.

That reminds of Hamlet's position on death: "... We defy augury. There is special providence in the fall of a sparrow. If it be now, 'tis not to come; if it be not to come, it will be now; if it be not now, yet it will come. The readiness is all."

I wish I could wrap up the past in an envelope and put it in my safe deposit box and forget it with my elementary school report cards. But in a small manila envelope there's a smaller plastic zip lock bag containing three items: a lock of brown curly hair; a swatch of fabric with a white butterfly on a black background; and a color photograph of Marta from 1969.

Three reminders of the fourteen-year old woman I have thought about every day since 1969: my sister, the beautiful Marta. I'm incapable of ignoring or destroying her love tokens: that would be a betrayal I could not live with. No matter how content I am with my life, I know I'll go to my grave haunted by the loss of Marta.

## West of Eden

Maybe all this crazy business has something to do with the Biblical expulsion of Adam and Eve from Eden. Perhaps there's something in our DNA that compels the human race to want to get back to that (mythic?) place to be truly fulfilled and happy.

Then again, if that story is much more primal than Adam and Eve, and I believe it is, it may be locked in our universal psyche: a vestige of the dream that drove our ancestors out of Africa: "the roots of heaven." They sought survival and a better life and perhaps always carried the hope that another Eden or Paradise could be found: one more hospitable than the first. I think some of our ancestors found it here.

My candidate is Yellowstone National Park, home to one of

the nearly intact ecosystems in the northern temperate zone of the Earth. The first national park in the world, Yellowstone was established by Congress and signed into law by President Ulysses S. Grant in 1872.

Inhabited by Native Americans eleven thousand years ago, this monumental land of lakes, rivers, canyons and mountain ranges was an Eden where the peaceful coexistence of humanity and nature flourished. Of course, this magnificent ecosystem sits on the Yellowstone Caldera and the continent's largest super volcano: alive with continuous geothermal activity; another looming beam?

Then there is Aetna, the ancient *muncibeddu*, as it was called, part of an island ecosystem that for ancient eyes resembled what Eden surely must have been like. The invaders and conquerors of the island did not always respect the land, but like animals and plants which provide manure and seeds for the next generation, they left their cultural DNA to mingle with that of the earlier inhabitants.

I believe these parallels between Sicily and America are apt. The Greeks found Sicily to be a paradise, especially compared to the rocky, inhospitable terrain of their homeland. For Rome, Sicily was the granary of the empire.

Millions of immigrants from Europe came with an illusion of paradise in their search for the American Dream. They found Democracy to be "waspish" and less tolerant than its creed. But those who stayed found it better than what they left behind, and many pursued that irretrievable "green light," improving their lot even if they couldn't quite grasp the golden ring.

## Shangri-la

Then there's the strange tale about *Shangri-la* and the great *Karakal* and "Valley of Blue Moon" amidst a mountain range somewhere in Tibet. The subject came up during my summer weeks at Camp Drum in 1986. My work for the Major in the National Guard increased as he had made full Colonel. After his three-month stint at the Pentagon that spring, we were having a beer at his residence in Drum, when the subject of Soviet ICBMs came up. That had been the area he was immersed in at the Pentagon.

"You teach college courses on literature, right?"

I nodded affirmatively.

"Well, I recently read a very interesting report connected to the novel *Lost Horizon* by James Hilton."

I perked up. My Colonel proceeded with an unusual narrative of a chapter in the "Cold War," mixing fiction and geopolitical reality. The tale began with efforts by a post-Great War peace organization to campaign for a better peace resolution than was found in the Treaty of Versailles. Known as "WarEnders International" and headquartered in London and New York, this group was established in 1923.

One of its tangential platforms was the "Preservation of all the arts through the archiving and safe keeping of their precious material and spiritual expressions." James Hilton, a founding member, published *Lost Horizon* ten years later, when fear of a cataclysmic war was rising. It was to his *Shangri-la,* hidden in the highest mountains of Tibet that this process of preservation had begun, not in 1933, but nearly three hundred years earlier!

One Father Perrault, a Belgian priest, was the first European to find *Shangri-la* in the early eighteenth century. He was still alive in 1933! Perrault, the High Lama of this lamasery was dying and stealthily brought Hugh Conway, a British diplomat and kindred spirit, there to replace him. Conway, an immediate convert, nonetheless left the lamasery with doubt and regret. Having subsequently discovered that *Shangri-la* was all it appeared to be, Conway apparently tried to find his way back.

Now in 1934, a group of eight WarEnders International members set out to find *Shangri-la,* convinced that Hilton's novel was based on a factual account. The group included scientists, journalists and a Catholic priest. Two of them were Americans, two were British, and the others were two Russians and two Chinese familiar with local Tibetan dialects. A Eurasian millionaire funded the expedition, so long as there was no publicity about the venture. Not even Hilton was told of the plan.

Once the group's plane landed in the last civilized outpost in Tibet, they prepared to travel on foot into the *Kunlun Mountains* with local guides. They posted letters to the secretary of the man funding the expedition. There was no further communication with the group. That is until the Soviet space station *Mir* was orbiting the Earth in June of 1986.

As its orbit moved over the *Karakal Mountain* range nearly six miles high, a radio signal was picked up by *Mir*. The signal lasted only minutes, and so it took four orbits before the crew of three Russians could record what was being broadcast. The crew recognized words in Russian, Chinese and English. Two of the crew concentrated on the Russian words, while the other, more familiar with English than his comrades, listened carefully to the English, which had a distinct British accent. After they pooled their notes, they came up with a brief statement in Russian, supported by the English words.

The statement was as follows:

War Ender's expedition of 1934 four survivors found Changri-la in 1936 this community is a socialist dream truly utopian High Lama Conway British over ninety years old looks to be forty none of us has aged much after fifty years no word from outside world since 1939 rumors of war from last contact with porters we are well and happy this is what we have dreamed and hoped for since man walked erect is the world ready for Changri-la are we alone in paradise if you hear this message you may be able to contact us. We hope you do.

The recorded message was on a loop playing continuously and alternately in English, Chinese and Russian.

The *Mir* crew listened for two more orbits to convince themselves they had heard what they recorded. Then the Russian hot line was used to pass the message up to General Trelenska, last stop before Moscow. The General decided not to send the news any further. His long career had weathered the hard lines and purges of many heads of the Soviet Union. He was not inclined to embrace the "perestroika" and "glasnost" policies of Mikhail Gorbachev.

General Trelenska ordered the *Mir* crew to make every effort to contact "Changrila" and maintain some form of direct line with the Russian member, or members, of the group. Under no circumstance was this matter to be revealed to any other Soviet personnel or other governments: it was coded as "unknown phenomena under maximum Soviet security."

The general took the unprecedented initiative to secretly contact his counterparts in Beijing and Washington, DC for a clandestine conference to determine what to do. His own inclination (which apparently convinced the others) was to eradicate this "Changrila" before news of it could reach the outside world. He was particularly upset by the description of *Shangri-l*a as "a socialist dream truly utopian" place and "paradise." And the references to longevity of life sent shivers across his broad shoulders. His reaction almost mirrored the comments by Mallinson to Conway in the novel. No belligerent regime, especially a communist one, could be comfortable with such news. But the United States also signed off on the decision to obliterate *Shangri-la.*

After several exchanges between the triumvirate of cold world powers, the following was decided:

1. Obtain exact coordinates for *Shangri-la's* location.
2. Order the discontinuance of the looped message, and any other attempts to communicate, now that a direct line to the world exists via *Mir.*
3. Assure *Shangri-la* transmitters that a UN (explain concept) air-rescue operation will soon allow the surviving representatives of the original expedition to be debriefed on site.
4. Identify a secret Soviet ICBM installation to carry out a non-nuclear mission to eliminate *Shangri-la* "with extreme prejudice."
5. Subsequently, have the *Mir* crew report what appears to be a volcanic eruption, and an unusually large number of avalanches, in the vicinity of the *Karakal Mountain* range in Tibet.

I was horrified at what I was hearing, whether fact or fiction: even a *mediocretan* sensed the cruel irony and indiscriminate callousness of the plan.

Suddenly, my mind transported me to the space station with the Soviet crew. They were preparing to celebrate the moment of impact, having coordinated their orbit with the launching of the ICBM. They passed around the sealed miniature bottles of vodka, and turned on some prerecorded music selected for celebrations.

I looked down from the station as the taped music was reaching a quaking crescendo mixing the concluding notes of apotheoses in both Mussorgsky's *Pictures at an Exhibition: The Great Gate of Kiev* and Tchaikovsky's *1812 Overture,* combining crashing cymbals, sustained grand pipe organ notes, reverberating thunder gongs, bells, chimes, smashing timpani and canon fire. It was orgasmic, and I was caught up in the moment; then a red-white ring of fire rose from the Earth marking the end of *Shangri-la:* a gigantic black crater filled with dead people, animals and millions of tons of ice and snow in continuous avalanche. The *Mir* crew sent out an international message about a volcanic explosion seen in the *Karakal Mountain* range.

My Colonel was looking me in the eye as he abruptly stopped his narrative. I was feeling queasy, wondering which one of us was hallucinating.

"It was all a joke," he blurted out, and he began to laugh and howl over it, uncontrollably. "You get it? Somebody made the whole damn thing up!"

But who was the joke on, I wondered?

"I have to pee, I said, as I squinted for effect. I ran to the bathroom and vomited into the open commode. In times of great stress and overwhelming sadness, I have always thrown up.

## The Name Above the Title

This sad episode did remind me of Frank Capra's film *Lost Horizon* from 1937. It was not one of his popular films; nonetheless it is an interesting take on *Shangri-la* shortly before the Nazi onslaught into Eastern Europe. James Hilton was concerned that destruction by airplanes in a new war could bring the future of civilization to the brink of extinction.

However, Frank Capra and Vincente Minelli are worth remembering as two of the century's great Sicilian-American film directors. It was Capra whose meteoric rise in Hollywood in the 1930s prompted his name to appear above the title of films he directed and/or produced.

Francesco Rosario Capra came from Sicily to America in 1903. Throughout his career in Hollywood and the U. S. Army during World War II, he reflected his passionate patriotism for his adopted land through commercial and military films that celebrated average Americans and the idealism of American Democracy, and reminded us why we went to war.

He won three Best Director Oscars in five years for *It Happened One Night**(1934), *Mister Deeds Goes to Town* (1936) and *You Can't Take it With You* (1938). His other great films include *Mister Smith Goes to Washington**(1939) and the perennial favorite, *It's a Wonderful Life**(1946). While early critics labeled his films "Capra-corn," more positive recent assessments prefer "Capra-esque." Three of the films cited* above were among the American Film Institute's fifty greatest American films of all time in a 1997 list.

Vincente Minelli was born in America in 1903, with a prominent Sicilian blood line of 1848 revolutionaries on his father's side. After becoming involved in theater in Chicago in the late 1920s, he came to Broadway as a designer/director and built a reputation as an imaginative director of musicals. MGM invited him to Hollywood in the early 1940s to direct musicals.

His successes included *Cabin in the Sky* (1943), *Meet Me in St. Louis* (1944), *An American in Paris* (1951) and *Gigi* (1958). He was nominated as Best Director for the latter two films, winning for *Gigi*. Both films received Oscars for Best Film of the Year: a rarity until the 1960s.

Although Minelli directed non-musicals to some acclaim, such as *The Bad and the Beautiful* (1952) and the wonderful *Lust for Life* (1956), his forte was working with colorful and stylized musicals. Alan J. Lerner, noted lyricist, who worked with Minelli on several films, said he was "the greatest director of motion picture musicals the screen has ever seen." Minelli, his one-time wife, Judy Garland, and their daughter, Liza Minelli, constitute the only Oscar-winning family in film history.

Now where was I?

## The Last of the Tommasos

As far as I know, Marta and Sylvia are the last of the direct Tommaso bloodline. From whatever depths our Tommaso lineage may have risen, they share a gene pool which helped them excel in physical beauty and extraordinary intellect: and now one of them has a royal title, too! It also means that the Sanfidele girls may have benefitted from Pop's liaison with Michela, whose own father remains mysteriously unknown.

One Tommaso line will play out its drama in Mallorca and Calatafimi, while the other's scenario will develop in New York and Pennsylvania. That's a good Sicilian-American story. No, a good Sicilian-American comedy, I think. Like a Shakespearean comedy with nuptials and incredibly attractive, bright and powerful females: that's for me!

## A Haunted Heart in Search of the Green Light

Why does Marta's image still haunt me, a happily married man at last? I must accept her being my sister for my own sanity. Rachel should not have to share me with a phantom from my past. But as Virginia Woolf once noted: "It is far harder to kill a phantom than a reality."

In the night, though we're apart
There's a ghost of you within my haunted heart
Ghost of you, my lost romance
Lips that laugh, eyes that dance

Haunted heart won't let me be
Dreams repeat a sweet but lonely song to me
Dreams are dust, it's you who must belong to me
And thrill my haunted heart, be still, my haunted heart

Dreams are dust, it's you who must belong to me

And thrill my haunted heart, be still, my haunted heart

## Prescriptions to Live By

More recently, I had a dream which bordered on being a nightmare. I stood on a crowded line in a pharmacy, waiting to pick up several prescriptions. Suddenly, gaunt Dr. Cassidy appeared in a white jacket looking at me directly.

"Who's next," he asked.

I looked around and I was alone standing before him.

"Tommaso," I said meekly.

"Tomm-ass-o: let me see? You have two prescriptions on file: A and B, my son" he said. He looked at a card then back at me.

"A is for another twelve month supply of 'Marta.' I'm afraid you've got no refills on that illusion. You need a new prescription from Dr. Michela, my son."

"What about B, I asked?"

"That's for another twelve month supply of 'Don Silvio.' You do have one more refill on that illusion. Please go to the dispensary for the drug, my son, and be quick, it's almost 4:45 and I have to go to New Haven. Good-bye, my son."

There are illusions that sustain us, as well as those that shackle us, in their power to influence events in our lives. It was time to say good-bye to Marta.

# THIS NEARLY WAS MINE

One dream in my heart,
One love to be living for,
One love to be living for:
This nearly was mine.

One girl for my dream,
One partner in paradise;
This promise of paradise:
This nearly was mine.

Close to my heart she came,
Only to fly away,
Only to fly, as day flies from moonlight.

Now, now I'm alone,
Still dreaming of paradise;
Still saying that paradise
Once nearly was mine.

Oh, Marta. Oh, *Paradisu pirdutu!*

## Gatsby's Last Words

Rachel and I will stay in Queens or maybe move to New Hyde Park, a mere fifteen minutes away from Kings Point. There the Merchant Marine Academy sits looking out to the Throgs Neck Bridge. I was there the first week in September for a conference.

One night, the conferees took a ferry excursion out into Long Island Sound. We looped around Kings Point and Sands Point, the two peninsulas jutting out into the Sound. I decided to close my eyes for a moment, as we sailed along the shore of Sands Point, trying to connect with Fitzgerald's wondrous words at the conclusion of *Gatsby:*

Most of the big shore places were closed now and there were hardly any lights except the shadowy, moving glow of a ferry-boat across the Sound. And as the moon rose higher the inessential houses began to melt away until gradually I became aware of the old island here that flowered once for Dutch sailor's eyes—a fresh, green breast of the new world.

... for a transitory enchanted moment man must have held his breath in the presence of this continent, compelled into an aesthetic contemplation he neither understood nor desired, face to face for the last time in history with something commensurate to his capacity for wonder.

I opened my eyes and looked out to the myriad docks punctuating the shoreline and I smiled. Like dim Chinese lanterns strung along the coast, no less than ten green lights blinked at me across the water. Is the symbol of the "orgiastic future" that's already behind us born anew, or are they just ten green lights? "So we beat on, boats against the current, borne back ceaselessly into the past."

As I lay my pen down, I see we have come full circle. My thoughts are with my parents whose bones rest an ocean apart, and I, their orphan, am riven by dislocation. I'm feeling sorry for myself, but Rachel is my constant star: the one indispensable person in my life. She loves me and that's my taste of paradise, the only one I will ever know.

To Shakespeare I give the last quote, in the oft' borrowed words of *The Tempest*:

> *We are such stuff*
> *As dreams are made on; and our little life*
> *Is rounded with a sleep ...*
> *How beauteous mankind is! Oh brave new world ...*
> *that has such people in it!*

Sunday September 9, 2001

Jerome Silvio Tommaso

# LIST OF ARIAS/SONGS AND PAGES

Most of the arias and songs referenced above may be seen and heard on "YouTube" in multiple versions, or direct from film soundtrack versions. Enjoy!